'He botched the operation – he killed the patient,' Sister Smith repeated softly. 'You see, sir, he was drunk.'

'Who was the surgeon who did this operation?' Matthew Armstrong asked her at last.

'Mr Parker Brown,' she said, and burst into tears.

THE AUTHOR

Max Marquis devised ATV's television series General Hospital, with his partner Dick Sharples. As well as originating the show he has been Story Editor, and he continues to write scripts. He based the Midland General on the real-life Luton and Dunstable General Hospital.

Max has been a journalist on several Fleet Street newspapers, and he has more than 400 TV credits behind him. Born in Ilford, Essex, he now lives partly in Barnes and partly in the South of France. He is married to a Frenchwoman, and he writes and broadcasts in French on his greatest love – soccer.

Also available in Everest Books

General Hospital No. 1 – The Care Takers

General Hospital No. 2
A Matter of Life

MAX MARQUIS

EVEREST BOOKS LIMITED
4 Valentine Place London SE1

Published in Great Britain by Everest Books Ltd, 1976

A paperback original

ISBN 0905018 168

Made and printed in Great Britain by
Hunt Barnard Printing Ltd., Aylesbury, Bucks.

Prologue

If the Good Samaritan had been an American doctor he would have passed by, head averted, leaving the man from Jerusalem lying there, for fear of a suit for medical malpractice.

In New York and many other big American cities these days, if there is a street accident – or simply someone quietly groaning in the gutter – the wise physician doesn't cry out: 'Stand back, I'm a doctor.' He keeps going, because he knows that one of the first actions of the victim, as soon as he can talk, may well be to call a lawyer, and sue for damages. He will claim that the free first-aid treatment – possibly life-saving – he was given as he lay bleeding in the road-way has made it impossible for him to raise his arm higher than *this*; caused him great anguish and suffering; and given him severe headaches. So, Good Samaritans are thin on the ground in U.S. city streets. After all, the premium for insurance against malpractice suits costs about £25,000 a year – nearly £500 a week.

William Parker Brown, senior surgical consultant of the Midland General Hospital, was never concerned for an instant with considerations of this kind. If someone needed his professional help, they were given it without hesitation. On one occasion this trait in his character spurred him into sudden, violent and dramatic action which had its even more startling outcome some months later: an outcome that utterly changed the rest of his life.

It is impossible to count all the myriad threads of chance and coincidence that fate brought together to contrive the meeting of William Parker Brown and Dominic Frayne on a motorway at 6.14 on a summer's evening. It was a crucial encounter.

Frayne, a tall, finely-drawn young man of twenty-five, was driving to Scotland for a brief holiday. A sports car travelling south on the other carriageway lost a wheel nut which a careless mechanic had failed to tighten when he changed the wheel a week previously. The driver, who was more concerned with looking flash than caring for his car, hadn't noticed it. The sports car was being driven above the legal limit – about 90 mph – when the nut shot off at a speed well in excess of 100 mph. It bounced once on the roadway, jumped over the low central reservation, and flew straight at Frayne's car, which was doing about 80 mph. The murderous piece of metal went through the windscreen at a combined speed of nearly 200 mph, nicked the side of Frayne's neck, and continued straight out through the rear window. The blow in itself was not enough to knock him out, but the shattering sound of the impact made Frayne briefly lose control. He veered over on to the hard shoulder, and hit the embankment. His seatbelt was not tight enough: he hit his head on the windscreen, and badly bruised his legs on the underside of the dashboard. Before Frayne lost consciousness he straightened the car and brought it to a stop. He wasn't even aware that he'd been cut – badly.

A few moments later Parker Brown was driving north towards Frayne's parked car. Idly, Parker Brown noticed there was a hole in the back window of the car on the hard shoulder. Alerted, as he passed the vehicle, he glanced at it. First, he noticed the hole in the windscreen, then saw a figure slumped sideways in the front seat. Parker Brown swung sharply on to the hard shoulder, braking brutally. He slammed the car into reverse, and screeched to a halt in front of Frayne. It was typical of Parker Brown's presence of mind in moments of extreme crisis that as he got out of his car, he took the keys from the ignition. People rarely steal elderly Rolls-Royces, but there was no point in tempting the law of averages by making things easy for thieves.

He wrenched open the car door on to a grisly scene. Frayne's entire front was covered in blood which was still pumping from the wound in his neck. As his life poured out from him in a terrifying crimson cascade, his face, made even more frightening by contrast, was taking on the waxy pallor of a corpse.

Parker Brown took three or four seconds to sum up the situation and decide on a course of action. He reached out with his left hand and found the carotid artery in the side of Frayne's neck. With his strong, stubby fingers, so unlike the classic surgeon's fingers of fiction, he applied pressure to it, pushing it against the transverse processes of the spinal column. The massive haemorrhaging stopped, but Parker Brown knew that the least relaxation of his fingers would let it pump out arterial blood once more.

Somehow, Parker Brown eased Frayne into the passenger seat, holding him by the neck, and under the arm. Adrenalin, rushing into Parker Brown's own bloodstream, made him capable of physical acts that would normally be beyond his capabilities. But for all his care, and all his temporary added strength, once or twice his fingers slipped against the neck, made so slippery by the thick, warm blood. As they did, Frayne's strong young heart sent blood jetting from the wound once again.

The car's engine was still running. Parker Brown roughly put it into third gear, and was about to let in the clutch when he had a sudden thought. He switched on the headlights, then looked into the ashtray and found a used match. He wedged it between the horn button and its ring. With the horn blaring continuously and the lights blazing, Parker Brown set off, the engine screaming in protest as it had to drag the car away in the high gear.

The motorway exit for the Midland General, fortunately, was the next one in the direction they had been travelling. Parker Brown lurched off it, down the sliproad and to the roundabout at the bottom. The car's headlong, swaying and transparently determined course towards the roundabout nullified all rules of right of way: other cars in the roundabout pulled up unceremoniously, missing each other by a whole succession of minor miracles. The crew of a police Land-Rover actually on the motorway saw and heard the confusion with some incredulity, then set off in pursuit down the sliproad with the hyper-powerful siren blaring, adding more tumult to the noisy confusion. At the same time it helped Parker Brown, for cars ahead of him were warned of his approach. He took full advantage of this, weaving in and out of the traffic, past drivers who sat shocked at their wheels when they first saw the wildly-driven vehicle approaching them, then made out what looked like a grim-faced maniac, holding up a bloody corpse as he drove one-handed, barely in control of the car. He couldn't spare a hand to change gear, so he slipped the clutch instead.

By the time Parker Brown came up to the traffic lights a mile from the roundabout where he had to turn right to the hospital, the smell of tortured clutch and brake linings were filling the inside of the car. Parker Brown hardly glanced at the lights: he caught a glimpse of green, and heaved on the wheel to bring the car to the right. An idiot driver coming in the opposite direction chose this moment to insist on his right of way – blazing headlights and screeching horn with a police siren in the background failed to register any sense of danger on his slow-moving mind. As Parker Brown turned across the front of him, the driver doggedly ploughed on.

How one car did not smash broadside into the other defied all logic. An extra tug on the wheel of Parker Brown's car, an involuntary movement born of subconscious self-preservation by the moronic driver of the other meant that the seemingly-inevitable disaster was avoided somehow. Parker Brown's car weaved crazily into a skid that sent up great clouds of smoke from scorching rubber before he managed to straighten it and head for the hospital.

The Casualty Entrance was visible for all of the last 500 yards. As soon as he came into view of it, Parker Brown was hit by a sudden icy shock. He could no longer feel anything with his left hand. It was numb, no longer under his control. He turned his head to look briefly at the unconscious man beside him. The left hand, holding in Frayne's life for him, was still there, pressing on the carotid artery, stemming the urgent pressure of blood that would prove fatal in a matter of moments if not contained. Parker Brown looked at the hand as if it belonged to someone else, or as if it were a lifeless surgical instrument: it no longer seemed part of him. For the first time since he had opened the car door on that horrendous spectacle, Parker Brown was frightened – frightened that the hand might release its hold of his own volition, and he would be unable to command it to grip again. He muttered what with him passed for a prayer that he might hold on until they could get to the hospital.

Bywaters was on duty in Casualty. Some time ago he had left Parker Brown's surgical team to become a senior medical registrar. However, it soon became clear to everyone that Bywaters, although a conscientious physician, was by nature a surgeon. Eventually he transferred back to the surgical division when a senior registrarship became vacant, and he was selected for the post.

With Bywaters in Casualty this particular evening was Arnold Yappe, a young surgical houseman of little experience, but all the bounce and self-confidence of a man twice his size. So far Bywaters and Sister Cunningham, a casualty sister as massively unshakable as a stone statue, had stopped Yappe doing any actual harm to a patient. Bywaters, with a self-control that surprised both him and Sister Cunningham, had even managed to speak quietly and patiently to a bumptious little man who was heading for a sharp-edged lesson. And soon.

While Parker Brown was careering spectacularly towards the hospital, they had a patient before them, a local farm-worker named Gareth Lloyd who had been injured when a horse being led down a ramp from the back of a lorry slipped and fell off the ramp on to him. In a panic, and struggling to get up, the horse had caused him painful and serious injuries. Gareth Lloyd was vast. He was so barrel-like and heavily muscled that it seemed surprising that one horse could hurt him. But he had five broken ribs on each side, and a great curved bruise on one side of his face. He was in so much pain that he could breathe only shallowly, and his lungs were barely expanding. Mucus was beginning to collect and there was a bubbling sound as he took each painful breath. Bywaters regarded him compassionately.

There is a rule of thumb in medicine that if you are considering whether or not you should do a tracheostomy, you should do it. There is a natural reluctance in most doctors (Yappe and cut-hungry surgeons excepted) to cut into a human throat, but failing to do a tracheostomy can rapidly make a bad situation worse. Bywaters remembered the rule, and said to Yappe: 'I think we'd beter do a tracheostomy.' As soon as the words were out he regretted the choice of one of them.

'Yes, of course,' Yappe replied. 'Tracheostomy. I was just about to suggest it. Right, I'll do it, then.'

That was the mistake Bywaters had made: he said '*We*'d better do' instead of '*I*'d better do . . . ' Yappe took it as an invitation.

Bywaters very nearly contradicted Yappe and said he would do it himself, but he checked. Basically, tracheostomies aren't very difficult, even if they do look pretty drastic to a layman. Yappe, with Bywaters at his elbow, should be able to manage it without too much fuss; and even though he was a bouncy little fool, he had to learn some time. Bywaters didn't want to cut him down to (even smaller) size in front of nurses and Sister Cunningham, despite the fact they knew exactly what Yappe was.

While Bywaters and Yappe put on surgical gloves, Sister Cunningham prepared the patient and washed his neck with Cetrimede. A nurse wheeled over a trolley with all the necessary equipment.

Bywaters looked down at Lloyd and wished he'd told Yappe he'd do the tracheostomy after all. The man had a short, heavily-muscled neck that was going to be a pig to do. He told Sister Cunningham to put pillows under Lloyd's shoulders, and bend his head back. This helped a little, but not much.

Bywaters injected the local anaesthetic. 'Go ahead,' he told Yappe.

The houseman took a scalpel, and cut through the skin along the midline of the neck. 'Give me a clamp,' he said importantly.

Bywaters, suppressing a remark, handed one to him. 'I'd better spread in one direction, and you spread in the other,' Bywaters said.

'I can manage,' Yappe said. After a moment he said: 'Hmm.'

Bywaters wordlessly took a retractor and started to spread the muscles on his side, and Yappe did the same on his. At about the fifth attempt, between them they spread the muscles enough to reveal the white ribbed tracheal tube, which moved as Gareth Lloyd breathed.

'Here's the tube,' Bywaters said to Yappe. 'I'll make the incision in the trachea, and you put the tube in.' He handed Yappe a dish containing a curved, hollow plastic tube.

Bywaters took a scalpel and made a horizontal incision at the level of the second ring of the tracheal tube. He took hold of the lower lip of the incision, and enlarged the cut into an inverted U-shape. 'Put the damn thing in,' Bywaters snapped. Air was spluttering into the wound from the hole in the trachea.

Yappe pushed the tube into the place that Bywaters had prepared. 'Not too bad,' Bywaters said mechanically. Nevertheless, Lloyd was still coughing and bubbling.

'I don't like his colour,' Bywaters added. He put a soft plastic suction tube down the main tube to clear out the blood and mucus in the trachea . . . but the suction tube jammed somewhere inside the larger one. 'What the hell . . . ' Bywaters muttered.

'My God, look at his neck!' said Yappe, his voice going up an octave. As they all looked at it, it began to swell like an over-inflated inner tube of a tyre.

Bywaters instantly realised what had happened. The patient was blowing air into his neck from his trachea: the plastic tube that Yappe had put into place was only resting on the incision. It hadn't gone properly into place. Bywaters wasted no time on niceties: he sharply elbowed Yappe out of the way. 'Light,' was all he needed to say to Sister Cunningham, who pulled down the Angle-poise lamp so it shone directly into the neck.

He pulled out the tube and held the trachea steady in a clamp, then carefully, but swiftly and firmly, inserted the tube properly. Blood and mucus sprayed out of the upper end, most of it catching the front of Yappe's white coat.

'His colour's better now,' said Sister Cunningham, referring to the patient, and not Yappe, who had turned a dirty white when things started going wrong. Lloyd indeed did look better: he was rapidly becoming less blue.

The main door to Casualty thundered open like the great drumbeats in Siegfried's Funeral March. The sudden crash stopped all movement in the area: everyone froze, as if caught by a photographer's flashlight. Nurses and ancilliary workers stood motionless.

Dr Alison Moxey, a junior surgical registrar, halted two stairs from the bottom on her way down from an upper floor; a porter froze in mid-movement of putting rubbish into a trolley bin.

Right in the centre of the group was the blood-streaked Parker Brown, standing by an emergency trolley on which lay the even bloodier Frayne, Parker Brown's hand still clamped to his neck. Two porters, at either end of the trolley, were clearly bemused from the bombshell of Parker Brown's arrival. From outside came the last angry growl of the police siren as the Land-Rover pulled up by the Casualty entrance. A moment later the hooter of Frayne's car, which had been blaring away unceasingly, finally stopped. The sudden quiet was even more shocking than the previous commotion.

Bywaters was the first to recover. He quickly grasped the essentials of the situation. 'Alison, take over here for me,' he said, indicating his tracheostomy patient. Alison Moxey hurried down the rest of the stairs and over to Sister Cunningham, who explained the position to her. Bywaters, meanwhile, moved swiftly to Parker Brown's side, stripping off his contaminated gloves as he went. 'Clamps, Staff,' he said to the senior of the nurses not with patients. 'Plasma,' he told another. 'What happened?' he asked Parker Brown.

'I found him on the motorway.'

Bywaters nodded. 'How's his heart?'

'You don't have much time.'

The Staff nurse arrived with the clamps, and Bywaters was able to clip the ends of the severed artery. Parker Brown could release his hold at long last. Next Bywaters ruthlessly ripped the jacket and shirt sleeves from Frayne's arm. The second nurse arrived with a bottle of plasma and a tray with the feed line. Bywaters took a swab soaked in alcohol, and rapidly cleaned the inside of his elbow. While he did this, the nurse hooked the bottle to the stand attached to the trolley. Fortunately there was a clearly visible vein for Bywaters to put the needle in. He managed it, exactly right, the first time, and plasma started dripping into Frayne's dangerously depleted circulation, gradually restoring the volume. The odds against his survival, which had been monumental before Parker Brown opened the door of his car, were now shortening by the second.

'Into the theatre with him,' said Bywaters. The porters wheeled Frayne away on the time-saving short journey to one of the special operating theatres next to Casualty itself. With a nod to Parker Brown, Bywaters hurried off to scrub up.

Parker Brown massaged the fingers of his left hand. As the feeling came back into them, they began to ache. The discomfort spread up into the muscles of his forearm; his shoulders and neck felt badly tense. For all this, he felt a sort of elation that was as great as anything he knew after a particularly difficult or lengthy operation. His part was done. He had complete confidence in Bywaters' ability to cope now.

He stretched, and sighed. It seemed hours since he had discovered Frayne. He glanced at his watch, and shook his head in disbelief, but it was acurate. From the moment that Parker Brown had started Frayne's car moving to the moment he arrived at the Casualty entrance was nine and a half minutes. It took less than a minute for porters, alerted by the non-stop horn of Frayne's car, the counterpoint of the police siren, and Parker Brown's trumpeting shout to them, to get Frayne out of the car and on to a trolley. It needed less than a further ninety seconds for him to be on his way to the operating theatre, his severed artery clamped off, and the plasma drip in place.

The fact that the Midland General was so close to the motorway inevitably meant that it had learned, the hard way, how to organise itself for a sudden rush of victims mangled by unyielding metal travelling at high speed, or smashed against concrete road surfaces which rubbed away flesh and skin like a giant rough file.

Efficiency and planning born of experience started at the moment the highly trained ambulance crews arrived at the scene of the accident and loaded the casualties on to stretcher trolleys. The ambulances had the powerful motorway horns that could blast a swathe through a knot of the most obdurate drivers, saving vital seconds. At the hospital, the emergency operating theatres were but a few steps from the Casualty entrance. They were odd-looking theatres, for they had no tables. The specially-designed stretcher trolleys were instantly convertible to operating tables, so the victim did not have to be moved from a conventional trolley to a conventional table. All this hard-won technological expertise and frequent practice of complex traumatic surgery under pressure meant that Dominic Frayne would survive. Another place, even another time, and he would have died like a candle blown out in a sudden wind.

'Sir, what would you like me to do?' Parker Brown stopped washing his hands, turned and looked over his shoulder. Arnold Yappe was waiting expectantly.

Parker Brown's long, long look was far more expressive than the obvious answer to that obvious question. He dried his hands and walked away without a backward glance.

Yappe alone in the middle of Casualty, as superfluous as a spare appendix. No one caught his eye.

'I think I'll just go for a coffee,' he said to no one in particular. 'If I'm wanted, I'll be in the canteen.'

'Don't call us, we'll call you,' muttered an anonymous nurse.

Three thousand miles away, a dark, powerful-looking man of about forty was finishing lunch. He glanced through the wide, armoured-glass window, but there was nothing to see but the dark grey waters of the Atlantic.

The steward served coffee. 'This your first trip, sir? I haven't seen you on the ship before.'

'My first trip east, yes.'

'Holiday?'

'No, I'm going home.'

'Ah. The States are all very interesting, but there's nowhere like England, I always say.'

'Yes.' The answer was unrevealing.

'Well, I hope you have a nice crossing, Mr Wallman.'

'How are you now?' Parker Brown asked.

'A bit sore,' Dominic Frayne told him. 'And weak.'

'You've only been here a couple of days. You'll soon be feeling stronger.'

'Yes.' Frayne paused. 'They told me what you did. There aren't any adequate words; but I think you know how I feel.'

'Rubbish,' Parker Brown said briskly. 'I only did what any doctor would have done.'

'But I suspect you did it rather better,' said Frayne. 'I shan't forget.'

Chapter One

It had been a crowded year for Parker Brown: crowded even for that man who frequently seemed capable of twenty-six hours' work in every twenty-four. First, he had spent some time on temporary attachment to a London hospital where he had made some of the senior surgeons glad that he normally worked at the Midland General. Parker Brown had gone there for some intensive retraining. In the earlier part of his career, he had done a lot of cardiac surgery, but typically of him, he had perversely moved from semi-specialising to doing general surgery. Practically every other surgeon did the opposite. He did not want to become, Parker Brown said frequently, an expert on a particular ten cubic centimetres of the human body. However, recently he had been regaining his interest in cardiac surgery. Nothing as spectacular (and short-term, he said disparagingly) as heart transplants, but reparative surgery on valves and on the arteries immediately surrounding the heart.

He had split his spell in London with a visit to the Middle East, where he helped advise a minor oil-rich Arab state on the setting up of a new hospital. It was a quite remarkable place, full of the most modern equipment, supplied without the least consideration of cost – far better than any British National Health hospital. Almost all its patients would be unsophisticated tribesmen, whose daily lives were not affected by any device even as elementary as the wheel.

Most of the other advisers were Americans, with whom Parker Brown got on remarkably well, tolerantly forgiving them for their frightful assaults on the English language. In fact, he quite enjoyed himself there, despite the cruel heat. He just ignored it. He thought cool.

There was only one jarring element. A Texan neuro-surgeon, interested to learn that Parker Brown came from England's Midland General Hospital, observed that he had already met one of Parker Brown's colleagues who was working in America: a Mr Wallman. 'It's a small world,' the Texan observed unexpectedly. (Texans reputedly ignore the existence of anything less than giant-sized.) 'Yeh, I met Guy Wallman. It's a small world,' he repeated.

'Much too small,' Parker Brown replied.

Parker Brown then returned to London to complete his advanced refresher course to bring him up to date with the latest cardiac surgery techniques. At the same time, he was able to give advice – which he did frequently and irresistibly – to the hospital's Casualty department on traumatic surgery. Just before he was due to leave London, he received a letter from Matthew Armstrong, Medical Administrator of the Midland General, and one of his oldest friends. It had not been an easy letter to write: it was rather like writing to tell someone that his house had burned down and his wife had taken all the money out of the joint account and gone off with the milkman. The letter said, in essence, that Guy Wallman was back at the Midland General. He was in charge of an immunological and transplant unit which was quite autonomous of the hospital, and largely financed by a private foundation. At the same time, the Area Health Authority had engaged Wallman as a part-time consultant to the hospital proper.

Parker Brown's feelings when he received the news were fairly equivocal. He was furious that Wallman had managed to insinuate himself back into the Midland General. But after all, it was Parker Brown's own fault to some degree. When he caught Wallman and Mrs Helen Grant conspiring against him* – even though Wallman denied it – he let them go without taking any action against them. Now, all this time later, it would be useless making an official complaint. Besides, Parker Brown had little stomach for that sort of thing, complaining to officialdom. At the same time he was pleased to know that Wallman would be a member of the Midland General surgical team: he was a quite exceptional surgeon, and he would be under Parker Brown's direct authority.

Finally, Parker Brown had learned what to expect from Wallman. So, he wouldn't turn his back on him.

Now, a little more than a year after the famous motorway dash, Parker Brown was putting to use the experience he had gained in London. He was operating on a young man of seventeen for coarctation of the aorta.

The aorta is the main artery leading up from the heart to distribute the blood to the entire body. It has branches off it,

*See *GENERAL HOSPITAL No. 1 – The Care Takers.*

like side roads off a trunk road. A coarction is a narrowing of this artery: a bottleneck. Instead of being about an inch in diameter, the interior of the aorta is constricted, sometimes to little more than the thickness of a pencil. Oddly enough, this constriction always occurs about six inches from the heart itself, *after* the branch off to the head and upper part of the body and *before* the branches off to the lower parts. So, the blood pressure in the head rises to dangerous levels. The patient frequently complains of headaches and a throbbing pulse in the neck. At the same time, little blood gets through to the legs. This often causes limping, cramp in the legs, and always low blood pressure.

The operation to cure the condition is theoretically straightforward. The aorta is clamped above and below the constriction, the narrow portion is cut out and the ends joined together. That's the theory. The practice is sometimes rather different.

'The diagnosis was quite simple,' Parker Brown explained to the young housemen who were watching him . . . *perform* would be a better word than 'operate'. 'Straightforward radiography revealed a prominent ascending aorta, a "double" aortic knuckle with the constriction between them, and rib notching which strongly suggested enlarged and somewhat tortuous intercostal arteries. Since the patient is seventeen, and otherwise in good health, surgery was clearly indicated.'

Some of the younger housemen nodded sagely in agreement. Over the top of his mask Parker Brown glared at them. He didn't need their confirmation. Rapt interest, mixed with a little surprise, was the appropriate reaction when Parker Brown was talking about a case.

'The best ages for this operation are between five and fifteen. After twenty-five it is inadvisable since the wall of the aorta has become friable and inelastic by then, making suturing difficult, even for an experienced – a *very* experienced – surgeon.' He turned to his regular anaesthetist, Dr Thompson. 'Is your end unconscious?' he asked.

'He's anaesthetised, and he's stable,' Thompson answered equably.

Parker Brown held out his hand. After a moment he turned to the Theatre Sister, Hilary Wilson. 'Why do you think I am holding out my hand, Sister?' he asked quietly, but penetratingly. 'To shake hands? Or perhaps as an invitation to the dance? I am waiting to start the operation, woman.'

'Sorry, sir, but you didn't say what you wanted.'

'Where were you before you came here?'

'St Mary's.'

'Oh, *St Mary's,*' Parker Brown said with inimitable contempt. 'Well, I don't know what they do before they start operating in that charnel house, but here, we disinfect the site of the operation. A swab on a holder, Sister, if you can find one.'

Staff Nurse Lucy Hobbs exchanged a quick glance with Dr Lewis, a junior registrar. *Oh, he's in one of* those *moods,* said the first glance. *It was marvellous last night, darling,* said the second. Lucy lowered her eyes and tried to concentrate on her work. She jumped as Parker Brown rapped out smartly: 'Keep your mind on the patient, if you will, Nurse, and not on your private liaisons, fascinating as they doubtless are.' What shook Lucy was that she was standing behind Parker Brown's shoulder. The only way he could have seen her was by extra-sensory perception. Sister Wilson, still red-faced under her mask, felt sorry for Lucy, but at the same time she was glad that attention had been distracted from her. She put the swab on a holder into Parker Brown's hand.

'This operation is high in the chest, which is not the easiest area for the inexperienced surgeon to expose,' Parker Brown continued, painting a generous expanse of the patient's chest with the yellow disinfectant. 'Once the aorta is clamped, the operation must be completed rapidly. If the spinal cord and kidneys are deprived of a blood supply for too long they may suffer irreversible damage. At the same time there are numerous badly dilated collateral vessels which may be cut across during the operation. It is the special duty of the assistant to watch for, and control any such bleeding vessels. Dr Porter?'

'Yes, sir?'

'You will watch for them, won't you?'

'Oh, yes, sir,' Porter said earnestly.

'I am reassured to hear it. However, I shall do my best to avoid giving the patient unnecessary incisions and resections.' He finished disinfecting, and threw the swab into a corner of the theatre. 'A scalpel, for cutting, please, Sister,' he said, with a voice like breaking glass.

As soon as Parker Brown made the first incision, his manner changed. There were very few bitingly sarcastic remarks: the earlier ones had performed their funtion of keeping the theatre staff on their toes. But even though he spared Sister Wilson any further barbs, he was deeply discontented with her. The Theatre Sister he had worked with for the past eleven years, Sister Wallis, had left his service when he went to London, and had been appointed Senior Nursing Officer (which is what they call Matrons now) in one of the better Western hospitals. He would have found fault with a paragon of Theatre Sisters replacing her – at least to start with – and Sister Wilson was far from that.

Concentrating on his work with a fierce intensity, Parker Brown removed the constriction in the aorta, and deftly sutured the ends together. It was in good condition, and putting in stitches was child's play for Parker Brown, who was accustomed to sewing together vessels thinner than the refill of a ballpoint pen with microscopic stitches of – there is no other word – *beautiful* workmanship.

'Blood pressure's equalising very nicely,' Dr Thompson, the anaesthetist reported.

'Mmm. How much blood did we use?' Parker Brown asked.

'Two hundred millilitres,' Thompson told him.

Parker Brown addressed the junior surgeons. 'As I mentioned, blood loss in this operation can be high and that is why we have a thousand millilitres of blood standing by ready, before we start. However, between us, Dr Porter and I have managed to keep the loss from the other vessels to manageable proportions.'

Porter beamed.

Parker Brown turned toward him. 'Do you think you can manage to close up the patient without sewing your gloves to his chest?'

Porter stopped beaming even more quickly than he had started. 'Yes, sir,' he said. It seemed an inadequate reply.

'Then kindly do so,' Parker Brown said in a voice that sounded as if it were coming from a throne, and left the theatre like a schooner under full sail.

Everyone at the hospital thought that everything there was to say had been said, every joke there was to make had been made, about the brown liquid loosely called coffee served in the Midland General canteen. So when Neville Bywaters, back from a fortnight's leave, took a large mouthful of the uncertain brew, drank it, then took a deep breath before speaking, no one expected to hear anything particularly original. But what he said caused an immediate silence as his words sank in. He looked up, surprised, and in case they had misheard, he repeated his remark.

'Mmm. This isn't bad.'

This heretical statement had its roots in Bywaters' holiday. Although the hospital was more than fifty miles from the sea, Bywaters was the proud owner of a 30-ft yacht, on which he spent as much time as he could squeeze away from his duties. In the summer he would even drive the return trip of one hundred miles just for an afternoon and evening on the craft. When he had a whole fortnight off, he spent every hour of his time aboard her – with a very attractive girl named Lynda who was keen on the idea of sun, sea, fresh air and the concomitant pleasures of being with Neville Bywaters. For all this she was fully prepared to put up with the cramped quarters – which in fact also had its credit side – and the frankly basic food. On the first day of their holiday, they found coffee made with slightly sea-salty powder and condensed milk almost poisonous. At the end of the fortnight they were enjoying it, which probably says something for the quality of their relationship. (So does the fact that despite hardly ever being out of each other's sight for the entire holiday, they parted with regret.)

So, after the noxious brew to which Bywaters had become accustomed the canteen coffee tasted very much like real coffee. Barbara Kennedy, the rather earnest-looking consultant psychiatrist, was going to ask Bywaters if he felt all right, when there was a loud burst of female laughter from near the serving counter.

A tall girl, whose most obvious natural features at first sight were her long, naturally honey-coloured hair and strange tawny eyes, was joking with Walter Wright, a middle-aged member of the administration staff. She seemed quite oblivious of the rest of the people in the canteen, but it was inconceivable that she was unaware of the impact she was having on them. She was wearing an unfashionably short denim skirt, which nevertheless suited her because of her long, sunburned bare legs. Her blouse was a man's shirt, most of it unbuttoned. It was very clear that she was not wearing a bra. This was evident every time she moved and the skirt gaped open. She was a big girl, but being without a bra was no disadvantage. On the contrary. Her make up was as startling as her clothes. Her eyes were emphasised almost to the point of grotesqueness, like a pre-Christian Egyptian courtier; her lips were thickly painted deep red and moist. There was no make-up on the rest of her face. The total effect was compelling, as challenging as a slap across the face, as blatant as a raucous dockside invitation.

Oddly enough, Bywaters decided, she didn't look physically coarse or vulgar; but after all, some of the most depraved and vicious patients Bywaters had treated had the faces of Botticelli angels, while one of the most honest and selfless men he had known had the face and shambling gait of a movie monster.

'Who is she?' Bywaters said.

'Wasn't she here before you went on holiday?' Barbara asked.

'I'd have noticed her,' Bywaters said wryly.

'Her name is Suzy Palmer. She's working on the new computer installation – you know, the one for all patients' records, and hospital accounts and income tax for our pay and everything.'

'How on earth did Armstrong give her the job, looking like an Arab sailor's dream of port?' Bywaters said mystified.

'I doubt if he did. She probably was hired by the computer firm. Anyway, I doubt if she turned up for interview dressed *quite* like that.'

'Hello, Neville,' said Gregory Knight, sitting at the table. 'Asking about our Suzy? I wouldn't have thought you had enough energy to be interested in another woman after a fortnight aboard with Lynda. What do they call her at the Yacht Club – "The Lay of the Ancient Mariner"?'

'You know what you are, Greg – coarse, uncouth . . . '

' – But dead sexy with it,' Knight added. 'I'll tell you this. If you want to have a date with Suzy, you'll have to take your place in the queue.'

'Don't you men ever think of anything but sex?' said Barbara, starting to get up from the table.

'Look who's talking,' Neville retorted. 'As soon as a man comes into your consulting room, it's "Up on the couch, Mr Bloggs and make yourself comfortable".'

'Here, hang on, Barbara,' Knight said. 'Did you hear about the eight-year-old boy whose parents took him to the psychiatrist because he was always talking about sex, even though he was only eight? The psychiatrist sat the lad down, and drew a circle. "What does that suggest to you?" he asked the kid. "A man and a woman making love." The psychiatrist drew a triangle. "What about that?" "Oh, a husband and wife and the lodger in bed together." "Uhuh," the psychiatrist said, and he drew a square. "And that?" "Two married couples having a wife-swapping party."

'Well,' the psychiatrist turned to the parents and said: "You're right. The boy is obsessed with sex." The boy looked up and said "*I'm* obsessed with sex – ?" '

' – "Who's been drawing all the dirty pictures?",' Barbara concluded for him. 'Men,' she said, moving away from the table.

Neville watched her go. His eyes caught Suzy Palmer, now sitting a couple of tables away with Walter Knight, who was clearly embarrassed by her brash manner and loud voice. 'God, I needed that coffee,' he was saying. 'We must have got through half a dozen bottles of wine. I can just vaguely remember somebody putting me to bed last night. I woke up feeling like death, and my head going like a Salvation Army drum.' As she finished speaking, she turned her head and noticed Bywaters staring at her. The way she returned his gaze was like a blow in the stomach. She looked at him, then right through him as if he weren't there. There wasn't the least hint of reaction. He was nothing, non-existent to her.

Beside him, Greg Knight chuckled derisively.

'I am not a difficult or intolerant man,' Parker Brown said grandiloquently. Armstrong blinked. 'Indeed,' Parker Brown continued, 'I flatter myself that I am a fairly equable person.'

'I quite agree,' Armstrong said. Whether he agreed that Parker Brown *was* fairly equable, or that he flattered himself in saying so, Armstrong did not specify, but Parker Brown saw no equivocation in the reply.

'I might say that I have a certain reputation in this hospital.'

'You do indeed.'

Again Parker Brown was totally unaware of any amphibolous quality in the answer. 'Nevertheless,' he began.

'William,' Armstrong tried to interpose.

'Nevertheless,' he continued, 'there comes a time when even my good nature reaches its limit.'

Armstrong gestured to all the papers and files piled on his desk. 'I do have – '

It was useless. Parker Brown steamrollered on. 'We are short of surgical staff in all departments, which is serious enough in itself. But when – '

'The Area Authority has – '

' – But when I am short of operating theatre staff, and such staff I *do* have is inexperienced, inefficient, incompetent and . . . ' The effect was spoiled when he could not immediately find a fourth adjective.

'Inadequate?' Armstrong suggested.

'Please don't interrupt, Matthew. When the quality of the surgical staff in this hospital is adversely affected by the deficiences of the theatre staff – moonstruck nurses and dull-witted sisters – we might as well close the entire place down. After all, what else does the hospital exist for?'

The sheer effontery of this, the staggering egoism of its implications, left Armstrong momentarily speechless. He started composing a stinging reply, but sighed and changed his mind. This was not the sort of argument anyone could win with Parker Brown. On major questions of pure medicine he was strongheaded and opinionated, but he could be reasoned with, and could even be persuaded to change his mind on occasion. But on minor, purely subjective matters he was as receptive as a brick wall.

'You're not being fair to Sister Wilson, William,' Armstrong said firmly. 'And you weren't this morning, either.'

'How do you know what happend in my theatre? And what has being *fair* got to do with it?'

'To answer your first question, there is a bush telegraph system in this hospital which has the KGB beaten hollow. To answer your second, I should have thought it had everything to do with it. Frankly, William, from what I understand, it was nothing more than a . . . clash of personalities and – '

'Clash of personalities!' Parker Brown gave a short bark of laughter. 'You can't have a *clash* of personalities when one person doesn't have a personality. You can't clash with a bowl of porridge. However, the point is, there must be a rapport between the surgeon and the theatre sister. I can have none with Sister Wilson, and we *need* another experienced theatre sister. When will we have one?'

'Tomorrow,' said Armstrong.

'Because I refuse to continue operating – What?'

'There's a new theatre sister coming tomorrow. A Sister Smith.'

'Smith. Probably not her real name. I expect when she turns up we'll see she's more used to handling assegais and knob-kerries than surgical instruments. However, I'm prepared to meet with a perfectly unprejudiced mind a woman I'm quite certain will very probably turn out to be useless.' The outrageous illogicality of this last statement did not seem to strike Parker Brown, or if it did, it failed to trouble him. He turned away to the door. *William is being* particularly *prickly today*, Armstrong thought, *even for him.*

Just before Parker Brown left the office, seemingly almost as an afterthought, he said casually, 'Where's Wallman this morning?'

Instantly Armstrong realised what was digging into Parker Brown like a thorn in a lion's paw. 'Gone to town for the day, I understand.'

'Hm. Making trouble, I've no doubt.'

'Another brandy?' Wallman asked Piers Cavenne Charles Marignan Frere Trenchman, eighth Earl of Dellamayne. They were finishing lunch at Wallman's London club, The Portals. It was not one of the most fashionable ones, but it had a good address, a fairly distinguished membership – an earl as a member's lunch guest caused not the least stir – an excellent chef, and a better than-average wine cellar. The subscription that Wallman paid as a Country Member was most reasonable.

Passing through the doors of the club was rather like stepping back, if not into the previous century, at least to the immediate pre- and post-World War I period. There was an almost palpable sense of class distinction, of protection from the harsh realities of the outside world, from problems like the difficulty of getting domestic staff. In other words, once inside the club, the member could retreat into a pleasant cocoon of unreality insulated from the cold wind of modernity, and be assured by his treatment by the staff of his natural-born superiority.

For all this, Wallman was usually somewhat ill at ease at The Portals. Vaguely, undefinably, he felt he should despise all this assumed sense of privilege by right. Parker Brown once said of him that he brandished his working-class origins like a badge. This was true to a point, which only increased the dichotomy of Wallman's feelings. He had a strong but subconscious sense of guilt, of being a 'traitor to his origins', because he enjoyed the quiet luxury and near-feudal deference he was given. On this particular occasion, his unease was heightened: Lord Dellamayne, whom Wallman had met once or twice, had accepted his invitation to lunch, and had been a model of courtesy. Wallman's discomfiture was due to his uncertainty how to address his guest. 'My Lord' clearly was unsuitable for an informal occasion. 'Dellamayne' seemed rather casual,

'Piers' assumed far too great an intimacy. So Wallman solved the problem by avoiding it. Like someone who has forgotten a casual acquaintance's name, he did not address Dellamayne as anything. If Wallman wanted to attract his attention, he said 'I say,' or 'Oh, by the way . . . '

'Another brandy?' Wallman repeated.

'No thanks,' Dellamayne replied. He paused, looking straight at Wallman. Without warning he said: 'So you want the Ghazarossiam Foundation to give you a grant.' There was no need for Wallman to say anything. 'Why come to me personally, instead of approaching the Board of Trustees? Or writing to me in my capacity as chairman?'

'A lawyer once told me that it's always three people in a jury who make the decisions and tell the rest of the jury how to vote.'

'I wouldn't know,' Dellamayne said. 'I've never served on a jury.'

'Peers are exempt from jury service, aren't they?' Wallman asked.

'Only if they want to be. If one is picked, one can serve. Actually, I'd rather like to.' He paused again. 'You think the other trustees do as I . . . suggest?'

Wallman smiled. 'I'm certain of it. Look . . . ' He hesitated briefly, wondering if this once he should use Dellamayne's name, but he decided against it. 'Look, I've explained the work I'm doing, and the importance of it. You have the outline of what we're trying to do there. What we want to do if we have more money.' He indicated a file of neatly typed sheets on the sofa beside them. 'I believe in going to the top man. If I've failed to persuade you – ' Wallman shrugged. ' – I shan't bother to tackle the other trustees. If, on the other hand, you think the Foundation's money would be well spent with me and my unit . . . ' He left it in the air.

Lord Dellamayne regarded Wallman steadily. *I don't like him much,* he thought, *but I suspect he's pretty damn good in his own field.* He stood up abruptly. 'I'll read this, and think it over. I'll give you my decision as soon as I can. Of course,' he said with the ghost of a smile, 'whatever *I* decide will be subject to the decision of the full board.'

Like hell it will, Wallman thought.

'Who?' Bywaters said into the telephone in the Doctors' Common Room.

'Lynda!' came the answer. 'Don't say you've forgotten me already. I've still got the marks from your boat's decking on my bum, and it was only two nights ago that you – '

'Of course I haven't forgotten,' Bywaters assured her hastily. 'I didn't hear your name properly, and your voice sounds funny: it's a bad line.'

'So's that,' said Lynda, but she was joking, only pretending to be peeved. 'Look, I'm coming over your way this evening. There's this new disco opening, and I've been invited. Would you like to come?'

'A disco,' said Bywaters dubiously. 'I don't know that I'm all that keen on discos.'

'You've aged all of a sudden. And we don't have to stay there for the entire evening.' Bywaters needed a little persuasion. He made arrangements to meet Lynda in town. Then the tone of his voice changed.

The Common Room suddenly went very quiet. All the other doctors began taking a keen interest in what Bywaters was saying. He became visibly embarrassed as he said into the telephone:

'Yes, of course . . . Yes, so do I . . . It's a bit difficult at the moment . . . You *know* I do . . . '

'Go on, tell her,' Gregory Knight called out across the room. 'Don't be shy.'

'Good God, I believe he's actually blushing,' said Barbara Kennedy.

Bywaters slammed down the phone. 'You know what you lot can do, don't you,' he said, rather inadequately.

'Chance would be a fine thing,' said Knight dolefully.

Bywaters wondered what on earth he was doing there.

The new disco was trying to show it was better than its rivals largely by being noisier. The nasally plangent music was woolly enough to start with; but it was amplified to the point where people near the loudspeakers risked permanent damage to their hearing. Bywaters marvelled that the electronic genius which made it possible to reduce the output of an entire opera chorus and orchestra to minute variations on a piece of plastic and then transmute those microscopic irregularities back into glorious music once more, could be so prostituted to produce the idiot's cacophony being spewed from the disco's sound equipment. If a customer managed to keep his wits despite the assault on his ears, he still had to survive the stupefying effect of flashing lights. In addition to the offensive against his eyes and ears, Bywaters was acutely aware that the converted cellar was full of hot, sweaty people. Very sweaty, and smelly. And a lot of them were smoking, vitiating the air even more.

Despite all the pollution of the local atmosphere, he became aware of an acid smell that he thought hard about, then recognised. *Cannabis indica.*

It'd be just my luck to get busted, he thought. *I can see the headlines . . . 'Doctor in drugs raid . . . '*

That was not the end of Bywaters' complaints. The drinks were absurdly expensive, and, he suspected, probably watered as well. Finally, although he was supposed to be dancing *with* Lynda, they were slowly gyrating and swaying, out of touching distance of each other. *What ever happened to that old fashioned cheek to cheek stuff when you could put your hands on the girl, pull her close to you and feel –*

The music came to a half-explosion, half-wail sort of end, cutting short his line of thought.

'You had enough of this place, yet?' Bywaters asked Lynda.

She looked at him in astonishment. 'We've only just got here.'

Bywaters looked at his watch, and was reminded once more that time is relative. For him the hour spent in the club had seemed an eternity; for Lynda obviously it had been just a moment. He picked up his lukewarm drink, a sort of Scotch that even the Japanese would sell under an assumed name. 'I can think of better ways of spending the rest of the evening, that's all,' he said mildly, although inside he was screaming with boredom.

'Oh, all right,' Lynda finally agreed. Another high-powered discordant jangle erupted from the speakers. *The anti-Concorde lobby don't know what noise is,* Bywaters thought. 'I'd like to hear this first, though. All right?' she shouted into his ear.

Bywaters nodded without speaking. He wasn't going to compete with the general racket. A tall youth, all dark hair, dark blue shirt and dark glasses, approached from the gloom. With a jerk of the head and a raised eyebrow he invited Lynda to dance. She was polite enough to look at Bywaters for permission. He could see no reason to be jealous: Lynda and the hairy youth would hardly be aware of each other while they danced. In fact, anyone who didn't actually know in advance would be hard put to it to decide who was dancing with whom in the slow-motion rugby scrum on the floor.

Bywaters leaned back as best he could in his uncomfortable chair, trying to reconcile himself to present discomfort by the thought of future pleasure. Abruptly, he sat up straight.

Moving round the floor was Suzy Palmer. She seemed to be with Dennis Porter, the young surgeon who had 'assisted' Parker Brown at the coarctation operation. He was facing her, watching her hungrily as she moved, but she seemed quite oblivious of the crowd around her and the overpowering noise. Although she appeared unaware of the other dancers, they were very conscious of her. Her honey-coloured hair hung down her back, concealing the collar band of her halter top and giving the impresion from behind that she was quite naked above the waist. From the front it was obvious she was wearing the halter top, but it was so sharply cut that the general effect was nearly as provocative as if she had been naked – perhaps even more so. From the side the swelling base of an only partially-covered breast could be seen. As she swayed from the hips, gently swinging her arms, each movement threatened to reveal a breast completely. Her flared slacks were of a fine, shape-hugging material.

Bywaters watched her intently. Despite her flamboyance, paradoxically there was something almost defenceless about her that he found instantly appealing; but that was not all – there was something else, strange and incalcuable. Like many of the other people on the floor, she had her eyes closed, and as the music continued, her movements became more pronounced, more jagged. He could not make out whether she was deliberately setting out to be sexually challenging, or whether it was all unconscious. Lynda inched past him, the hairy youth somewhere in her wake, but Bywaters was hardly aware of her.

The music crashed to its finale. Suzy opened her eyes, and followed Porter back to their place near a corner. As they went, Suzy again glanced in Bywaters' direction, and again she looked right through him. Porter said something to her, and she laughed shrilly.

'Bloody hell,' Bywaters said to himself. 'That's what it is! She's bombed out of her mind.'

'Miss me?' Lynda asked from beside him. Her face was glistening with sweat: the disco was like a sauna. Bywaters looked at her blankly. 'Okay, Sinbad, shall we go?' she said.

Bywaters failed to meet her eye.

'Might as well stay for a little longer, now we're here.'

He looked across at Suzy Palmer.

What the hell's got into me? he thought angrily.

Bywaters picked unenthusiastically at his lunch. The dubious liquor at the disco the previous evening had unsettled his stomach, and his mediocre performance with Lynda had done as much damage to his ego. 'Look, darling,' she had said eventually. 'I don't know what it is you've got on your mind, but it's not doing the rest of you any good. I think we'd better call it a night. Better luck next time, and all that.'

Gregory Knight and Dennis Porter came and sat with him. Knight indicated Bywaters' meal. 'Are you going to send that to the path lab, or have they just sent it to you?'

'Look out, I think it moved!' Porter said with mock alarm.

'I saw you at the new disco last night,' Bywaters said with assumed nonchalance. 'Quite a place.'

'You at a disco, grandad?' asked Knight. 'Must have been hell on your rheumatics.'

'With that new girl, er, Suzy Palmer, weren't you?' Bywaters continued to Porter, ignoring Knight.

'Uhuh.'

Knight looked at Porter with new interest. 'Floozy Suzy? What was she like?'

Porter grinned. 'I tell you: she makes you feel you've just given three pints of blood.'

'I didn't think you had that much,' Bywaters said. There was an edge in his voice neither Porter nor Knight seemed to notice.

'Did you get to bed with her?' Knight asked. 'Silly question. Of course you did: she's basic. Come on, how was she?'

Porter hesitated.

'What's the matter? Don't tell me you're shy!' Knight put on a 'posh' accent. 'Or is it that gentlemen don't speak about ladies in the Mess? Well, that's all right: Suzy's no lady.'

'Why don't you shut up, Greg?' Bywaters asked.

Knight looked at him in surprise, but before he could say anything, his bleeper started sounding. He got up from the table. 'I only hope you enjoyed it, mate, because that was your lot. It'll be somebody else's turn tonight,' Knight said, and walked away.

Porter kept stirring his coffee without looking up. Bywaters stared at him, but Porter refused to be drawn. After a moment Bywaters pushed his uneaten meal aside, and got up himself. As he went out of the canteen, he heard a familiar laugh. Coming round a corner towards him was Suzy Palmer, outrageously dressed as usual. Two laboratory technicians were with her, devouring her with hot eyes. Behind her back, one of them winked salaciously at his colleague.

Bywaters walked past without a word or a glance.

'You wanted to see me, Matthew?' said Parker Brown, entering Armstrong's office like an invading army. 'I don't have much time, of course: I've a mitral stenosis in half an hour, but . . . Oh, good afternoon, Matron,' he said to Senior Nursing Officer Lanning, who was seated to one side of Armstrong's desk. Seeing her there, he prepared himself for a battle about some complaint from a member of the nursing staff that he had been sharp with, but for once this was not the reason for the meeting.

'The new theatre sister,' Armstrong began, and then Parker Brown saw her for the first time, as he closed the door that had been concealing her from his view.

'Good heavens,' said Parker Brown. 'Sister *Smith*. It didn't occur to me for an instant that it would be *you*.'

'Hello, Mr Parker Brown,' said Sister Patience Smith. 'It's been a long time.'

'Sister Smith,' Parker Brown repeated. He turned to the others. 'She was my theatre sister for – what, eight years? – at Parkway Hospital. My first theatre sister, and my best.' (If he had been talking to Sister Wallis, his most recent theatre sister, he would have called *her* his best, and meant it equally sincerely.) 'You know, Sister, you've hardly changed.'

Sister Smith was between forty-five and fifty. Her dark hair, streaked with some silver, was neatly cut. Her makeup was subdued, but adequate. Parker Brown probably didn't realise she *was* wearing makeup. She looked trim: she had not put on more than four pounds since she was twenty-five. Her features were strong, but not unfeminine; her dark brown eyes regarded Parker Brown levelly.

'She was the youngest theatre sister in the hospital, and the best,' he repeated. 'Do you want to join my service?' he asked.

'William, that is a matter to be arranged between Matron, Sister Smith and myself,' Armstrong interrupted.

'Well, she wants to come and work for me again, and I want her on my team,' Parker Brown said forcefully, taking the wish for the fact. 'What's to be arranged?'

Armstrong looked at the Senior Nursing Officer, and then at

Sister Smith. 'This could be embarrassing for Sister,' Armstrong pointed out. 'She may not want to – '

'If I may, sir, Matron, I'd like to join Mr Parker Brown. Subject to your approval.'

'That's settled then,' Parker Brown said before the others could speak. And, effectively, it was. Sister Smith had returned to Parker Brown's life from the past.

She was going to affect his future more than he could ever have dreamed.

Chapter Two

Black Friday, as it became known at the Midland General, started innoculously enough. The weather was good, and the most seriously ill patients had managed to survive the dangerous passage of the immediately pre-dawn hours when human resistance is supposed to be at its lowest: no one had died overnight. There had been no sudden access of the technological human's equivalent of the lemming syndrome: motorway madness, when men unaccountably hurl themselves to a messy end at enormous expense. There had not even been an unusual number of minor, run-of-the-mill emergencies like acute appendicitis, or premature birth.

In fact, Black Friday was also Dr Armstrong's birthday, although that piece of incidental information might as well have been marked 'Top Secret' for all the stir that the anniversary caused. His personal post had been as heavy as ever, but it contained only two cards; one from his son, in general practice in the south; one mysterious one which he opened with great interest, only to find it was a standard printed card from his insurance company. Yet Armstrong had no one to blame but himself. He rarely mentioned the date of his birthday, and gave no heavy hints that one was coming up soon. His closest friend, Parker Brown, invariably ignored all birthdays as pointless irrelevancies anyway. In fairness, he adopted the same attitude towards his own birthdays, although Armstrong sometimes wondered uncharitably whether Parker Brown did this less from meanness (which he didn't suffer from) than from an unwillingness to concede he was getting any older. As he sat alone at a table in the Consultants' Dining Room, his breakfast rapidly congealing on its plate, Armstrong admitted to himself that although logically he had no right to feel dejected about the lack or response to his birthday, his reason failed to overcome emotion.

'Good God, Matthew. What day were you born?'

Armstrong was shaken out of his gloomy reverie by Parker Brown, who was carrying an enormous breakfast over to Armstrong's table. Armstrong warmed to him. 'Why do you ask, William?'

'Because you look so damned miserable you must have been born on a Wednesday. "Wednesday's child is full of woe." You know the old saying.'

Armstrong's spirits plummeted again. Rather acidly he said 'I suppose you were born on a Sunday. And a child that's born on the Sabbath day, is fair and wise and good and gay.'

'That's right.'

Armstrong thought furiously, but he could find no answer to that.

Parker Brown ploughed through his breakfast. 'Good, this kedgeree,' he said, making one of his disconcerting digressions that so often threw people who did not know him. 'Kedgeree; from the Hindi *khichri*. In India they make it with rice, split pulse, onions, eggs . . . It's only in England that we use fish. Mm, it's very good.' He paused. 'What's wrong with you, Matthew? Off your food?'

'Just thoughtful. I've come to a decision.' He coughed. 'I think you'll agree I'm still fairly fit . . .'

'For a man your age,' Parker Brown admitted.

Armstrong breathed deeply through his nose, counting up to twenty under his breath. When he had done that, plus a further ten for good measure, and he felt his blood pressure go down again, he said 'My reflexes are still quite good . . .' Parker Brown looked at him, astonished. 'And I have all my faculties. *All* my faculties,' Armstrong said meaningly. 'But I'm letting myself get into a rut. I'm starting to live like a middle-aged bachelor with nothing to look forward to but my pipe and slippers.'

'You don't smoke,' said the literal-minded Parker Brown.

'I was speaking metaphorically. I mean, I'm not a bachelor, either,' said Armstrong, who was a widower, as Parker Brown well knew.

'No, but you *are* middle-aged.'

To be a Medical Administrator demands great powers of self-control. In the pressure-cooker atmosphere of a large hospital, where staff are forced into daily life-and-death decisions as a matter of course, where emotions often rack the soul, tempers are as eruptive as nitro-glycerine and rivalries can be traumatic. The Medical Administrator has to preserve objectivity and calm along the raging torrents of animadversion and vituperation. Sometimes Armstrong thought that it was a job Solomon would have refused. He was a particularly good Medical Administrator, steering a precarious course between the Scylla of the surgeons and the Charybdis of the physicians. Nevertheless, Parker Brown sometimes tried even his temper. It wasn't only what he said but how, and when.

'True,' said Armstrong eventually, to Parker Brown's *No, but you* are *middle-aged.* 'Still, I've decided to do something about it. What in my youth we used to call "Cut a dash". The only trouble is, they can be very expensive.' He checked, realising he had said more than he meant to. His embarrassment alerted Parker Brown. 'What can?' he demanded.

'Oh . . . ' replied Armstrong vaguely. He nodded and smiled at someone over Parker Brown's shoulder, before turning to him and saying 'How are you getting on with Sister Smith?'

The ploy was successful. 'I suppose you mean how is Sister Smith getting on with me,' Parker Brown replied grandly. 'Very well. Very well indeed. After the first couple of days it was just as if we were still at Parkway Hospital, and we'd been working together all these years. She knows exactly what I'm going to need before I have to say a word. Save minutes in every operation. And she's no clockwatcher. If there's work to be done, she does it, irrespective of the time.'

'I wonder how her husband feels about that?' Armstrong said. 'I take it she *is* married?'

Parker Brown stopped his fork a matter of inches from his mouth. 'What on earth has that got to do with anything?'

'Well, if she keeps working long hours and going home late her husband might not like it very much . . . ' A thought struck him. 'No, of course she's not married. She's still Sister *Smith.* That was her name at Parkway Hospital, wasn't it?'

'It doesn't follow that she's not married. A lot of women keep their maiden names. Frankly, I couldn't be less concerned whether she's married or not. She does her work admirably; the theatre runs like a new Rolls Royce . . . staff, equipment, everything. And nothing's too much trouble for her. I don't care if she has a husband, a lover, or whether she's the head of some polyandrous household, as long as she continues to do her work as she does it now.'

'Of course she's not married. I've just remembered: she's living in the Nurses' wing,' Armstrong said. He was still feeling a little waspish from his unremarked birthday. 'But there's always the chance that she will find some man – '

'And give up working with me? I doubt it. She's dedicated, Matthew.'

Armstrong had a sudden thought. Dedicated to what? *Or to whom*?

The first shadows of Black Friday were cast over Casualty, just before lunch, and darkened the day of Mr Dennis Porter. He was far from being as catastrophically inept as Dr Arnold Yappe, who had left the hospital at Parker Brown's 'suggestion' and then found a job writing medical advertising literature for a drug manufacturer. Nevertheless, Porter was going through the stage when he was convinced he knew a great deal about everything, and everything about a great deal. His first case of any importance in Casualty was the admission (or more accurately, the re-admission) of a six-months old Pakistani boy, Nazim Hanij.

Porter had seen the child at midnight the previous night when his distraught mother had brought him in. Her family G.P., also a Pakistani, was off duty that night. When she rang his number, she became confused by the operator answering and referring her to the deputising service's number. So Mrs Hanij decided to take the boy to the hospital. She guessed, reasonably enough, there would be someone there who could speak to her in her own language.

With a Pakistani nurse helping with translation, she explained to Porter that the boy had been vomiting profusely for more than an hour. Porter could find little enough wrong with him, apart from a temperature of a little over 99°, which was by no means extraordinary for a baby. At that age the blood-temperature regulator in the brain is over-sensitive and a little erratic. Perhaps it was the tedious business of having much of the conversation translated that made Porter slightly careless. In the event, he didn't ask the mother all the questions he might have done.

He gave the boy promethazine elixir, which had the effect of calming the child, and the mother. To be fair, he did make sure before she left, that she was going to contact her own doctor first thing next day. In the meantime, if her child started vomiting again, or developed any other symptoms, she was to bring him back right away.

As the mother left the hospital, the child was sleeping peacefully in her arms.

What Porter had not realised was that the child had an ileocaecal intussusception. This is a blockage of the intestine: a length of the tube is telescoped into the next section, and the natural action of the abdominal muscles draws the 'folded' length farther into the tube. The effect is rather like what happens to the fingers of a too-tight glove that turns inside out as it is pulled off. No one quite knows why it happens; or why it happens almost exclusively to children under the age of five – but medicine is full of mysteries.

One of the standard textbooks on childhood diseases says that it is of the utmost importance to make the diagnosis of intussusception within twenty-four hours of the onset of the symptoms. But, the textbook continues, the family doctor rarely sees cases of intussusception. He may see only one or two cases in his entire career, and so make a serious – indeed fatal – mistake if he relies exclusively on the classical symptoms of severe abdominal pain, vomiting, and the passage of blood in the stools.

Next morning young Nazim started vomiting again, and he was obviously in pain. By the time Mrs Hanij got him to her G.P.'s group practice he was momentarily quiet again, and the receptionist took her insistence that her child was dying as a typical case of an immigrant's mother's hysterical overreaction. In fact, although the mother did not realise it herself, that was nothing more than the brutal truth. The child was careening downhill towards death; soon it would reach the point of no return. If his true condition was not correctly understood very soon and an operation performed, Nazim would be dead before another night had passed.

The critical moment in his short life came when he was seen by Mrs Hanij's G.P., an insignificant-looking little dark man in a shiny blue suit, whose English was always uncertain, often unconsciously funny. His unpretentious appearance could not have been more deceptive. He was very acute. He had seen only one case of intussusception before, and even then only as an assistant, but he recognised this one without too much difficulty. When he learned how long the boy had been suffering, he arranged for his instant admision to the Midland General as an emergency case. Bywaters admitted little Nazim. Minutes later he was being X-rayed and having tests; within the hour he would be operated on.

Normally Bywaters was a pleasant, equable young man – even under pressure – without the irascibility that seemed to come automatically with some surgeons' promotion to registrar. This past week, however, he had been unaccountably prickly, ready to snap at his colleagues – although he kept his temper with the nursing staff. (Shouting at one's subordinates is less a sign of bad temper than of bad manners, or of a sense of inferiority, Parker Brown once observed.) If anyone had hinted that Bywaters' irritability had anything to do with Suzy Palmer, he would have advised a hurried visit to the Psychiatric Wing. He had seen her about the place, usually with a man, usually a different one each day, and usually looking the worse for wear; but she had not spoken to him, nor he to her. Perhaps that explained Bywaters' atypical behaviour.

While Nazim was in the X-ray Department Bywaters spoke to Porter about his examination of the boy the previous evening. It started as a simple discussion, but Porter's self-satisfaction aggravated Bywaters' ill-humour. Very quickly the discussion escalated into a major row. Bywaters made the reasonable point that the first person to see an acute abdomen has the least excuse to miss it, and Porter was that first person. In any case, he should have kept the child in for observation. Porter countered by suggesting that Bywaters had an exalted opinion of his own abilities and himself. When Porter had seen Nazim there was apparently nothing more seriously wrong with him than an over-anxious mother. Porter had nothing to reproach himself over, he said with more than a little arrogance.

Bywaters took Porter into the corridor outside Casualty so that the patients and other staff wouldn't hear what he said.

'Now listen to me, you cocky little bastard. Everyone makes a mistake in diagnosis, misses something, from time to time. The thing to do is learn from it, not try to justify your own ineptitude. If a bright G.P. hadn't picked up your mistake, that child could have died. So keep your eyes open and your mind on your work in future.'

'You can't talk to me like that,' Porter began, with a marked lack of originality.

'Thank your lucky stars it's not Parker Brown who's talking

to you,' Bywaters said grittily. 'If he knew you'd made a balls up like that he'd have – '

'Like what?' came Parker Brown's voice. He had come up unnoticed on the two younger men, who were facing each other like fighting cocks.

Parker Brown was not to be put off with evasions, equivocations and half-truths. The story of the boy with the intussusception which Porter had missed, and sent him home again, came out to the last detail.

'I will see you in my office at two-thirty,' Parker Brown told Porter in the sort of voice guards of the French Revolution used to call out the names of aristocrats due to get aboard the tumbril.

As Porter turned away, he gave Bywaters a look of unadulterated dislike.

But Black Friday was only beginning. In the canteen another piece of news went from table to table like bushfire, and then throughout the hospital. It concerned Louise Betts, a young nurse in the Paediatric wing. She worked in the most harrowing ward of all the hospital: the ward for children suffering from incurable diseases. To see these youngsters smiling happily, unaware; to see them growing uncomprehendingly weaker; to see their shattered parents pulling themselves together to present a cheerful face to their children on visiting days, and then breaking down again . . . all this is more than the human spirit can stand for very long. Only the deeply compassionate and spiritually strong can undertake the work.

Louise Betts seemed to have enormous reserves of character and strength; her compassion was apparently boundless. And yet . . . perhaps there was more to it than that. Certainly she looked like a sentimentalised painting of a Christian martyr: delicate features, blonde hair and an unworldly expression. Her sympathy for her young patients left her little emotion for anything else.

Recently a new patient had been admitted to her ward: an abandoned baby girl with myeloid leukemia. Louise became deeply, personally involved with this child, at enormous spiritual cost to herself. At the same time, she at last fell in love – with a young electronics technician who maintained the hospital's radio broadcast system and other communications.

The child died, as Louise knew it must; and in the same week her boyfriend told her he was going to become engaged to another girl. Just like that. Louise was so shattered by the twin blow that she was given a week off to help her recover. But she didn't return to duty.

It is commonplace now that most would-be suicides subconsciously want their 'attempts' to fail. Nearly always, someone manages to find them, and so they are saved, after having made this desperate cry for help. But occasionally one of these 'attempts' goes wrong: the expected flatmate doesn't turn up; the warning letter doesn't arrive, or is read too late. Louise's suicide was no mistake, no death by default. Her self-destruction was very deliberate. When she was found, she had been dead for six days, exsanguinated in the bath. Her death was nearly as rapid as it was final.

The news of it plunged the nursing staff into deep gloom.

Compared with this, Gregory Knight's accident, in which he broke a bone in his foot, seemed ludicrously insignificant; yet this was another of the more important elements in the making of Black Friday, whose happenings were to cause such reverberations in people's lives and deaths for months afterwards. What happened was that Knight got into his car and started to drive away. He thought he had a flat tyre, stopped and got out . . . leaving the automatic gear in Drive. The car inched forward and ran over his foot.

The next incident again involved Bywaters and Casualty – if 'incident' is the right word for an occurrence that nearly shut down all the hospital's emergency and ancillary services. It started with a call that a man had been found unconscious or dead near the town centre. The ambulance sent to fetch him screamed out of the hospital, blue lights flashing, headlights ablaze, and siren shrieking. It raced toward the traffic lights a hundred yards from the hospital gates, picking up speed all the way, even though the lights were at red. The driver and his mate knew that before they arrived there, the lights would turn green automatically. When an ambulance left on an emergency call the despatcher pressed a special button which set lights flashing on the gates, and changed the traffic signals in favour of the ambulance.

The man they went to collect was against a wall on a piece of waste ground, surrounded by his own filth and empty cheap wine bottles. A policeman and a few lugubrious sensation-seekers were standing near him.

'He's dead,' the policeman said.

The driver, Sam Pickard, bent down and gingerly touched the side of the man's neck. He felt no pulse. 'Reckon you're right. Ritchie, let's get him out of here,' he said to his mate. They heaved the body on to a stretcher, into the back of the ambulance. They drove back slowly and unspectacularly to the hospital.

The coincidences which were to give this day its sombre name were accumulating like compound interest of a debt. Shortly after the first ambulance set off there was another call from a nearby hotel, where a man was suffering 'from cardiac arrest', as the agitated telephone caller said. As soon as this second ambulance team arrived at the hotel, resuscitation attempts were started on the motionless man. He was about thirty-five, and expensively dressed. The strenuous efforts to revive him were continued in the back of the ambulance by the driver's mate and another policeman: the classic rhythmical pressure on the sternum and mouth-to-mouth artificial respiration. At the same time, the driver called up the hospital on the radio to warn them he had a heart-attack case aboard.

The two ambulances arrived at the entrance to Casualty in a photo-finish, although the arrival of Sam Pickard's ambulance went practically unnoticed in the drama of the other one's flamboyant approach. The 'cardiac arrest' patient was rushed into Casualty, with Porter and Sister Cunningham walking beside the trolley. Work on trying to revive him had gone uninterrupted since the ambulance crew first arrived at his side.

As the group hurried to the first cubicle, Porter saw Pickard.

'Who have you got?'

'A DOA* case, doctor. A tramp.'

'Right,' said Porter, 'leave him in the ambulance. I'll see him later.'

Alison Moxey came out of a cubicle. She saw the commotion going on round the trolley, and Sam Pickard standing away to one side. 'Shall I see to the other patient?' she asked.

'No. He's had it. A DOA. Give me a hand with this one.'

'But – ' began Alison.

'Come *on*,' said Porter.

The trouble-making fates played another card. Bywaters, who had just come from seeing Nazim Hanij in the High Dependency Unit, where he had been moved after his operation for intussusception, walked into Casualty again. He heard the intense activity in the cubicle, and went to join the others. He could do nothing more than Porter and Alison were doing, and had already done.

*DOA: Dead On Arrival.

'It's no good,' said Porter eventually.

'How long have you been at it?' Bywaters asked.

'More than half an hour,' Porter replied.

Bywaters nodded. 'Then I'm afraid you're right. He's gone.'

So, they gave up. Although the patient was only thirty-five, apparently healthy, a non-smoker and an only occasional drinker, he had been killed by an absolutely unpredictable heart attack.

Exhausted and depressed, they all trooped out of the cubicle.

Sam Pickard was sitting on a bench, waiting.

Ambulance drivers are mostly hardworking, underpaid men who do a frequently responsible and unpleasant task with some sense of dedication. A few – as in all jobs and professions – are like Sam Pickard: sour, belligerent, looking for bones to pick and rules to stand on. This was going to be the day for it.

'Oh, I'd forgotten you. I suppose I'd better have a look at the customer in your wagon,' Porter said wearily. 'Come on.'

Bywaters looked at Porter, surprised. 'You've got a casualty outside in an ambulance? How long's he been there? What's wrong with him?'

'He came in the same time as the other one, but he was DOA. No point in bringing him in here messing up a cubicle.'

'You saw him?'

'No, but – '

'Then how do you know he was dead on arrival?' Bywaters asked, pushing past Porter and Sam Pickard to go to the ambulance.

'He was dead when we picked him up, doctor,' Pickard said. 'Looked like heart attack.'

'How do you know he was dead?' Bywaters repeated slowly and distinctly.

'Well, I felt for the pulse in the neck. I mean, I've seen dead 'uns before.'

By now they were at the ambulance. Bywaters jumped up and inside. The dead man's filth and stale alcohol stank it out. Bywaters needed only to make a cursory examination: the body was already noticeably cooling. Bywaters came out of the ambulance again. 'Well, he'd dead now, all right.' He turned to Porter. 'But you just left him. You didn't even look at him?'

'The other case came in at the same time. The cardiac arrest.'

'What's the bloody difference between cardiac arrest and Dead on Arrival? The fact that one man was decently dressed and the other was a drunk?' Bywaters could feel his blood pressure rising. For a moment it seemed that he would be able to keep cool, but the thin thread of control snapped. 'Wasn't there any doctor to have a look at him? Where was Dr Moxey?'

'She was helping me with the cardiac – with the other patient,' Porter admitted reluctantly. 'I mean, this one was dead.'

'How do you know!? You didn't even *look* at him!'

'I told Dr Porter the man was dead,' Pickard said belligerently. 'Blimey, I seen enough of them. Besides, he was only some old . . . ' He checked.

'Yes?' said Bywaters icily.

The driver kept quiet.

'So you decided he wasn't worth making an effort for, I suppose.' Bywaters looked at Porter. 'Doctors say when patients are dead, not ambulance drivers, or roadsweepers or fortune tellers. That's the law, apart from any ethical considerations.'

'Now look here,' Pickard said. Bywaters turned to him.

'And there's a rule in this hospital that all emergency cases are to be treated the same. We don't differentiate between old tramps and young executives or down-and-outs and . . . trade union officials. Remember that.'

'I'm not going to be spoke to like that. I'm seeing my shop steward right away to make an official complaint. Until I get a ruling, I'm withdrawing my labour. And so will my brothers.'

What had provoked Bywaters into this imprudence with a junior doctor and a permanently disgruntled ambulanceman was the fact that he had recently read a study of the factors affecting the treatment of a moribund emergency patient. According to the author, the probabilities are that if you suddenly collapse, someone other than a doctor will decide not only whether you are dead, but also if you are going to live. And the important factors in deciding your fate are your age, social class, appearance and sobriety. The younger you are, the higher your social background seems to be, the neater and cleaner you are, the better your chances of being given prompt, determined and prolonged attention. The situation that had occurred at the Midland General was almost a perfect illustration of the writer's contentions. Unhappily, it was not the only case of a pair of patients arriving at the same time in much the same condition where one patient was given intensive treatment at the expense of the other, who was virtually ignored. With the report fresh in his mind, Bywaters was seething.

Porter, of course, was not simply indifferent to the fate of the tramp – who, in all fairness, would probably not have survived whatever treatment he was given – he just didn't think about the situation. Porter acted instinctively, as most other young doctors would have done, because that is what they had always seen happen, and because it seemed reasonable behaviour.

Whatever the other consequences of Bywaters' diatribe might be, at least it had made Porter think. If ever the same situation presented itself, he would remember the equal 'rights' of the second patient to the best care available. But for the moment, it seemed that the lesson had been rammed home at a high cost. The hospital teetered on the brink of a strike, not only by members of the ambulance drivers' union, but by members of other unions who were either misled about the 'dispute', or were malcontents. Actually to avoid a stoppage needed all the diplomacy of Dr Armstrong and Ken Fosdyke, the senior shop steward of Pickard's union, and some carefully composed memos between the various parties of great cunning and subtle nuances which could be interpreted in a number of different ways. What also helped was that Bywaters was generally popular, and Pickard was not.

Nevertheless, Bywaters was given a verbal sandpapering by Armstrong that left him badly smarting. This did not improve relations between him and Porter. They did not speak to each other for days, except on the most essential professional matters; and when they did, their over-polite conversation was heavily sprinkled with phrases like 'Yes, *doctor*'; 'No, *doctor*'; 'Of course, *doctor*, if you say so'; 'Thank you, *doctor*'. (The over-employment of the title 'Doctor' between two doctors is a fair indication that each would like to stuff the other's instruments up his jumper.)

(Eventually, after about six days, Bywaters gruffly said to Porter, 'Dennis. Come and have a drink.'

Porter stared at him. Equally gruffly he replied, 'All right. As long as it isn't hemlock.'

They both burst into laughter, and that was the end of that.)

But Black Friday still had some desperate hours to run.

Late that afternoon, during the homegoing rush hour, a lorry skidded and ploughed into a queue waiting at a bus stop. Miraculously no one was killed, but there were more than a score of seriously injured people, and as many walking wounded and shocked who needed some degree of attention. The hospital's resources, both of surgeons and equipment, were strained to the breaking point. Shortly after this major influx had been dealt with, Alison Moxey received a mysterious telephone call.

Alison was a strange, equivocal figure in the hospital. She was a not particularly attractive young woman – at first sight. Perhaps the very regularity of her features, and the fact that she used a strict minimum of make-up, gave this impression. The white coat she was always wearing over a practical, rather than eye-catching, dress or suit effectively disguised her slim figure. Yet occasionally someone caught a glimpse of a very good-looking young woman, wondered who it was, then suddenly realised it was 'only' Alison.

Alison's beauty, in fact, was more than skin deep. It was just that in the constant rush of the hospital, no one had the time to look beneath the surface, or the imagination to see what she could really look like. This could have been because Alison seemed to have no life outside the hospital. Once she went out through the main doors, she might just as well have ceased to exist. Occasionally one or two people had speculated on what sort of place she lived in, and what she did in her spare time . . . but it was only a short-lived curiosity. Because her appeal was not immediately obvious, and she never responded to the standard sexual overtures, interest in her atrophied. It was a sad reflection on the perception of some of her contemporaries, but there it was.

So, when she asked permission to go off because someone in her family was ill, briefly Parker Brown thought 'What family?' but did not pursue the matter and allowed her to go. He had not yet heard that Knight had broken the bone in his foot. Nor could Parker Brown know that Dennis Porter was going to start sniffling and sneezing in the first stages of influenza at any moment, which would make him quite unfit for operating.

It had been a long day, and Parker Brown would be pleased when he had finished operating. This last patient was a man of fifty-odd, a chartered accountant. He had become seriously alarmed when his speech became slurred and his right arm and leg were weak. It may have sounded comic had it not been part of a much more serious situation, but the accountant, Bernard York, could not hold his ballpoint properly. There had been other, previous attacks, initially less severe, but of increasing seriousness. He had been subjected to a formidable battery of tests before finally Armstrong and Parker Brown agreed on a probable diagnosis.

'Before long he's going to have a stroke,' Armstrong said. 'I think he's got an atheroma of the left carotid artery.'

'Looks very much like it,' Parker Brown conceded. 'Well, we'll do an ateriogram and find out.' This is a technique in which defects in arteries are shown up by X-rays when an (opaque) iodine compound is injected into the artery immediately before the film is exposed. If there is any irregularity in the shape of the artery – constriction or ballooning – it shows up.

The arteriogram of York's left carotid artery plainly indicated that it was choked with fat and calcium like a furred-up old kettle, cutting down the blood supply to the left hand side of York's brain – the part that controlled the right hand side of his body.

Now Parker Brown, with Sister Smith at his side, was performing a carotid endarterectomy, to ream out the spaghetti-like plug from the artery: an inert, but deadly, snake. Within twelve hours of Parker Brown's removing it, York would be able to use his ballpoint again; the strength would return to his right side and his speech would lose its imprecision. Parker Brown held out his hand. Sister Smith put a needle holder and needle with the correct thickness of suture into it wordlessly. Parker Brown began to close up the artery: not hastily, but without wasting time. The brain cannot live long without a proper blood supply. And damage to it is irreversible.

As Parker Brown, white coat over theatre green, entered his office the phone was ringing. He moved to the desk but when he picked up the receiver there was a click and the dialling tone started. He shrugged, and hung up.

He sat down, tipping back his chair and putting his feet on the desk. It was an extraordinary acknowledgment of his need to relax. Although he was alone, the gesture was akin to a War Office general appearing in public with his uniform unbuttoned. He leaned over precariously and took an unmarked bottle and a glass from the bottom of a filing cabinet near the desk. He poured himself a half-glassful and drank it gratefully. It was a pale straw colour, and could have been anything from a plain ginger ale to a whisky and something. In fact it was a bone-dry sherry.

The phone rang. 'Hello?' Parker Brown didn't announce his name. The only person who answered the phone in his office was Parker Brown himself. Bywaters was at the other end.

'Oh, it was you,' Parker Brown said after a moment. 'I heard the phone ring as I came in but I was too late picking it up.' He frowned as Bywaters spoke rapidly for a moment.

'What about Knight?' Parker Brown said eventually. 'Broke a bone in his foot? How inconsiderate of him. There's Dr Moxey – oh, no, I gave her permission to go off. Have you tried Porter? . . . I see. And what are *you* doing yourself, Bywaters? . . . Oh, very well. I'll come along in a few moments.'

He hung up peevishly and swung his feet on to the floor.

There was a knock at the door. Parker Brown's 'Come in!' was so savage that the unfortunate on the other side was almost afraid to. Dr Archie Seton, the hospital's youngest and most inexperienced anaesthetist, stood there. His eyes swivelled from Parker Brown to the bottle and glass on the desk and back to Parker Brown again.

'Sir, Dr Bywaters told me to try to find you. There's an emergency case come in – '

'I know,' Parker Brown cut him off. 'He just called me. I've agreed to take the case for him. Surgeons seem to be going down like flies this evening,' he added hyperbolically. A thought struck him. 'Are you going to be my anaesthetist?'

Seton admitted that he was.

'Good God,' said Parker Brown. It didn't do Seton's confidence much good.

The emergency admission was a man with a classic abdominal obstruction. Bywaters had seen him when he was brought in, obviously seriously ill, after having collapsed outside a cheap pub. He was left for some time before the befuddled drinkers leaving the place began to realize that something more than celebratory drunkenness was wrong with him. At last he was sent to hospital, where Bywaters admitted him – only to be forced to leave him when another, even more urgent, emergency case was brought in.

This one was a deckhand from a river tugboat. The boat belonged to a near-bankrupt company which managed to keep afloat financially and literally only by cutting costs to the bone. Some of the economies actually put the crews in jeopardy. The towing cable had not been regularly inspected, as it should have been, for example, and on this day it parted suddenly with a noise like a giant Jew's harp. It snaked back and caught the man above the knee. He was lucky: only the last four inches of cable caught him, half-severing his leg. A few inches more, and it would have taken off his leg like a cheese-wire ripping through soft camembert. Three feet or so higher, and it would have decapitated him.

The other men on the tug, not knowing better, put a tourniquet on the leg, and a narrow one at that. If a tourniquet needs to be applied, which is rarely, it should be a broad one: a scarf rather than a wire. At least someone had known enough not to leave it on permanently. From time to time it had been released, but before the vessels had had time to seal themselves. By the time the boatman was brought in, he had lost a lot of blood, he was shocked, and the wound in his leg was filthy. Bywaters' spirits sank when he saw it: he knew it would be a battle to save the leg. In the meantime, the man with the intestinal obstruction was moaning gently in another cubicle. So, he sent out the emergency call for assistance. Only Parker Brown was available to help.

Shortly after Parker Brown started scrubbing up, Sister Smith hurried in to join him.

'I got your message, sir,' she said calmly.

'Ah, there you are, Sister. I'm glad you've got here. We have an inexperienced anaesthetist, and no one to assist.'

'What's the operation?'

'Obstruction, of the large intestine from the look of it. The abdomen's badly distended, and the pain is hypogastric.' In other words, it was in the lower middle area of the abdomen, below the umbilical region. In obstruction of the small intestine, the pain is usually around the navel or higher, and the distension is often less marked.

Sister Smith began scrubbing up beside Parker Brown. They had no need to say much more. She had seen more operations for intestinal obstruction than most surgical registrars, and given the opportunity, could probably have done it herself better than most.

When the abdomen was opened, Parker Brown quietly said 'Good God. Look at this.' Seton, at the patient's head, looked up. 'Not *you*,' Parker Brown hissed at him. 'Concentrate on *your* end.'

Sister Smith looked inside the abdomen. She could see that the intestine had an obstruction that was as total as if it had been tightly sewn across. Gas had formed inside it, and the intestine had ballooned up grotesquely. And there were some very tricky complications. At some time or other the patient had been operated on for appendicitis and for a strangulated hernia. As a result, the intestines were a mass of thick adhesions.

'It's like Spaghetti Junction,' Parker Brown grumbled. What had promised to be an urgent, but relatively rapid operation, was now going to be a long, fiddling and complicated one. And as he worked, Parker Brown was grimly aware that it was going to be touch and go whether the patient would be strong enough to survive an operation of that length and complexity.

Three hours later Parker Brown walked wearily into the surgeons' rest room. (Bywaters had already finished his operation, and was back in Casualty, dealing with an unmomentous case: a cyclist who had a piece of grit in his eye.)

Parker Brown slumped on to an easy chair, and passed a hand across his eyes. It did not occur to him that he did not even know the name of the man on whom he had just performed the difficult, necessarily untidy operation.

He had no inkling that the operation, on Harry Wingate, fifty-five, human derelict, was the one that would have the greatest effect on his life of any single operation he had ever performed.

Black Friday ended, in effect, at three o'clock in the morning of the next day, Saturday. The final element was the death from post-operative complications of Parker Brown's patient Harry Wingate.

Chapter Three

It was the sort of civilised party that Bywaters enjoyed. There was none of the relentless noise of the discotheque, and anyone showing a bright light would have been considered guilty of a gross lack of *savoir faire*. This was because there were a considerable number of people at the party, but they were neatly divided into well-united pairs, and none of the pairs was much interested in the activities of the others. Everyone was doing much the same sort of thing, anyway.

The party was being held in a large, moderately dilapidated Victorian house with large rooms and sparse, threadbare furniture. There were no wild shrieks of dismay if someone spilled a little wine on any of the fittings. As the owners, Steve and Nicky Sharpe said of their divan: 'If that thing could speak, it would hiccup . . . or let out a long sigh of deep pleasure.'

Steve and Nicky were engaged in some undefined self-employed gainful employment. As it was honest employment it wasn't very gainful. However, the Sharpes enjoyed entertaining, and had a lot of friends. So they made the most of their one asset, the large house, and threw bottle parties. *Bring a bottle and your partner, and we'll supply a comfortable floor* was their attitude.

Bywaters was with a new girlfriend, Prue. Lynda was still slightly off him after his undistinguished performance on the night of the discotheque, despite the previous demonstration of his abilities on the yacht. 'Well,' Bywaters told himself, 'you're only as good as your last show.'

He met Prue briefly a week or so earlier when he was at a tennis club he went to occasionally. She was with a rather dull young man who looked rather as if he were being pulled around behind her on a little trolley, the way he always kept within range. Not quite always. Prue managed to say a few words to Bywaters, and give him her telephone number. He called her, and she invited him to this party.

They were sitting on the floor near open french windows, giving on to a long, unkempt garden which looked its best at moonlight. Most things do.

Bywaters offered her another glass of a pleasant *Moulin-à-Vent*, but she refused. 'I'm just right now,' she said. Bywaters was self-controlled enough not to ask her what she was right for. 'What do you do for a living?' she asked.

'I'm a doctor. A surgeon at the Midland General.'

'Really,' Prue said. 'Well, that's a bit of luck. You see, I've got this sort of funny feeling that starts here, and goes round here . . . ' She made a vague movement that encompassed practically all her abdomen. 'What is it?'

'I can't tell you without an examination,' he said, keeping a straight face and level tone. 'You'd better take your clothes off.'

'Here, or at my place?'

They got up slowly, and walked, hand in hand, towards the front door. To get there, they had to pass through another room and a lengthy corridor which could have been used for a bowling alley by day and for haunting by night. And just before they got to the front door, it happened again to Bywaters. Coming down the stairs and nearly bumping into him, was Suzy Palmer. Even in the flickering light of a few candles he recognised her instantly. With something between admiration and illogical anger he had to admit that she practically seemed to glow in the dark. She was dressed in a light-coloured Chinese-style dress which is pronounced something like *ch'ang-sam*. The main feature of this tight fitting dress is that it is split up the side, to the thigh. Following her downstairs was a beefy-looking man, who was fondling her back. Suzy had a glass of wine in one hand, which she turned and handed to the man following her. Bywaters noticed that her heavily-applied lipstick was smudged. In the semi-darkness her make-up made her eyes look enormous.

Involuntarily, Bywaters squeezed Prue's hand. Unaware that the pressure was due to surprise rather than affection, she squeezed his back again. 'When do you have to be back at the hospital?' she asked.

He paused, not sure why. 'Not until tomorrow.' She squeezed his had again. A thought struck Bywaters. 'By the way, what do you do?'

'Practically everything,' she said. 'You'll see.'

America shook slightly, and started moving towards Europe with increasing speed. But before the New World collided with the Old, Africa bestirred itself, and shot rapidly northwards and swamped them both. Then the headlit car passed, and the shadows on the ceiling, which had looked very much like Mercator's Projection of the World, reassumed their proper shapes and positions. The shadows were cast by the lamp post in the street outside shining through the branches of the cedar tree in the garden.

Bywaters turned his head and looked at Pru, lying beside him, only half-covered by a single sheet on the bed. It was a warm evening, even for people sleeping on their own. She was an attractive girl, there was no doubt about it. She was lying on her side, her back to him, and her head slightly raised on her hand, resting on a high pillow. He was vaguely reminded of the Valasquez painting 'The Rokeby Venus'. Except that the *Rokeby Venus has got a podgy face, as far as you can tell from the reflection in the mirror*, he thought, *but Prue hasn't*. She stirred gently, turning towards him, and instinctively reaching out a hand for him. As soon as she touched his bare flesh, she sighed, and settled down again.

He continued to lie on his back, staring wide-eyed and completely awake, at the patterns on the ceiling. He couldn't understand his sense of . . . lack of tranquility was the best way he could describe it. By all normal standards he should be sleeping peacefully and deeply. Instead of which . . . He turned and looked at Prue, her ripe young figure. There was a faint gleam of moisture between her breasts, perspiration on this warm evening. His gaze travelled up to her face. He let out a faint cry of shock, his heart thumping. Prue's eyes were wide open as she stared wakefully at him.

'Anything wrong?' she asked.

'No. Why, was I – ?' he began, but her chuckle cut him off.

'I didn't mean that. You were quite good. Actually, *very* good. But don't let it give you a swollen head,' she said with a wicked smile. 'Like some coffee?'

'I'd prefer tea,' Bywaters said. She leaned over, kissed him swiftly and lightly, and they both swung out of bed. They went to the small kitchen where they talked as she made tea.

'Are you in love?' she asked him abruptly. Bywaters looked at her, taken aback for the moment. 'Oh, I don't mean with me. We like each other – quite a lot. And that's all that counts, at the moment,' she said. He nodded. 'I mean, are you in love with somebody and she's not in love with you?'

'Not that I know of,' he said.

'Are you married?' He shook his head. 'Why not? Haven't you met anyone you want to marry? The . . . "right woman"?'

'I've been engaged twice.'

'Then neither of them was the right woman. Otherwise there'd only have been one.'

'One of them was killed. The second one.'

Oh, Janie, Janie, he thought. *I haven't forgotten.* A moment of blind panic overcame him: he couldn't remember what she looked like, He tried as hard as he could, concentrating almost until it hurt, but her face evaded him. Then, as suddenly as the image had gone, it came back again.

'You'll always be in love with her, then,' Prue said. He looked at her uncomprehendingly. 'She'll always be young and beautiful, desirable . . . No crows' feet round the eyes, no sagging figure . . . ' She smiled, and pushed at her own still-firm flesh. 'You won't even have had time to quarrel properly . . . '

'D'you know,' Bywaters said wonderingly, 'it hadn't occurred to me until now. I never saw her outside the hospital. I met her there, fell in love, became engaged there . . . And the first day she walked out, she was killed. We never had a life outside; not one second.'

Prue put his tea in front of him. 'As long as you don't ruin your life out of some mistaken sense of loyalty to a memory,' she said.

He shook his head. 'No. I've been through that stage and come out the other side.' He sipped his tea. 'As a matter of fact, I think you're rather super yourself, darling,' he said. 'That's a very shrewd head as well as a pretty one you've got there. Not to mention the rest of you.' She smiled and leaned over to kiss him. As she wasn't wearing any clothes, it was an exciting movement.

'I'm free again next Tuesday,' Bywaters said eventually.

Prue shook her head, and gave him his biggest shock of the evening.

'Sorry,' she said. 'I'm getting married on Saturday.'

The man was about thirty to thirty-five, quite handsome, with an indefinable air of at least moderate prosperity. His clothes, although tending to be slightly conservative, were clearly not bought from a chain store. His hair had been cut by someone who had talent and who had taken his time about it. In the luggage rack above his first-class corner seat was a well-used, but good quality, large leather suitcase. Beside him was a man's leather handbag – the sort of possession that could have had equivocal implications about the owner's habits. However, even though he was sleeping, there was no mistaking his heterosexuality.

It was mid-morning and bright, but he did not wake as the train rattled noisily over the points outside the station, nor when the train's hooter sounded mournfully. It was the final jerk of pulling up, together with the station's public address system suddenly booming into noisy, incomprehensible life that shook him into wakefulness. The man looked out of the window and saw the name of the station. He started, snatched up his handbag and suitcase and jumped out of the train.

The man stopped a few yards from the station exit, put down his suitcase, and started searching through his pockets for his ticket. After a moment, he realised where it was, and found it in his small handbag.

A moment later he came out of the station, walked to the edge of the pavement in the station courtyard . . . and stepped out in front of a moving taxi. He let out one short, sharp cry as his leg was broken, then passed out.

Parker Brown knocked on the door of Armstrong's office and walked straight in without waiting for an answer. 'Your secretary said you had no one with you,' he said as he entered. His tone changed in mid-stream, as it were. Armstrong was turning over the pages of a newspaper – but it was clearly not one of the better-known ones. This in itself would not have aroused Parker Brown's interest, but Armstrong's curious reaction certainly did. As soon as the door opened, but not before his gesture had been remarked, Armstrong quickly slid a couple of files over the newspaper and tried to give the impression he was enthralled by them. His uncharacteristically furtive behaviour, like a small boy being caught with his hand in the biscuit tin, or a spy with a minicamera pointing at secret documents, caused Parker Brown's formidable eyebrows to rise in astonishment. If the paper had been open at Page three of one of the tabloids, or had been one of the glossy magazines with photographs of girls who were revealing their ultimate physical secrets, Parker Brown would have understood Armstrong's reaction, if not his absorption.

However, the paper was open at the page of classified advertisements.

'What on earth is that?' asked Parker Brown.

'A patient's file. Why?'

'No, the newspaper. The one you tried to hide when I came in.'

'Don't be ridiculous, William. Why should I want to hide a newspaper?'

'Exactly.'

The telephone, that contrary instrument which always seems to ring at the most inconvenient moment, or refuse to ring when it is most needed, for once came to the rescue. Armstrong answered it, resting his forearm with studied casualness on the files which covered the newspaper.

As soon as he had finished the conversation, which for once he was in no hurry to end, Armstrong asked Parker Brown: 'How did the inquest go?'

He was referring to that morning's inquest on Barry Wingate, the patient who had died after the operation for an intestinal obstruction. Like many purely formal inquests on patients, this one had been held in the hospital itself, and had lasted only a few moments. There were no relations of any kind, no friends present. Harry Wingate had none. Only Bywaters, who admitted Wingate, and Parker Brown, who had performed the operation, gave evidence; without delay the Coroner returned the obvious verdict of Death from Natural Causes.

'Good heavens!' Armstrong exclaimed with patent hypocrisy. 'Look at the time, William. I must get along to the wards. I expect you must, too.' He rose and made for the door. 'Oh, what did you want to see me about?'

'As a matter of fact, I intended to ask you what you meant when you said you were going to . . . "cut a dash" again.'

'Just a manner of speaking,' said Armstrong, every pore oozing insincerity. 'Come along, William.'

With unexpected docility Parker Brown followed him out of the office and along the corridor. They parted company when Armstrong stopped at the lift. Once around a corner, Parker Brown stopped dead, and as soon as he heard the lift move off, he doubled back to Armstrong's office. Miss Fletcher, Armstrong's current secreatary, was at the desk. 'Excuse me,' said Parker Brown, moving the files aside, to Miss Fletcher's astonishment. 'I think I left something here.'

He stared at the newspaper Armstrong had concealed. It was *The Advertisers' Gazette,* a newspaper containing only classified advertisements, most of them of one particular group. For example, at the top of the page was the heading:

Ladies Under 39. The first advertisement read:

> Divorcee (innocent party), 30, good figure, happy disposition, warm, affectionate, intelligent, cultivated, seeks professional man, 35–45, widower or divorcee, view friendship, initially. Must be a stimulating companion, mentally and physically.
> Interests music, theatre, quiet dinners for two. Fuddy-duddies need not apply.
> Write to The Good Companions Bureau, Box . . .

Parker Brown stood as if he had been mumified.

Good God! he thought. *It's happened to Matthew: the male menopause; the middle-aged-man-chasing-his-lost-youth syndrome. Matthew Armstrong, of all people . . . !*

Alison Moxey was on duty in Casualty. Despite her apparent youth – she looked considerably younger than her twenty-seven years – she had little trouble even with rabid believers in male superiority – the type who believe that women can't count up to five, and that their only place is either in the kitchen or the bedroom. She had a daunting self-possession that the most belligerent masculinity could not dent, but there was more to her than that: she very obviously knew her job and was good at it.

Alison had in large measure that indefinable quality that can most easily be seen in those who are expert in dealing with animals. The moment an experienced vet or zoo-keeper, for example, picks up a frightened or dangerous animal, it quietens. The expert's touch wordlessly and soundlessly communicates something to the animal; gives it an instinctive sense of security. Equally with Alison Moxey. Simply the way she took hold of a limb, studied an injury or started to give treatment formed an instant bond of confidence between her and the patient. He was aware, without knowing *how* he was aware, that he was in good and competent hands.

When the man from the railway station was brought in, he was in no condition to appreciate any niceties of his treatment, or special qualities of the casualty officer. He was in some considerable pain from his left leg, where the broken fibula had come through the muscle and skin, making an unpleasant-looking wound. His ribs ached badly, and his head was spinning. Alison first lifted the sterile dressing the ambulancemen had put on his leg, and studied the injury. Next, she asked him if he had any pain anywhere else.

'My side, here,' he told her.

She gently felt his ribs. 'I don't think you've broken any ribs,' she said, 'but we'll make sure after we've taken care of that leg. Anywhere else?'

'My head. I think I must have given it a crack.'

She ran skilful fingers over his scalp. 'Yes, you've got a nasty bump there. We'll check that, too, as soon as we fix that leg.' She turned to the porters who had pushed in the trolley. 'Theatre, please. We'll send him to X-ray later.'

Sister Cunningham approached, a clipboard in her hand. 'What about the admission form, Doctor?' she asked.

'Oh, leave it until afterwards, Sister. I want to get this cleaned up as quickly as I can, and I don't think he feels much like talking yet.'

When the man had been given a local anaesthetic in the leg and an analgesic for his aches and pains, Alison prepared to to clean the wound. The object of the operation was to ensure that the wound was lined only with living tissues, with a proper blood supply, capable of destroying bacteria. She left the sterile dressing until the surrounding skin had been properly cleaned with antiseptic, then she and the theatre sister, the unfortunate Hilary Wilson, screened it off with sterile towels. Alison held out her hand, and the sister passed her a scalpel. She lightly trimmed the edges of the wound and enlarged it by about two-and-a-half inches above and below, along the length of the leg. Next, she trimmed the deep fascia – the sheath of connective tissue around muscles – and opened it up throughout the length of the wound. The sister handed Alison a pair of curved scissors. She trimmed each layer of muscle in turn, and finally the periosteum – the fibrous tissue over the bone. Last, Alison thoroughly scrutinized the wound to make sure there were no fragments of dead, crushed or non-contractile muscle left in it. The bone fragments she left there: the less bone removed from the wound the better. Finally, she tied off a ruptured artery with fine catgut and removed the pressure forceps that had been stopping it bleeding. 'All we have to do now is set the bone, put on a plaster, X-ray his ribs and do a scan of his head,' Alison said. That was all.

When the man was ready to be taken to a surgical ward, Alison went over to him. 'You don't seem to have done yourself any more damage than break your leg,' Alison told him cheerfully. 'Now, what happened?'

'I was knocked over. A taxi, I think.'

Sister Cunningham bustled up, her clipboard in her hand again. 'We had the taxi driver in,' she said. 'He kept saying it wasn't his fault.'

'It wasn't. I stepped in front of him without looking. Though why . . . ' His brow furrowed with puzzlement.

'Well, there's no need to worry about it now,' Alison said briskly.

'Is it all right to get the details for the admission form, doctor?' Sister Cunningham asked, brandishing the board. Alison nodded, and the sister turned to the casualty. She clicked her ballpoint importantly. 'Name?' she said.

There was a long pause. *'Name?'* Sister Cunningham repeated, raising her voice to the level she used for dealing with those hard of hearing, or rather thick. There was another long pause, then the man said:

'I know it must sound stupid, but . . . I can't remember my name . . . who I am . . . anything.'

Surgeons work hours that would make most trade unionists blench. They are frequently up as early as postmen; and emergency surgery aside, they often are still operating while most people are having their evening meal, or switching off their minds as they switch on television. Another difference between surgeons and members of some other professions is that the more senior and celebrated they become, the more work they do, not less. By comparison, a journalist, for example, begins his life by writing, it seems, non-stop. He covers weddings, funerals, church fetes, court cases, sports days, prizegivings . . . The list is endless. The higher he rises in the newspaper hierarchy, the less writing he does. If he ever reaches the dizzy heights of Editor, he will find he need write absolutely nothing at all. If he actually becomes a member of the board of directors of a newspaper (where journalistically-trained executives are rare as hen's teeth) it is doubtful if he will be required to read, either.

Guy Wallman was operating rather late this evening because he was trying to clear his list for the following morning, so he could concentrate on some work in his special research unit. He had already done a number of extra operations: removal of a lung, the repair of a hare lip and cleft palate, and the removal of a gall bladder. He was now on his last one: the removal of a kidney stone, or nephrolithotomy, from a patient who had developed renal colic – an agonising pain which made it impossible for him to lie still. Special X-ray examination had revealed the presence of a stone or calculus in the kidney.

When the patient was being prepared for the theatre Wallman personally marked out on the patient's skin with indelible pencil the area of the operation. He wanted there to be no possibility of a mistake.

The operation was being performed with the patient on his side on the operating table, his affected right side uppermost, just over the 'break' in the table, which was raised in the middle. His right arm was drawn forward across a support, his left knee and thigh drawn up with the right leg across it. Finally, the patient's pelvis was turned back and held in place with a broad band of adhesive tape.

'Right,' said Wallman. 'All we have to do is dig this one out, then we can all go home.'

Matthew Armstrong drove back towards his home, humming cheerfully, more or less in harmony with his car radio. He had just been out to call on one of the advertisers of *The Advertisers' Gazette.* When he got there, it wasn't quite all he'd hoped for, but at least he'd started looking, and he felt sure it wouldn't be long before he found exactly what he wanted. In hopeful anticipation of better luck next time, Armstrong still had a faint smile of pleasure on his face. Parker Brown, with the licence of friendship, would have called it a foolish smirk.

Armstrong's light euphoria was suddenly punctured by the sight of flashing blue lights and waving torches ahead.

In the lives of hospital staff, road accidents inevitably play a large part. A recent Government survey showed that there are nearly 18,000,000 vehicles on Britain's roads. The survey also came up with a fascinating measure called vehicle/kilometres. In other words, if one vehicle did 1,000 kilometres in a year, that would count as 1,000 vehicle/kilometres. Ten vehicles all doing 1,000 kilometres in the year would count as 10,000 vehicle/kilometres. In Britain in 1974, our traffic accounted for 237,000,000,000 vehicle/kilometres. In the same year there were nearly a quarter of a million road accidents, causing nearly 7,000 deaths and more than 317,000 injuries.

In hospitals, they know all about motor vehicles and the damage they do.

Armstrong pulled up short of a side road so he could turn off and drive around the blocked road if his help were not needed. He got out of his car and walked to the scene of another crash.

Police cars and an ambulance were already there. A white sports coupé had its crumpled nose and awkwardly splayed front wheels nudged well into the badly distorted side of a small family car. A young man in a dark velvet jacket and flowered shirt, both covered with blood from his lacerated face, was being helped into an ambulance. The shattered windscreen of the sports coupé, most of the broken pieces outside, on the bonnet, hinted strongly that he had not been wearing his seat belt when the cars collided, and had paid the inevitable price in pain and injury by going right through it.

Two flat-capped policemen were taking a statement from an

angry-looking man of about the same age as the injured one, but much more conservatively dressed. A pale-faced girl sat in the front seat of a police car.

Armstrong approached a police sergeant. 'I'm a doctor. Can I help?'

'Thank you, sir, but I think everything's all right. There's only one injured, and he doesn't seem to be too bad. They're taking him off to hospital.'

Armstrong nodded, and walked over to the ambulance. The driver recognised him, and saluted, which impressed the police sergeant. 'All right?' Armstrong asked the young man, who was sitting up.

He nodded without speaking.

'Sure?' Armstrong insisted.

The young man made an effort. 'Ribs hurt a bit.' He seemed breathless.

'Well, you'll be at the hospital in a few minutes,' Armstrong told him. 'They'll take care of you.' He could see no obvious signs of serious injury, haemorrhaging or shock. The best thing for the injured man would be to get him to hosital quickly for a thorough examination there, rather than have a superficial once-over by the roadside which would only delay proper treatment under favourable conditions. Armstrong nodded to to him and turned away.

As he started walking back to his own car, he passed a policeman going to the ambulance. Armstrong did not see him take something from his pocket, nor hear him say to the young man: 'Will you blow into this, sir? Try to fill the bag with one continuous breath.'

The policeman held out a breathalyser.

Chapter Four

By the time the young man in the car accident reached Casualty, he was looking rather more sorry for himself. He was pale and sweating, and his voice had become much quieter. Occasionally he shivered, and the movement caused him to wince with pain. He had picked a bad time to be injured. When he was admitted Casualty was full, having one of its busy evenings. Casualty duty, many doctors never tired of saying, was like war – long periods of boredom interspersed with unexpected moments of intense activity.

Bywaters was dealing with two men who had become involved in a drunken brawl. Normally drunks don't do each other much harm – their movements are too imprecise, their punches damage little more than the circumambient air. Their major hazard is from falling over, particularly in front of moving traffic. However this pair had whacked each other with bottles which broke, causing some nasty-looking scalp lacerations. They were followed almost immediately by a man with an arm injury sustained in a factory working night shifts, and a small child with scalds, who had pulled a kettle of hot – fortunately not boiling – water on to herself from the cooker. The distraught mother had plastered the scalds with butter, thinking this would help; but in fact had only complicated the doctors' task. Burns and scalds should be covered with non-greasy, clean dressings – clean paper if nothing else is available – until medical help is available.

Dr Porter had answered an emergency call to help in Casualty and was on his way there when he bumped into Wallman getting in his lift. As they went down, Porter explained the reason for his haste. On an impulse that he was never able to understand, Wallman decided to give a hand as well.

Bywaters, coping with the noisy, frightened child and her mother, was grateful for the help. He told Porter to deal with the arm injury, and politely asked Wallman if he'd take the road accident. Away in a corner a staff nurse was finishing off the two drunks, while a policeman stood massively beside them, ready to 'calm' them if they became obstreperous.

The young man in the car crash was lying on a trolley. His jacket was off, and his shirt was open, revealing some ugly bruising over the left ribs. His face seemed vaguely familiar to Wallman, but when Sister Cunningham told him his name, it meant nothing to him: Julian Charles.

'We've sent blood for cross-matching, and the wet plates should be here any moment,' Sister Cunningham said. 'Mr Charles has also got rather heavy bruising in the region of the left kidney, so Dr Bywaters asked for a full set of X-rays of the abdomen, as well as a head scan.'

Wallman picked up the chart. Charles's temperature, blood pressure and respiration all confirmed the outward appearance of mild shock, but his condition – so far – was by no means serious. Wallman leaned over the young man for a closer look at the injuries, and became aware of a strong smell of alcohol – whisky, probably.

'You didn't hit your head, did you?' Wallman asked.

'I don't think so,' Julian Charles replied weakly, 'although I don't know how it all happened, exactly.'

'That's quite usual,' Wallman said reassuringly. At that moment the more-or-less-controlled chaos in Casualty increased sharply. Staff nurse Chalmers came over to Wallman. 'There's a man on the phone who says he's Mr Charles's father, and he'd like to speak to you about his son,' she told him.

'Take his number and say we'll call him back. At the moment his son is . . . say he's being examined, but is giving no cause for concern.' It was a good formula.

'He said he particularly wants to speak to you, sir.'

'You shouldn't have given him my name, then,' Wallman told her irritably. 'Go and say what I told you to say.' Staff Nurse Chalmers seemed on the point of replying, thought better of it, and went back to the phone.

Coincidentally, a man walked into Casualty with the brutal assurance of an army of occupation. He was large, had been powerful once, and was still to be reckoned with despite a thickening and coarsening of his body. His grey hair was naturally unruly, even though it was cut almost convict-short. He had cold, unfriendly eyes; you could not imagine him whispering soft gentle words to a woman. His mouth, a sword-slash in his craggy face, had the corners turned down in a permanent affirmation of bitterness.

A pace behind him was a Police Sergeant, the one from the scene of the accident involving Julian Charles.

'Where is he?' asked the large man.

'Who are you looking for?' asked Sister Cunningham, who was not easily put out.

'That young bastard who hit my boy's car.'

Wallman came over. 'Who are you?' he asked.

'My name is Alderman Tindall. Some drunken young swine drove right into him – '

'Are you hurt?' Wallman asked him.

'I wasn't in the accident,' Tindall replied impatiently.

'Then is your son hurt? Are you making enquiries about someone? If you see Sister – '

It was Tindall's turn to interrupt.

'I've come to make sure he doesn't get away with it.'

Wallman, that excellent judge of good and bad character, that perceptive assayer of a person's value and use to him personally, considered Tindall. The way he called himself *Alderman* Tindall said volumes in itself. In fact, as he looked at the man, Wallman was surprised that he didn't call himself *Alderman* Tindall *JP*.

Old school Labour politician, a bully. A committed enemy of 'class', which he in fact perpetuated by his own attitude to anyone who did not work with his hands for wages and did not have an impeccable working class ancestry, Wallman decided. *He'll never do anything to help me, but on the other hand, he can't do anything to harm me. Not worth wasting time on.*

'If you're not here to see a relative, and you're not a patient, I'm afraid you'll have to leave,' Wallman said. 'We're rather busy.' He turned and walked away before Alderman Tindall could say anything more.

'Sister, have the patient prepared for theatre, in case, and have the drip set up right away. I want to have a look – '

'One moment, sir, please. Before you do that . . . '

Wallman turned. What he saw both astonished and angered him. The police sergeant stood beside the trolley, where it was clear he had been talking to Charles. The sergeant stared back at Wallman with a policeman's professionally unimpressed regard.

'Sergeant Harris. Doctor, I'd like a blood or urine sample from Mr Charles before you start giving him a transfusion. You could do that, couldn't you?'

Wallman looked dubious. 'Did you give him a breathalyser?'

'No. He said he was too breathless to blow up the bag.'

'I can understand that.'

'But I explained the legal position and said that when he got here I should require a blood or urine sample. And I've just asked him if he'll now provide the sample.'

Before Wallman could say anything, a nurse hurried up with the wet X-ray plates on their metal frames. It didn't take long to see why Charles was breathless, and mildly shocked. The wonder was he wasn't more so. He had three broken ribs, two of them bent at an angle that suggested they might have torn some soft tissue and caused internal haemorrhaging. It is difficult to tell much about kidneys from ordinary X-rays. An IVP (intra-venous pyelogram), where an opaque liquid is injected into the system rather like with an arteriogram, is needed.

Nevertheless, Wallman could make a shrewd guess that the left kidney had been damaged as well.

'Sister Cunningham – have him taken into theatre right away. I want to see if those ribs have caused any internal haemorrhaging, and have a look at that kidney.'

'Sir,' Sergeant Harris said.

'And leave the transfusion for a minute, Sister.' She nodded and moved off, organising a nurse and a porter to take the trolley to the ante-room of an emergency theatre.

'Sir, this could be important,' Harris insisted. 'There's been an accident, and certain allegations have been made.' He grimaced. 'You heard the alderman. Mr Charles might want the opportunity of a blood test to clear any doubts. You only have to ask him. Is he fit enough to give blood? Or urine, if he prefers?'

Wallman nodded reluctantly.

'Then there's no harm, is there? And as I say, Mr Charles may think it's to his own advantage. Because I've explained that if he refuses, he could be guilty of an offence – '

'I know the law,' Wallman broke in. 'Very well, I'll ask him. But I won't put any pressure on him.'

'I shouldn't want you to, doctor,' Sergeant Harris said. 'Er, you know the procedure? Enough for two samples, which you seal and label yourself. One for us, one for him.'

'Yes, all right,' Wallman said, his irritability returning.

Staff Nurse Chalmers, who had taken the original call from Julian Charles's father was on the phone again. This time the man at the other end did not just say he was Julian Charles's father, he gave his full name. It nearly startled her into dropping the telephone. She began to move towards Wallman, but he was already on his way to the scrubbing-up room, and Sister Cunningham called out to her to come and assist with the scalded child.

Unfortunately, when she was asked to recall some time later the exact sequence of events of this agitated evening, she was unable to do so.

'Unfortunately' . . . for a number of people.

The ward was quiet at this time. The livelier patients were in the day room watching the last permitted hour of television, the less mobile ones were reading in bed, or listening to radio on the earphones. The sicker ones were just resting or sleeping, thankful to be alive. Alison entered the ward, and waved to

Sister Washington, on duty at the nurses' station, to stay put. She went over to the bed where the man from the train was lying. He had earphones on, but he wasn't listening to the programme.

Alison picked up his chart from the end of the bed and glanced at it briefly. 'How are you feeling?' she asked, putting on an encouraging smile.

'The leg aches a bit, but . . . ' He shrugged. 'The trouble is, I still can't remember anything. My name, who I am . . . '

'I shouldn't worry too much about it. People often lose their memories of the period just before an accident. Bit by bit the blank period gets shorter, until at last it all comes back.'

He shook his head. 'It's not like that – ' He checked. 'What about the things in my pockets! Haven't they got a name or address in them?'

'Apparently your pockets were practically empty. The taxi driver said he thinks you were carrying one of those men's handbags when he ran into you. I expect somebody quietly stole it in the confusion.' She gave him another smile. 'In the meantime, we're calling you John Smith. Not very imaginative, I'm afraid.'

He didn't respond; he was too deep in his own thoughts still. 'What troubles me is that I can remember that I couldn't remember, if you see what I mean. I know that when I woke up, and got off the train, *I'd already lost my memory.* I didn't know who I was, what I was doing on that train, where I was going. Nothing.'

Alison took his wrist and felt his pulse. It was over 110. 'I'll have Sister give you something to relax you,' she said. Her hand slipped from his wrist down to his hand, and she held it for a moment, then released it suddenly, surprised by her own gesture. 'I know it's easy to say, but you must try not to worry too much. I'm sure it'll all sort itself out quite soon.' As soon as she spoke, she knew how stupid it sounded, but 'John Smith' was still full of his own thoughts.

'Someone may be wondering what's happened to me, worrying . . . '

'Yes,' she said flatly. 'Well . . . I'd better take care of those tablets.' She paused. 'I'll come and see you again tomorrow. If there's anything . . . ' She didn't know how to finish it. On sudden, inexplicable impulse, she squeezed his hand again, and turned away quickly.

Alison took his chart from the bottom of the bed, and

marked *Nitrazepam 10 mg* on it, with the date and the time. She walked over to the nurses' station, where Sister Washington unblinkingly watched her approach. Alison had the uncomfortable feeling that she had heard everything she had said – but that was impossible, she vigorously told herself. Sister Washington's handsome, dark and usually mobile face was expressionless, which was a significant expression in itself.

'I've written him up for some Nitrazepam, Sister. He's still rather agitated.'

'Very good, doctor.' She turned and called out to Staff Nurse 'Doris Day' Holland, who came bustling up, took the chart and drugs cabinet key, swept up Student Nurse Nicola Stevens like a mail train picking up a trackside mailbag (drugs are always dispensed by two nurses, to eliminate errors), and went off to get the tablets – all in one complex, non-stop operation.

'Any idea who he is yet, doctor?' Sister Washington asked. Alison shook her head. 'Well, he's not exactly down and out, anyway. His clothes are off the peg, but from Harrods. Beautiful material. And he had £45 in a gold clip in an inside pocket. Somebody's soon going to be asking for a good-looking fellow like him, that's for sure.'

Alison walked out without saying anything.

'Are you sure?' Wallman asked.

Julian Charles nodded. 'Quite sure.'

'Frankly, I'm not at all sure you're quite fit to give a specimen, or come to a rational decision – '

'I *want* to give the sample. If I'm guilty, I should be punished for it.' Wallman said nothing, but it wasn't the sort of remark that would give him any confidence that Charles was completely rational. Or anyone else for that matter.

Charles was lying on the trolley in the ante-room to the operating theatre. Dr Mark Perryman, an anaesthetist, Sister Malden and a couple of nurses were all standing by, just waiting for Wallman's instruction to start.

'Take the blood – please,' Charles added. 'Come on, let's get it over with.'

Wallman looked at the others in the room. They had all heard what Charles had said. He shrugged; there was no way of avoiding taking the samples. He picked up the swab, cleaned the inside of Charles's elbow with a non-alcoholic disinfectant, and expertly took a blood sample, which he injected into two sterile bottles. While he was at it, he prepared the vein to take the drip. As he wrote on the labels and signed his name he spoke to Perryman. 'You can start now, Mark. And Sister, connect up the drip.' Perryman gave Charles his first injection. This would swiftly make him unconscious, not deeply enough to be operated on, but sufficient for Perryman to be able to put the endotracheal tube into his throat. This is a fearsome looking piece of chromium-plated ironmongery with a handle, seemingly, to the layman, much too weirdly and massive to go in comfortably. It is an essential piece of apparatus, for it keeps the airway open, makes for easier breathing in thoracic operations, and allows the anaesthetic gases to be passed into the lungs without difficulty. Putting in the tube is a skill anaesthetists finally acquire after practising on newly-dead patients. *Some* patients: the 'better-class' patient, even though dead, stands a good chance of escaping being a post-mortem guinea pig. The drunken derelict is an odds-on bet for a session of tube-passing practice.

Wallman called to a theatre porter. 'As soon as the patient's been taken into theatre, deliver one of those bottles to Sergeant Harris in Casualty, and put the other one on the desk in my office,' Wallman instructed him. He got on with his preparations to go into theatre: he was already scrubbed up; all he needed now was help in getting into his operating gown.

One of the theatre nurses said to her colleague, as they helped wheel the now-unconscious Charles into theatre: 'Do you know who his father is? The patient?' And she told her.

The porter finished his chores, and went over to pick up the two blood samples. On his way out he passed behind Wallman, who stepped back, adjusting the tapes of his facemask. His elbow caught the porter's hand and sent the two bottles crashing to the floor, where they broke and spilled their contents.

'I'm sorry, sir,' the porter said, scared. 'You moved so quickly.'

'Never mind,' Wallman said without inflexion. 'Can't be helped. And we can't get any more from him now. Tell the sergeant what happened, will you?'

'Fancy that,' Sergeant Harris said with monumental unsurprise. 'So we can't get a blood sample from his lordship after all.' The porter looked at him blankly. 'Oh, didn't you know? He's the Hon. Julian Charles, Viscount Trenchman. His father's Earl Dellamayne. That's why that nurse . . . '

'Staff Nurse Chalmers,' the porter volunteered.

'Staff Nurse Chalmers practically curtsied to the phone the second time, when Dellamayne said who he was.'

'How do you know?'

'She's been running all over the place telling everybody she could get hold of.'

'Viscount Trenchman, Earl Dellamayne's son, eh!' said the porter, impressed. He looked in the direction of the operating theatre. 'I wonder if Mr Wallman knows it's him?'

Sergeant Harris said, slowly and mirthlessly, 'Ho, ho, ho.'

When Wallman opened up Julian Charles (or Viscount Trenchman) he found the broken ribs had caused more damage than he had suspected. The kidney needed three very fine sutures, but with luck it would heal. The patient was also given four pints of blood – the ordinary red kind.

'How did it all go?' Bywaters asked him as he got out of his theatre green.

'A good night's work,' Wallman said. 'Yes,' he repeated, 'a good night's work.'

Bywaters looked at him sharply.

Wallman was smiling a quiet, secret smile.

Chapter Five

The return of Mr Guy Wallman to the Midland General did more than simply strengthen the hospital's surgical team. There were techniques and practices which he had learned during his stay in America; there was his research on transplant surgery and immuno-suppression, which, although carried on in the special autonomous unit not part of the Midland General proper, still added to the hospital's store of knowledge and experience. There was another, less tangible but nevertheless valuable contribution that his presence alone made. Parker Brown himself described it as a 'useful stimulus to keep me on my toes; the grit to my oyster'.

Normally Parker Brown kept this sense of rivalry from the younger man under control. Occasionally, however, an unguarded remark would get through to him like a dart. One young surgeon imprudently said to another that it was time Parker Brown overcame his vanity and used spectacles that he must surely need at his age. Someone else remarked that Parker Brown was showing signs of flagging when the pressures of long hours in theatre were exceptional. Parker Brown – whose hearing most certainly was not failing – overheard these observations, and seethed.

One of his customs that infuriated everyone in the surgical department was his insistence on making out the surgical schedules himself, for everyone. This meant, as Dennis Porter said bitterly one day, 'You never bloody know what you're going to do the next day until eight or nine o'clock the previous evening.' Not that Porter was allowed to do anything that was much more than elementary on his own.

Parker Brown had taken the afternoon and most of the evening off on the day that Wallman operated on the Hon. Julian Charles, Viscount Trenchman. He returned to the hospital and made out the next day's operating schedule even later than usual. It was a solid list, with a couple of back-breaking, eye-boggling, very serious operations for himself included: two coronary by-passes. Oddly enough, this formidable programme caused a lot less sourness than might have been expected. The reasons for the lack of adverse reaction became evident during the course of the next day.

As Parker Brown scrubbed up at 7.30 a.m., Bywaters mentioned that Wallman was not coming in today: he'd rearranged his work so he could spend the day at his special unit. Parker Brown reacted with annoyance at this; but it seemed rather half-hearted and Bywaters could not really believe that he had forgotten the arrangement. Equally, Bywaters could not accept that Parker Brown had overlooked the fact that Porter, who was down to perform some straightforward, run-of-the-mill surgery, was going on a week's holiday.

'Never mind,' Parker Brown said when Bywaters 'reminded' him. 'Knight can do some of his cases.'

'Greg Knight's foot is still in plaster,' Bywaters said.

'Good God, that shouldn't stop him operating! When I was his age we'd operate with both legs in plaster, propped up on a shooting stick or a bar stool, after a weekend rugby match.'

Bywaters had another piece of news for Parker Brown, but thought it best to keep that back for a while.

Parker Brown's first operation was another cleaning out of the carotid artery. It was a relatively simple operation – compared with what was to come – and could be likened to an athlete's warm-up lap before a steeplechase. Bywaters, meanwhile, was dealing with a woman's hiatus hernia. In this condition part of the stomach bulges up into the space in the diaphragm through which the oesophagus passes. The patient, Mrs Kyle, had been steadily and remorselessly getting fatter for the past thirty years, since she was twenty-five, and the extra weight pressing on her slack abdominal muscles were the last straw. She suffered heartburn, and sometimes severe pain, especially when she bent or stooped down (as much as her straining girdle would allow her). Sucking antacid tablets and sleeping propped up on pillows didn't help her. Now the surgeon's skill and knife would put right in a matter almost of minutes much of the damage that three decades of overindulgence had produced.

When Bywaters had finished, he returned to the scrubbing-up room where Parker Brown was preparing for his next operation: the first coronary by-pass operation.

'Well, I'm off, sir,' Bywaters said with an assumed hearty nonchalance.

'Will you be good enough to translate that into moderately grammatical and comprehensible English?' Parker Brown said acidly.

'I'm leaving now. I have to be in court in London today.' He coughed. 'You remember, sir. I'm giving evidence in that High Court action for damages. I *have* to go,' he admitted unnecessarily.

Parker Brown's face became even more like a disapproving Apache chief's. 'There used to be a time when surgeons actually did a little surgery,' he said. 'Have you any idea where Dr Moxey is? Giving ballroom dancing lessons, perhaps, or taking the day off to concentrate on her raffia work?'

'She's on Casualty duty.'

Parker Brown nodded, completed his preparations, and went to the second theatre, where he was going to do the fearfully taxing and high-risk conorary by-pass operation. The patient was Brian Fearn, a forty-five-year-old financier, who was two stones overweight, smoked forty cigarettes a day, and frequently had cholesterol-packed business lunches accompanied by liberal quantities of alcohol, not to mention dinners that were even more deadly. He had suffered a number of minor heart attacks, but three children at expensive boarding schools, two large cars and a house which his bored wife always seemed to be redecorating, refurnishing and redesigning with extensions and patios, meant that he couldn't stop overworking. The truth was, he didn't want to. He had enough money to retire right now and live a comfortable, if rather more modest life, but he was a workaholic. He was a prime candidate for being the richest man in the cemetery in the next few months.

His arteriograms had shown an unmistakable blockage in the left upper coronary artery. The blood supply to the heart was badly reduced, and one part of it was completely starved of blood. Effectively a section of the muscle was dead from earlier heart attacks. When the heart was exposed, that ischemic part, as it is described, would be a dirty grey.

What Parker Brown intended doing was to take a large vein from his leg and put it into his heart to add to the blood supply and give it a better chance. During his year in London, Parker Brown had seen a considerable number of these American-devised operations performed, had assisted at quite a lot, and had done one or two himself. However, it was the sort of operation that not the most megalomaniac surgeon would approach without some trepidation. Fearn, the patient, knew this operation was dangerous, but less dangerous than going on in his present state. He would have been shocked into another heart attack if he could have seen himself now: he made the Bionic Man look positively human by comparison. There were probes of every kind stuck to and into his body. He had electrodes stuck to his shaved skull to monitor the brain activity – the operation could be a technical success yet leave the patient a vegetable because the brain's supply of oxygen-bearing blood had been cut down. So, the brain's condition was observed all the time. There were probes to measure his venous pressure and arterial pressure; a catheter for the drip to keep his fluid level topped up, a self-retaining, balloon-ended Foley catheter in his penis to remove the urine; yet another to monitor his temperature . . . Of course, there was the usual endotracheal tube down his throat to take the anaesthetic gases and the tube attached to the machine that would do his breathing for him.

With Parker Brown were Sister Patience Smith, Dr Wim van Kroll and Dr Terence Leakey.

Van Kroll was a young Dutchman, with experience roughly equivalent to that of a Midland General Registrar, on an exchange posting from a hospital in Leyden. He seemed a pleasant young man, even if he did talk football at the least provocation, and often with none at all. Although Dutch, he was as swarthy as a southern Mediterranean. He had been at the hospital long enough for Parker Brown to assess his abilities and be well satisfied with him. However, there was nothing on this day's schedule that Parker Brown would allow him to tackle on his own.

Dr Leakey was a fairly new houseman from Africa, whose ambition was to go back to his own country as a consultant surgeon and teach other young doctors. He had the blackest skin and whitest smile that Parker Brown had ever seen. Parker Brown was also aware he had an enormous potential talent for surgery. He had not only beautifully deft hands, but also that human instinct that separates the good surgeons from the great ones. At the moment, however, Leakey's career was coasting along in neutral. When he had discovered that standards of sexual morality in England were non-existent compared with his own country, where women's rights were roughly equivalent to those in Britain before the Renaissance, he had neglected his work to concentrate on the pursuit of young women. Sooner or later he would calm down: it was a law of nature. New workers in a chocolate factory stuff themselves witless at first, but the very availability of the sweets quickly makes them less desirable. Besides, a man can only do what a man can do, and Terence Leakey was doing it right up to the hilt.

There were others in the theatre, of course. It was crowded with nurses; the anaesthetist, Thompson, was there; and so were the technicians who would operate the complex heart-lung machine. Its invention two decades ago had made possible open-heart surgery, and dramatically increased the range of surgery that was feasible.

'Are we all ready?' Parker Brown's voice broke through Leakey's reverie about a young West Indian lady he had met, whose pliability suggested she would be an excellent limbo dancer, even with her clothes on.

At 8.36 a.m., Parker Brown made the first incision, in the fleshy part of the middle of the upper thigh. About two or three centimetres under the surface Parker Brown found a solid, healthy-looking vein. He gradually worked it out, like a sparrow pulling a worm from a flower bed. When he had enough, he clamped off either end, cut it, and put it into a metal dish. Leakey took this, and began washing it through with saline solution to clean it. At the same time, he examined it minutely for tiny holes. If he found any, they would have to be sewn up.

Now Parker Brown made a long incision from just below the neck to just above the navel – more than a foot long. To stop the tiny blood vessels which feed the skin from bleeding, he sealed the length of the incision with an electric cautery. A thin cloud of acrid-smelling smoke – it smelt like burned steak – briefly hung above the body on the table.

He held out his hand, and Sister Patience Smith handed him an electric saw. A nurse in the corner switched on the current; Parker Brown began cutting into the sternum, or breastbone. Retractors pulled back the ribs and held them apart to reveal the pericardium: the heart's fibrous sheath, which contains a lubricated membrane – like the lining of a joint – allowing the heart to beat almost without friction.

Sister Patience put a pair of surgeon's scissors into Parker Brown's hand – no word had passed between them since the operation had started – and he cut open the sheath, to reveal the slowly-beating heart.

This double muscle, weighing less than one pound, and about the size of a large clenched fist, is a spectacular sight: under the brilliant, shadowless theatre lights it is almost gold, with traceries of blue and black and areas that are wine coloured and mauve . . . In this particular heart there was an ugly dark grey patch of dead muscle near the apex.

'I don't like the look of that,' said Parker Brown, that master of meiosis. (It was almost equivalent to General Custer remarking: 'I say, what a lot of Indians.')

'Well, let's get on with it.'

And so started a day that went down in Midland General history.

'There's a telephone call for you, sir,' Miss Fletcher told Dr Armstrong over the intercom system. 'It's about your reply to the advertisement in . . . The Advertisers' Gazette.' There was an unusual note in her voice. Armstrong, that excellent diagnostician, noticed it at once.

'Something wrong, Miss Fletcher?'

'Well, sir . . . The caller. It's Capper.'

Arnold Godfrey Capper had left the Midland General – left, it should be added, entirely at his own initiative. No pressure had been applied, unless the silent prayers and unspoken wishes of a great number of the staff could be taken as pressure.

Although there were many perks to be had by an enterprising, imaginative porter, although there was considerable profit to be made with a man with commercial enterprise, and although there was a fair amount of unidentifiable hospital property that was not screwed down, Capper felt that he could do better in the outside world. Some activity that would not involve time clocks and PAYE would be better suited to his peculiar talents.

'Besides,' he had confided to Sister Washington, Doreen Holland, Nicola Stevens and one or two others when he announced his departure, 'they don't understand me any more. It's not like the old days. And they don't seem to appreciate my sense of humour now.'

There was a strained silence. Then Doreen proffered: 'Be fair, Capper. Sometimes it was a bit . . . '

'Rudimentary,' Sister Washington helped her.

'Yes, a bit rudimentary. I mean, there was that time when you hid in the mortuary behind one of the corpses, and when poor Mr Johnson came in, you said in that horrible voice: "Help! I want a second opinion!" '

'How is Mr Johnson now?' asked Nicola.

'Recovering,' said Doreen. 'Lucky he had a strong heart.'

'But he'll never go into a mortuary again,' said Sister Washington. 'Well, maybe once more.'

'Besides,' Capper said, 'there doesn't seem to be a niche for me. The whole place has changed.'

The three women looked at each other. To them the Midland General seemed as immutable as the Pyramids.

The truth of it was that Capper's ingenuity in making money inside the hospital was not up to inflation and a general growing suspicion of everything he did – even when it was honest. So, at last he had succumbed to the overtures of Big Harry to join him in one or two ventures outside.

'It's Capper,' Miss Fletcher repeated. 'Capper, who used to be here,' she added unnecessarily.

'Calling about my reply to the advertisement?' said Armstrong, a little disconcerted. 'All right, put him through.'

Of course, before Capper had been put through to Dr Armstrong's secretary the switchboard operator had asked who was calling. When she heard the answer 'Come off it, Lil. You haven't forgotten me already, have you?' she was so surprised that she quite forgot to operate the key that cut her off from the conversation, and accidentally overheard what Capper and Dr Armstrong had to say to each other. She was so surprised that she was unable to pull herself together sufficiently to operate the cut-off key for the entire three minutes of the talk.

'Hello, Dr Armstrong. Mister Capper here. I got your answer to our advertisement, under Box Number 935.'

'Hello, Capper. Mr Capper. I didn't realise you had put it in.'

'Me and my associates,' Capper said comfortably. 'And I must say I was very pleased to hear from *you*. You're the sort of gentleman we cater for. We've got what you might call quite a high class clientele. Now, what exactly was you looking for?'

'Well, the one in your advertisement – '

'To tell you the truth, that's just to arouse interest, as you might say. We got all shapes, sizes and colours available; English, foreign, whatever takes your fancy. Look, why don't I come along and have a word with you, get an idea of what you'd like and tell you what we can supply you with? Then we could take it from there.'

'Well . . . ' Armstrong said doubtfully.

'Of course, you can rely on our complete discretion. You know me, Dr Armstrong,' said Capper in his 'sincere' voice. Armstrong felt there was no answer he could reasonably give to that. 'But just one last word . . . '

'Yes?' said Armstrong, hoping desperately it *would* be only one, but knowing that it was a vain hope.

'Nothing cheap. I mean, if you're after something cheap that's going to cause you trouble before you know where you are, I'm not your man.'

'Quite,' said Armstrong. He felt he was losing the encounter.

'For an ex-colleague and gent like you, I'll personally find a lovely little trouble-free model,' Capper continued.

Capper proposed a time for a meeting later that day. 'I'll just see,' said Armstrong, looking for his diary. Miss Fletcher, listening on the extension, just stopped herself taking it in to him, unasked. She put her phone back on the hook as Armstrong called to her, took in the diary, and whizzed out again to carry on listening.

Armstrong reluctantly confirmed the rendezvous, and hung up. He was not naïve enough to believe that no one else would be aware of his date with Capper. Armstrong himself had said it often enough: the hospital had a secret information gathering and disseminating system that whacked the KGB hollow.

'Still,' he said to himself, 'why shouldn't a man of my age cut a dash a little, if he feels like it. Why *shouldn't* I buy a sports car?'

The rest of the hospital – Parker Brown excepted, perhaps – would probably agree with him. The trouble was, by the time the garbled story, becoming more lurid each time it was passed on, became general knowledge, everyone believed that Dr Armstrong was looking for something very different from a car . . . something very much more exciting and unmechanical.

Shortly after eleven o'clock, Parker Brown was nearing the end of the coronary bypass. After opening up the patient, he had inserted the transparent plastic tubes to connect him to the heart-lung machine, which would take over his life-maintaining functions. Brian Fearn's gallon of blood was no longer driven round his body by his ailing heart, but by the machine. Every forty seconds or so the entire supply of blood circulated through the machine where it was oxygenated – the job the lungs would normally do – and back into the body. The heart, meanwhile, was motionless, inert, and Parker Brown could work right inside it.

He took about 12 cm of the big vein from the leg, and started a task of such minute precision that it almost defies belief. His intention was to sew one end of the by-pass into the aorta, the largest blood vessel in the body; and the other end to the coronary artery beyond the 'bottleneck' in the aorta. The needles and sutures required to do this work are so incredibly fine that some people cannot actually see the suture itself with the naked eye. Only recently has it been possible to manufacture these sutures and (curved) needles, which are held in a sort of pair of tweezers. Their existence is one of the things that have made this and similar operations, possible.

As Parker Brown stitched on – he would be nearly fifty minutes on this alone – he was deciding that he would do some more training in London, if he could arrange it later, this time on the techniques of operating while using a special microscope. The young surgeons who were brought up on it, and the older ones who were not too reactionary to want to learn, all sang its praises long and loud.

But it'll have to wait for the moment, Parker Brown thought. *First I have this day to get through.*

When he was finished, when the vein was securely in place, the moment of truth arrived. The clamp would be taken off the aorta, and the heart-lung machine stopped.

Sister Smith was ready with the two big defibrillation discs connected to an electricity supply. Sometimes, when the heart has been stopped and then started again, it 'forgets' how to beat regularly, and begins a rapid, unco-ordinated twitching. Ventricular fibrillation, the twitching of the muscles which actually pump the blood, is highly dangerous, but it can sometimes be corrected by a mild electric shock.

Parker Brown's voice was steady as if he were ordering a cup of tea. 'I'm taking the main clamp off . . . now.' He paused for half a second that seemed like an aeon. 'Stop the machine.' Everyone in the theatre held his breath. It was a moment of supreme tension and drama.

Fearn's heart twitched once, then almost immediately began to beat regularly and strongly.

'Hm,' said Parker Brown. 'I think that'll do.'

There is no applause in operating theatres, not even in the gallery; but there was some thunderous silent cheering by the young doctors and the nursing staff.

'Who's in Theatre B?' Parker Brown asked.

Van Kroll looked at him for a moment, then went to study the copy of the day's schedule. 'Mr Mount, sir. The porta-caval shunt.'

'Very well. Close up this patient, please, doctor. When you've finished, come and join us there.'

The rest of the theatre staff looked at Parker Brown. Thompson, the anaesthetist, who knew Parker Brown better than anyone – except possibly Sister Smith – had the first niggling suspicion of what Parker Brown might be up to. But his wildest guess wouldn't have been right.

Chapter Six

'We've tried everything we could think of to find out who you are,' Alison Moxey said. 'But . . . ' She smiled wryly. 'Have you remembered anything since I spoke to you?'

Alison and John Smith were in the Day Room of his ward: the room where patients who could leave their beds went to read, watch television, or gossip. Normally there were quite a few people using it, but the sight of a doctor talking confidentially to a patient inhibited them from entering. Alison was sitting on the arm of an easy chair to put herself at the same height as John in his wheelchair, his plastered leg carefully propped up. It was the fourth time she had been to see him since he had been admitted to the ward, a fact which had not escaped the nursing staff. Nothing much did. As Alison walked into the ward, Sister Washington and Doreen exchanged a wide-eyed 'innocent' look.

'Everything before I woke up in the train, and saw the name of the station, is still a complete and utter blank. That's the first thing I can remember: Middleton Central,' he replied.

Alison had an idea. 'We know you came off the London train, but had you booked to here, or somewhere farther on? What did your ticket say?'

'I know it sounds silly, but I don't think I even looked.'

'It's not silly. You don't look at your ticket when you give it up. The collector does,' she said.

John smiled. 'That's true.'

'Apparently you had a handbag and a suitcase, but it now seems certain that when you were knocked down they were stolen. No help there.'

'I'm putting you to an awful lot of trouble,' he said, looking worried.

'Of course you're not,' Alison said, touching his hand. 'Anyway, it's not very original, but trouble is a hospital's business.'

John smiled vaguely, but didn't say anything. Unconsciously, he was rubbing the third finger of his left hand with the fingers of the other. He caught Alison's eye as she watched him, and held out his left hand. 'I don't know why I was doing that. It was as if . . .'

'If you were turning a ring round and round on your finger.' Alison nodded.

'But I don't have a ring. Besides, men don't wear wedding rings.'

'Some do,' Alison said, making quite sure that her voice was neutral, and wondering why she *was* making sure it was neutral. She looked more closely at the finger. 'You used to wear a ring,' she said. 'I can see the mark it left.'

'Then what happened to it?'

She shrugged. 'You took it off. Or perhaps somebody stole that, too.'

'No, I don't think so,' he said positively, then paused, surprised by his own certainty. His face became puzzled. 'I don't understand how it is I can lose all my memory about myself up to a couple of days ago . . . ' He broke off, as if saying this had at last really brought home his situation to him, as if he hadn't really fully comprehended it until now. He became sad, and more than a little frightened. After a moment he pulled himself together. 'If I can't remember who I am, where I come from, what I do, anything, why haven't I forgotten words, how to count, days of the week – things like that?'

'That happens with amnesia. It *is* selective: the sort of amnesia where *everything* is wiped out of the mind does happen, but it's very rare.'

'Yes. Oddly enough, I seem to know that,' he said.

'John,' Alison said slowly. 'You don't mind me calling you John?'

'I wish you would. It gives me some sort of identity. And it makes me feel . . . less alone. As if I have a . . . sort of friend.' He smiled to cover his embarrassment.

'Yes,' Alison replied in a tone that made him look at her sharply. Then he smiled, but with warmth this time. 'John, I can take care of your leg, and cure that, but I can't do anything for your amnesia. So, will you see one of our psychiatrists?'

His face darkened. 'Do I have to?'

'No, of course you don't *have* to. But if you want to get better . . . ' He still seemed unenthusiastic. 'Most people do resist seeing a psychiatrist at first,' she said. 'Even these days "being seen by the psychiatrist" seems to have some sort of stigma about it – quite wrongly.'

'I don't think it's because of that,' John said.

'And perhaps, subconsciously, you don't want to get your memory back,' she said. There was a long, still silence. 'John, sooner or later . . . ' She left it in the air.

'Very well. Who will it be?' he said at last.

'Dr Bauer. He's a German. Oh, quite young, and pleasant. I'm sure you'll like him. I thought you'd probably get on better with him than Dr Kennedy – Barbara Kennedy, that is. Man to man, and all that.' She was aware that she was talking too much, but couldn't stop.

Alison's pocket bleeper came to her rescue. It sounded, making them both jump a little. 'I've got to go. I'll arrange for Dr Bauer to come and see you as soon as he can. Take care of yourself.' She hurried out, astonished with herself for that last remark.

She hurried to the nearest phone and called the switchboard operator. 'You're wanted in Casualty, doctor,' the operator told her.

As Alison hurried along the corridor to the lift, she wondered what on earth had got into her.

'Take care of yourself'? What sort of remark was that? she asked herself. *Look, you know all about doctors getting involved with their patients, so what are you doing?* Another part of her mind told her not to be stupid. Good lord, she'd only known him for something like a couple of days. How could she be 'getting involved' *with him? Her final thought* was a bombshell.

'Only' *a couple of days? Just how long does it take?*

The portacaval shunt operation Parker Brown performed next had certain basic similarities with the coronary by-pass operation. It is relatively less complicated – no heart-lung machine is needed – but it carries nearly as much risk for the patient; and that inherent risk is increased because the patients who need this operation are nearly always in a terrible physical state. In a portacaval shunt the surgeon makes a communication between the portal vein and the inferior vena cava. (This is a big vein that is not affected by the disease of the liver that causes all the problems.) This procedure relieves the back pressure on the veins of the oesophagus. It is always a very bloody operation, because the very high back pressure means that the minutest injury can cause the veins to bleed massively. It's not unusual for a patient to need two and a half gallons of blood during the operation.

Parker Brown operated for little less than an hour and a half, which took him and the surgical team up to lunchtime. When he prepared to close up Mr Mount his portal hypertension was already significantly lowered. There was no more leakage of fluid (oedema) into the abdominal cavity, but Mr Mount's alcohol-induced cirrhosis of the liver, which had caused the trouble, was irreversible. Parker Brown had improved his condition, but he could not cure him.

'Who is in Theatre C?' he asked Terence Leakey unexpectedly.

Leakey went over to the schedule. 'Mrs Jacobson, sir. Mitral stenosis.' This is a heart valve which has become tight and sticky. The blood passes only with great difficulty, and frequently back pressure builds up, as in portal hypertension; in this case, enlarging part of the heart which has to cope with the extra strain. Putting it crudely, the surgeon sticks his finger into the heart, and unsticks the valve by prodding it with his finger. If that doesn't work, he puts in a curved knife and slits the valve open.

'I don't suppose Mrs Jacobson's actually in the theatre, sir,' Leakey said.

'And why not?'

'Well, she was on Dr Bywaters' list. I expect she's not been sent up.'

'I assure you she has, Dr Leakey,' Parker Brown said.

'Oh,' said Leakey, inadequately. 'Then shall I have her sent back to the ward?'

Parker Brown checked in the final stages of his work. 'Sent back to the ward?' he said in a voice that was a superb orchestration of utter astonishment. 'Why?' he added after a moment.

Dr Leakey made an indeterminate gesture. 'She was on Dr Bywaters' list, sir,' he repeated.

'Since Dr Bywaters is by now in the vicinity of the Royal Courts of Justice, London WC2,' Parker Brown continued, in his most histrionic style, 'I wonder, Dr Leakey, that you do not suggest the patient be sent *there.*'

Once again Staff Nurse Lucy Hobbs thought *Oh, so he's in one of* those *moods,* but she wisely kept silent; and as there was no young Dr Lewis there to exchange hot glances with, she went unnoticed.

'*I* shall perform the operation on Mrs Jacobson,' Parker Brown announced. 'What about the other patients on the schedule?' Leakey asked diffidently. 'Shall I tell the wards – ?'

Parker Brown interrupted. 'I have already sent round instructions that *all* patients on today's schedule are to be sent up to theatre unless I give express instructions to the contrary.'

'Are there any patients I can take, sir?' van Kroll asked politely.

'Thank you, Dr van Kroll, but I shall need you – both of you – to assist me in my own operations. All of them.'

A sudden silence descended on the theatre, broken only by the hum of the air conditioning and the soft bleeping of electronic monitors. Even the normally absolutely unflappable Sister Patience Smith turned to look at Parker Brown in astonishment. Wim van Kroll thought his English must have let him down and he had misunderstood something.

Thompson, the anaesthetist stared hard at Parker Brown, too. His earlier wild suspicion suddenly seemed rather less wild.

But not even Parker Brown . . . ? thought Thompson. *Surely, not even him.*

Miss Fletcher, Dr Armstrong's secretary, was a young woman of considerable resource and aplomb. She had to be: in hospitals, like in law courts, prisons and football ground terraces, humanity is not seen at its best. She was not unused to seeing loving families in screeching arguments over the disposal of a parent's goods before that parent had gone through the formality of dying. She had seen people with little more than ingrowing toenails behaving as if they'd been condemned to the meat-grinder. She had also seen many instances of quiet self-sacrifice and unostentatious courage. There are two sides to every coin.

Julie Fletcher, then, was accustomed to keeping the barrier of a straight face between her thoughts and the people she was dealing with. This time her self-control had slipped: her mouth was open with dazzled disbelief as she regarded the visitor.

He had introduced himself quite ordinarily. 'Arnold Capper to see Dr Armstrong by appointment,' he had announced in a plummy voice, as if they had not known each other for years. The new, somewhat strained accent was not what rattled her. It was Capper's *appearance.*

His thinning locks had suddenly become suspiciously luxuriant and immaculate. His clothes were . . . well, they were expensive, for a start. The shirt had a collar with points so large that if Capper ran into a stiff breeze he would run the risk of taking off. His suit – his *three-piece* suit, with *a waistcoat*! – was admirably cut. There was no denying it, even if the man who had cut it was either hopelessly colour-blind, or wearing very dark glasses at the time. On Capper's left wrist was a watch that told the time in hours, minutes and seconds, the date, day, and probably the time of high tide at Greenwich as well. On his right wrist was a gold identity bracelet, although a man dressed like Capper needed an identity bracelet as much as a funfair needed a sign saying 'Funfair'.

'Good afternoon, Capper . . . Mr Capper,' Julie Fletcher managed to say at last. 'You look very . . . ' A suitable word escaped her, and she had to settle for ' . . . very prosperous.'

Capper gave her a smile that was meant to be modest, but which came out smug.

She called Dr Armstrong on the intercom to announce Capper, then showed him in. She was bursting with curiosity, and it became almost insupportable when Armstrong told her 'See that we're not disturbed.'

Julie Fletcher decided to interpret this as 'See we're not disturbed . . . *by anyone else*' and set to thinking what excuse she could find to burst in and perhaps overhear something. When Dr Reuben Garrison, the senior pathologist, arrived with an urgent réquisition that needed Armstrong's signature, Julie decided to take it in immediately although it could well have waited until evening post time. As soon as Garrison had left, she walked silently to the communicating door, took a deep breath . . . then knocked and walked in with one movement. Her worst (or best?) fears were justified.

Capper was saying: 'Just you leave it to me, Dr Armstrong. I'll find you the sweetest little number you could imagine.'

And Armstrong started to say: 'Look, Capper, I don't want anyone to know about it – ' before he noticed Julie Fletcher, and stopped dead.

She got the signature and went out, her head whirling. If she hadn't heard it with her own ears . . . the final piece of irrefutable evidence . . . *Capper was fixing up Dr Armstrong with a girl!*

Julie went all over it again. There *couldn't* be any mistake.

But of course, there was.

By late afternoon, the surgical teams in the operating theatres realised that Parker Brown was going to do the entire operating schedule alone. The certainty dawned on them after the mitral valve operation.

Wim van Kroll had seen several of these operations, and had assisted at a few; Leakey had seen Parker Brown himself do some.

The tight valve in Mrs Jacobson's heart had caused so much back pressure that one of the ventricles, or chambers, had swollen monstrously. Parker Brown put a purse-string stitch about five centimetres above the tip of the dilated chamber, and van Kroll put a clamp below the chamber. Then Parker Brown cut off the tip of the appendage, took his glove off and inserted his bare finger into the beating heart, feeling for the valve. At the same time van Kroll pulled the purse-string stitch tight round his finger.

Parker Brown found the valve, and gently applied increasing pressure on it. The two leaves of the valve were badly stuck together by calcified deposits, and Parker Brown had no success for nearly two minutes. His brow was beaded with sweat, and twice Patience Smith had to dab it dry.

Then at last he gave a grunt of satisfaction. 'That . . . has . . . done it, I think,' he said. The valve had been freed, and was working nearly normally again. He slowly withdrew his finger, and as he did it, van Kroll pulled tight the silk suture with the purse-string stitch, closing the hole, to prevent any leakage of blood from the heart.

Equipment for use in operating theatres is rigorously checked and rechecked during manufacture, but there are weaknesses and faults that no amount of inspection and examination can reveal.

The silk suture being pulled by van Kroll broke.

A hole as big as a tap appeared in the heart, and blood sprayed out of the beating heart in a terrifying cascade. Even the most experienced nurses and other doctors were appalled by the sight of it.

Van Kroll quickly pulled himself together and reached for a clamp, just about the same time that Sister Smith picked one up to hand to him. But already Parker Brown had pinched together the hole in the heart, cutting off the killing jet of blood.

'Put another purse-string stitch in for me, if you will, Dr van Kroll,' he said with no audible signs of concern. 'I think I'd better hold on to this for the moment.'

When Mrs Jacobson had been sewn up she was taken to Intensive Care. Some of the nursing staff looked as if they'd like to join her. Parker Brown turned to Staff Nurse Hobbs. 'Have one of the porters go down to the canteen and bring up coffee and sandwiches, or whatever the other doctors require, please Staff,' he said. 'We shall be carrying on in Theatre A.' He turned to Leakey. 'Who is there now?'

Leakey looked at him like an ebony statue of Disbelief. Parker Brown had to repeat the question. 'Mr Maskell. Cholec – ' He tried twice, but couldn't manage 'Cholecystotomy.' 'Gall bladder,' he finished lamely. In other circumstances it would have been a music hall joke, but everyone was too shattered to see any humour in it.

'Very well,' said Parker Brown. 'I'll use the theatre team

already there. Sister, you and your nurses can all go to eat, or whatever you want to do. Back in an hour, please.'

'I'll stay, if you don't mind, Mr Parker Brown,' Patience Smith said without expression.

'As you like, Sister,' Parker Brown said cheerfully. He had expected no less of her.

When Parker Brown was in the Middle East, the Texan neuro-surgeon who had met Guy Wallman in America told him of an exploit by one of the world-famous Texas heart surgeons. It had gone into medical mythology, even though it did actually happen. At the age of sixty-two this man had gone through the whole day's operating schedule on his own. He had operated for an unbroken eighteen and a half hours on eleven patients.

It was now clear what Parker Brown was going to do: he was going to emulate this American, and do the entire day's schedule, solo.

At least, he was going to try, even if he died in the attempt.

Or someone did.

Neville Bywaters arrived back at the Midland General in a filthy mood. He'd been given a very tough time of it in the witness box by a highly skilled barrister whose savage sarcasm, under a veneer of politeness thinned out with deliberate incredulity, made Bywaters smart. What made it seem all so bitterly unfair to Bywaters was that he was not allowed to answer back. Answer, yes; but not answer back. There is a difference, and the judge made that plain to Bywaters on the one occasion when his calm deserted him.

When Bywaters left the box his look at the barrister said louder than words: 'If I ever get you on an operating table . . . '

He had caught the last train back from London by the skin of his teeth, and found that it did not have a dining car. The euphemistically named buffet car – a sort of snack bar and rubbish tip on noisy wheels – could offer only lukewarm tea in plastic containers, and highly suspect pies or limp rolls containing two microscopically thin slices of anaemic tomato. To give the whole thing a *je ne sais quoi,* the attendant had a jacket and trousers that was a sort of walking history of the buffet car's menus for the past month, complete with samples.

The journey had steadily become worse. There were no taxis at the station, and on the walk back in the humid summer night, heavy with thunder, Bywaters had been caught in one of the many sudden bursts of torrential rain.

His spirits began to revive fractionally in the canteen with some cold consommé and a crisp salad, but then Geoffrey Nollet, a medical registrar, came and sat with him. Bywaters disliked Nollet, who was a foul-mouthed, shifty-looking individual with all the earmarks, as Barbara Kennedy once observed, of a failed masturbator. Bywaters privately believed that Nollet had become a doctor only to be able to look at the nasty pictures in medical books. Not the least of his unlovable features was his determined refusal to know when he wasn't wanted.

He followed Bywaters out of the canteen and to the glass-walled corridor connecting the main hospital block with the residential block, still talking. As they walked along it, a couple came running through another downpour towards the door in the middle of the corridor. They rushed in, not seeing Bywaters and Nollet in their headlong dash with rain streaming into their eyes.

They were Suzy Palmer and a young physician, newly arrived to the hospital, whom Bywaters knew only by sight, not by name. Bywaters did not spare a second's glance for the man.

Suzy was wearing a thin, nylon blouse and a short cotton skirt. The torrential shower had completely soaked the blouse and plastered it against her; her dark nipples, made prominent and hard by the cool rain, were as evident as if she were completely naked. In fact, the effect, once more, was more arousing than ordinary nakedness: there was an extra wet, smooth, silken quality of the skin suggesting all sorts of tactile sensations. Her skirt, too, was plastered against her, outlining her legs and thighs. It was transparently obvious that she was wearing little more than a G-string.

She looked Bywaters directly in the face, and laughed, then hurried down the corridor. He turned and watched her go, his mouth suddenly dry. He didn't even hear Nollet's coarse remarks, which was just as well.

'Bloody hell,' said Nollet. 'I reckon she'll leave him for dead before morning. Did you see those tits! Poke your eye out! Christ, I wouldn't half like to – ' His drooling was cut off by the slamming of a distant door.

Bywaters at last moved on.

'Oh, by the way,' Nollet said, 'you've been in town all day, haven't you? Then you haven't heard about your chief.'

'What?'

'Parker Brown. He's gone mad.'

The saga was almost ended: Parker Brown was with his last patient. By now the entire hospital had heard what he was doing. Those who hadn't heard the story from the nurses who were given an hour's break, learned from ward sisters, who were astonished to be told to keep sending patients up to theatre at extraordinary hours.

Sister Smith was still at his side, but even that nerveless woman had needed one brief spell away from the theatre while Sister Wilson, half terrified, replaced her. Leakey and van Kroll had also had short breaks, technically on stand-by duty in Casualty while Alison Moxey took over for them in turn. Thompson, the anaesthetist, had handed over to young Seton for two of the less taxing operations while he got the crick out of his back.

Parker Brown dropped a gallstone into a small metal dish like a gold nugget into a prospector's pan. It clinked noisily. Others followed it. Thompson looked up sharply as a strange, soft noise became audible. He could not identify it, and was just about to mention it to Parker Brown when he realised with a shock what the strange sound was. *Parker Brown was humming.* No one, ever, had heard him *hum* in theatre. But this was not an ordinary day.

When the patient was being wheeled out, Parker Brown turned to Leakey. 'Who's next, Dr Leakey?'

'That's the last one, sir. There aren't any more.'

Parker Brown feigned astonishment. 'No more? Are you sure?'

'Quite sure.'

Parker Brown surveyed the theatre staff. 'Well, I suppose we'd better call it a day. Goodnight.' And he hurried out.

It was nearly a quarter to twelve. Parker Brown had been on his feet for seventeen hours, and had performed twelve operations, at least three of them enormously difficult ones. Van Kroll had an excruciating headache; Leakey felt his eyes were going to pop out. He said afterwards he was squinting like a bag of nails, looking at Parker Brown's stitches.

Next morning when Parker Brown entered the Doctors' Common Room, a group of surgeons were talking noisily: van Kroll, Leakey, Seton, Alison Moxey and Thompson among them. Wallman was also there. As soon as they saw Parker Brown they became silent, as if someone had pulled a master switch.

He walked to the coffee table. Wallman came over to him and said quietly:

'What were you trying to prove?'

Parker Brown took his time about answering. He poured his coffee, added sugar, and stirred. Then he replied. 'I was not *trying* to prove anything. I *did* prove one thing. It would be unwise to order any tombstones for me yet.'

Pride, of course, goes before a fall.

Chapter Seven

Dr Paul Bauer was a tall – 6ft. 2in. – blond, imposing man of just under forty years of age, and undeniably handsome. His family originally came from Munich, which is famous for its industries, famous old buildings and university; and infamous for being the headquarters of the Nazi party and for the Munich Agreement of 1938. His father was a psychiatrist and taught at the university as well as practising at the hospital. After a while the family moved to Dresden, also famous for its industries (but not porcelain – Dresden porcelain is made at Meissen) and less happily known for the horrific Allied air raid in World War II.

Ironically, the Bauers did not die in that raid because they were in a concentration camp: Dr Hans Bauer Senior had made no secret of his detestation of the Nazis. (It is worth recalling that before the war the majority of prisoners in German concentration camps were Germans.)

The mother did not survive the war; father and son did. They were somehow reunited, and returned to Dresden where Dr Bauer Senior continued practising, and Paul studied medicine. Shortly after Paul qualified his father died. Paul escaped from Eastern Germany and came to England.

Unlike Latins, Germans can often learn to speak English without accent. Bauer spoke it fluently but could not eliminate the last trace of German intonation. Almost all his women patients found his accent attractive; the older ones found it reminded them irresistibly of Anton Walbrook. Suggestions that Bauer deliberately cultivated his foreign accent like Maurice Chavalier, were unfounded. His delivery was idiosyncratic: measured, deliberate. It was a style that you found either fascinating, or maddening.

Bauer was reputed to be humourless; when he did make a wry, amusing remark, it was put down to chance. This was unfair: he was much sharper-witted than people gave him credit for. They underestimated him, perhaps because of his stern, Heidelberg dueller's face. This too, was deceptive. He was a gentle man who abhorred violence, physical or mental.

His interest in psychiatry came less from a desire to serve his fellow-man than a sort of crossword-puzzle interest in solving problems.

Bauer was at John Smith's bedside, the curtains drawn around the bed. He had given his first consultations there so John would perhaps feel a little more secure in what were to him his most familiar surroundings. There was no real lack of privacy; somehow the thin material managed to give an effective sense of isolation from the rest of the cubicle: and if anyone spoke quietly behind the curtain, it was almost impossible for other patients in the ward to make out what was said.

Not that there was much from John Smith to be overheard, either now or at the other consultations. He tried to cooperate, but Bauer could find no subjects which caused John even the most minute discomfort or reaction. The well-known word-association test had proved unilluminating. To 'wife' John had instantly replied 'husband', which was about as neutral as you could be. He didn't answer 'anger', or 'hate', or 'sad'. Later in the test Bauer had said 'Husband', and John replied 'marriage'. The key-word 'home' had brought the reaction 'comfort'.

Bauer closed his notebook and rose. 'I'm sorry, I'm not being very helpful, am I?' John said.

'You are doing what you can. No one can do better than that,' Bauer said, then spoiled it by adding 'You are not *trying* to be obstructive. At least, not consciously,' he concluded, utterly annihilating the effect of his first sentences. He pulled back the curtain. 'I shall see you at the same time tomorrow.'

Alison Moxey was waiting near the nurses' station. Bauer was somehow quite certain she had been waiting there for some time.

'How's it going?' she asked. 'Has he told you anything?'

'To your first question, no progress; to your second, no,

nothing of significance.' Then with the most plumb of straight faces and a fractionally stronger German accent he said 'But we have ways of making people talk.' Alison looked at him, bewildered. She couldn't believe he was unaware of the funny side of what he had said, yet his face was utterly humourless. She decided to let it pass.

'I've seen him in the ward here a number of times. Perhaps it would help if we transferred him to one of my wards in the Psychiatric Wing,' Bauer said.

'I don't think that would be a good idea at all,' Alison replied instantly.

Bauer permitted himself a major demonstration of surprise. He raised an eyebrow and said 'Oh?'

'I want to keep an eye on that rather tricky fracture,' Alison explained. Sister Washington, who was passing, barely managed to hide her own astonishment. The fracture of John's fibula (which is not even the weight-bearing bone of the lower leg) was healing remarkably well, thanks to Alison's early treatment. 'Besides,' Alison went on, 'I'm sure – I hope you'll agree – that he stands a better chance of quick recovery in the more . . . normal atmosphere of this surgical ward.'

Bauer looked up and down the ward corridor. 'In this ward I've noticed patients with ulcers, one who's had his appendix removed, two who've had gall-bladder operations, one with a compound fracture of the leg and severe abdominal injuries . . . Is that *your* idea of normality, Doctor?'

Alison looked ill at ease. 'I meant . . .'

'You meant, I suppose, that *my* ward is full of gibbering neurotics and psychotics.'

'No, of course not.'

'I don't suppose it will make a great deal of difference one way or the other,' Bauer said. 'He might as well stay here; I'm short of beds, anyway. I'll keep you informed of any progress I make with him.' He gave Alison a nod that was meant to be friendly, and left her.

Alison walked over to John's bed. When he saw her approaching, his face lit up. Alison returned his smile. If she had any more thoughts about 'becoming involved', she quickly suppressed them.

Dr Bauer sat in the Doctors' Common Room, staring at John Smith's file. He was giving it a great deal of attention, considering there was so little in it. Barbara Kennedy came and sat beside him. He was unaware of her until she said: 'Any problems?'

He turned and looked at her. 'No, thank you. I have enough.'

'You know that thing about the shortest books in the world?' she asked. ' "The Book of Italian War Heroes"; "The Book of Irish Thinkers"; "The Book of German 19th Century Humour" . . . That sort of thing?'

'No. Why?'

Barbara was going to say: 'Because it should be altered to "The Book of *20th* Century German Humour", but changed in mid-thought, and said instead: 'Because you seem to have one there. There isn't much in that file.'

'John Smith, the amnesia patient,' Bauer said. 'I can't imagine *what* he's refusing to remember. There's no physical reason for the amnesia. There aren't any physical indications that he's suffering from stress – indications like heart trouble, or digestive disorders, anything like that. He's obviously not short of money.'

'A woman,' suggested Barbara.

'I don't think so. There would be some signs of stress, I should think. Somehow . . . And . . . it doesn't sit right with him.'

'Perhaps he's a poor little rich boy, fleeing from a golden cage.'

Bauer looked at her. 'I sometimes wonder what you read, apart from technical journals.'

Barbara grinned, then a thought struck her. 'You said you didn't think it was a woman. Is he a homosexual?'

'Even more improbable. Which reminds me: are you a friend of Alison Moxey?'

Barbara looked at him. 'I don't see the connection, but never mind. I'm friendly with her, but we're hardly intimates. We don't have-to-heart chats, exchanging secrets and all that.'

'I should hope not.' Bauer paused. 'You might keep an eye on her. I think she may be taking too much interest in John Smith.'

'What on earth do you mean?' Barbara asked.

'Exactly that. Didn't I make myself clear?'

He got up and walked away, leaving Barbara looking very thoughtful.

'Oh, by the way,' Alison told John. 'We've informed the police about you, to see if there are any missing person reports that could fit you.' He looked suddenly worried. 'Have you remembered something?' she asked. Then, 'What's the matter?'

'There's nothing the *matter*. It's simply the idea of involving the police, I suppose. I mean, having them asking questions the way they do, trying to find out . . . ' He left it.

'Find out what?'

'I don't know.' He was quite irritable now. 'Find out about you, your past, and that.'

'I'm sorry, but it was the obvious thing to do.'

'Yes, I suppose it was. It shouldn't have upset me. Unless . . . '

Alison knew what he meant. 'No, I can't believe you'd be in trouble with the police. Not you.'

'It could be a reason for my amnesia, though, couldn't it?'

'It's not. I'm certain.'

He smiled wryly. 'Feminine intuition?'

'No, it's more than that. I can tell.' It was her turn to smile. 'Well, perhaps it *is* feminine intuition. Emotional, rather than rational. But I can't believe that you've done anything wrong. I wouldn't be – ' She stopped, appalled by her line of thought, and the unthinking admission that she had almost made.

But she might just as well have voiced it. He knew exactly what she was going to say.

The young physician's name – the one who had been with Suzy Palmer the previous evening – was Tony Callie, Bywaters learned. When he saw him in the canteen, eating lunch, he asked Jeannie, the cashier, who he was. Jeannie knew everyone.

Callie looked as if he'd been out in the rain all night, instead of coming in with Suzy. He didn't look pleasantly exhausted; more miserably washed out. Bywaters went to his table. The moment he had sat down Bywaters realised something for the first time. Suzy lived in town, not at the hospital, so she must have passed the night in Callie's room. There was a sudden acrid taste in his mouth, quite putting him off his own food. It couldn't have been caused by normal indigestion: every heterosexual doctor in the place must have had a girl in his room from time to time, including Bywaters himself. There was a legend that Tom Jones was going to have a revolving door fitted to his room, until he set up a permanent establishment with Penny Byron. So whatever the emotion was that stabbed Bywaters, righteousness it couldn't be. Anger? Bywaters instantly dismissed the possibility, and stopped indulging in introspection.

'Hello. I'm Neville Bywaters,' he said.

'Tony Callie. You're surgical, aren't you?'

'That's right. Parker Brown's my chief.'

'Oh, yes. I've heard a lot about him. And about him trying to get into the Guinness Book of Records, last night.' He saw Bywaters' frozen expression. 'Sorry. I'm not feeling very bright today.'

'I'm not surprised. I saw you coming in last night. With Suzy Palmer.'

'That's right, you were with that other fellow, that creep – Oh, Christ, have I done it again? Sorry – is he a friend of yours?'

'I don't think Nollet's anybody's friend.' He paused. 'She's a very attractive girl.'

'Yes. Very.' Callie attacked his food, and looked away from Bywaters as he chewed it. A shutter had come down, just as it had when Bywaters spoke to Dennis Porter about Suzy.

What was it she did to her men friends, that made them suddenly become so secretive? Bywaters wondered.

One thing was certain: she didn't spellbind them with her good nature, Bywaters decided later. He'd gone to the administration section to make enquiries about some overtime he felt had been wrongly calculated. Lorna Meadows, head of the section, had to go and find some records. She left open the door into the next office, where Suzy Palmer worked on preparing data for the computer, and getting readouts from it. Betty Galton, a nurse in the Geriatric wing, had come in to ask whether she could get her salary cheque for her holiday. Theoretically her leave didn't start until after duty tomorrow evening, but an understanding Ward Sister had let her add a day off to her leave period. Lorna Meadows had explained to Betty that the only person who could help her was Suzy.

'Sorry, but it'll take half an hour at least to get authorisation through the computer, a cheque drawn and then signed,' Suzy said with finality.

'I don't mind waiting,' Betty said, not really grasping Suzy's point.

'I do. I'm due off in quarter of an hour. Come back at ten o'clock tomorrow morning.'

'I'd be awfully grateful if you could manage it for me today. I'd like to get away early tomorrow.'

'And I'd like to get away early this evening.'

Betty Galton made one last effort. 'Look, it'd save me quite a bit of time.'

Suzy Palmer looked at her hard and said with icy venom 'You've got enough of it.' And she turned her back on Betty, leaving her standing there indecisive and rather angry. After a long moment Suzy turned back again. 'You still there?' she said acidly.

When Bywaters left a little later, his problems sorted out, he paused by Suzy.

'Couldn't you have stretched a point to help her?' he asked.

'Do I tell you how to operate?'

Bywaters wanted to hit her.

The group in the corner of the canteen looked as conspiratorial as Guy Fawkes and his bonfire boys: Barbara Kennedy, Bywaters, Greg Knight (still limping when he moved about the hospital), Alison Moxey, Seton the anaesthetist . . . Nollet wanted to join them, not because he knew what they were talking about, but because they were there. He was told there wasn't room for him, and when he said he could find a space, no one seemed to hear him.

'Just because Dr Armstrong's acting a bit . . . ' Barbara tried to find the right word.

'Potty,' said Knight.

'A bit gay – '

'What?' Alison exclaimed.

'Not *that*,' said Barbara. 'Anyway, there's probably some very simple explanation. He's won a prize, or some money – something on the pools. Yes, that's it.'

'Pools, in midsummer?' said Seton.

'Do you have to split hairs?' Barbara retorted.

'When I saw him today he was wearing a bright tie and a rose in his buttonhole,' said Alison Moxey. There was a respectful silence as everyone visualised the new, brighter Dr Armstrong.

'Look,' said Knight, 'it's obvious. He's at the funny age – '

'How old's that?' asked Bywaters.

'Depends on the individual. In your case, about now. As I was saying, he's at the funny age, and we know what Capper said to him on the phone: *"We can fix you up with whatever you like; young, old, English or foreign, blonde, brunette, you name it . . . "'*

'Are you sure that's what he said?' asked Alison.

'We got it from two seperate sources,' Knight said.

(Thus are born 'true stories' from 'reliable sources'.)

'And there was that newspaper, "The Advertisers' Gazette" – the one with all those dodgy "Lonely Hearts" ads,' Bywaters said gloomily. (Neither he nor any of the others bothered to remember that there were many other kinds of advertisement in the paper: property for sale, holiday homes, *cars . . .*)

'And *Capper's* involved,' Bywaters went on. That quashed nearly all doubts. 'Have you seen him recently? He looks like a Hong Kong pox doctor's clerk.'

'You mean he's pimping?' said Seton.

They all turned to look at him as if he'd laughed during a burial service. It was all right to think things like that, but it was very bad form actually to say them out loud.

'What are we going to *do*?' asked Bywaters.

'Somebody ought to talk to him, and warn him for his own good,' said Knight. The others round the table stirred uneasily.

'Are you volunteering?' asked Seton. Knight didn't bother to answer; he just looked at Seton.

'How *do* you tell someone like Dr Armstrong that he's making a fool of himself, getting mixed up with a younger woman?' asked Barbara Kennedy. 'I can't even get it through to some of my patients, who *want* my advice.'

'A friendly chat, man to man?' said Alison, emphasising the first 'man'.

'Supposing we draw lots,' Seton said brightly.

There began an immediate minor concerto with the sound of chairs being pushed back as the dominant theme and muttered harmonics of 'I've got to get to the ward,' 'I'm needed in Casualty,' and similar excuses as counterpoint.

Dr Armstrong, the object of his junior colleagues' concern, was in his office with Parker Brown, Kirby of the Area Health Authority, and Wallman. These last two were looking rather pleased with themselves, although Kirby's satisfaction was purely vicarious. Parker Brown sat impassively in a corner.

'The Ghazarossiam Foundation have made my unit a very handsome grant,' Wallman explained to Armstrong, not bothering to keep the gratification out of his voice. 'Lord Dellamayne phoned me unofficially today to let me know.'

'He also told the Authority,' Kirby said, 'as we are affected as well.'

'How?' said Parker Brown, not sounding at all like an Indian.

'The grant will mean that our research unit will be enlarged, and we'll take on extra staff,' Wallman broke in. 'And I'll be spending more time in the unit.'

'Are you leaving here then?' asked Parker Brown, without much real hope.

'The Authority felt that although he will have less time available for his part-time consultancy at the hospital, it would be a pity to lose his services altogether. So we have agreed to modify his contract so he can remain here.'

'Well, we can do with him,' said Parker Brown. Whatever he felt about the man personally, Parker Brown always acknowledged Wallman's surgical skills. 'Is that all?' Apparently it was, so he nodded and turned to leave. At the door he checked. 'Oh, congratulations,' he said to Wallman over his shoulder.

Armstrong spoke for the first time. 'Yes, indeed, Mr Wallman. I'm very pleased for you. It's a considerable distinction: the Ghazarossiam Foundation people are very selective.'

'It reflects on us all,' said Kirby, determined to emphasise his championship of Wallman's cause.

It was to prove a highly unfortunate remark.

Bywaters sat alone in the canteen. At least being left on his own meant the others weren't going to try to con him into having a friendly chat with Armstrong – a chat that would undoubtedly end with Bywaters being made to feel he'd gone through an automatic potato peeler.

Someone came and sat beside him. He ignored them for the moment, then looked to see who it was. He barely managed to conceal his surprise.

It was Suzy Palmer.

'D'you mind if I sit here?' she said, her tone making it obvious she didn't give a damn whether Bywaters minded or not. She wasn't even going to listen to his answer.

'I thought you were in a hurry to get away tonight,' he said coldly. He would have got up and left the table, but he still had most of his meal in front of him, and it would have looked childish.

'Only from the office. We haven't been introduced. I'm Suzy

Palmer. I know who you are.'

'I know who you are, too,' Bywaters said acidly. 'I should think everybody does.'

'Very likely,' she said, completely unconcerned.

'I thought that you weren't very helpful with that nurse.'

'I'm not paid to be helpful. Just to do my job.'

'Let me tell you something, Miss Palmer. This hospital exists to help sick people, and without nurses it couldn't function. It wouldn't have cost you much to help Betty Galton. I know one thing: she doesn't clockwatch when a patient needs help.'

'I'm sorry, I've forgotten my violin,' said Suzy nastily.

Bywaters looked at her steadily for a long while, oblivious of the fact that others in the canteeen were staring at them. Some barely concealed sniggers.

'You were a bitch to that nurse, and you carry on like some dockside tart. You come from a decent family and yet you – '

'You've been checking up on me, have you?' she said, amused.

'Somebody mentioned it,' Bywaters evaded. In fact, he'd 'casually' called into the Personnel Department and glanced at her file. It was something he didn't even want to admit to himself. 'Why do you do it, behaving like that? What the devil's wrong with you?'

'And what the devil's it got to do with you? Are you setting up as a keeper of public morals? You're free with criticism about me, Dr Bywaters; well, let me tell *you* something. Your trouble is you'd like to ask for a date yourself, but you're *scared*. You needn't be: all you have to do is ask.'

'Maybe that's the trouble,' said Bywaters. 'That's all anybody has to do: just ask. Anybody.'

Suzy laughed coarsely. 'Wrap it up any way you want, you're just plain jealous and . . . you're afraid I'd be too rich for your blood. You'd like to, but you're dead scared.'

'Don't be ridiculous!'

'For a man who's in the right you're shouting awfully loud.'

'Because you're so damned infuriating with your stupid remarks. "Scared of you" . . . ' He laughed, but not very convincingly.

'Oh, not the way you think I mean. You're afraid that if you go out with me, you may like it too much. Afraid of the brush-off afterwards.'

'You're out of your mind.'

'I'd have believed that if you'd got up and gone away when

you said I was ridiculous. Or when you said I infuriated you with my stupid remarks. But you're still here, Dr Bywaters, and so I know I'm right.'

He was hit with a double blow: the fact that she *could* be right, and the fact that she had the perception to understand him before he had understood himself.

She taunted him again with his desire to go out with her, and all that 'going out with' implied, and his lack of determination, but now she did it subtly, effectively. She achieved her end all the more easily because of Bywaters' loss of his temper. Before he quite realised what he was saying, he was agreeing to take her out. She took something from her handbag and put it on the table in front of him.

'It won't even cost you much,' she said. 'Two free tickets for the dinner show at the Wharton Towers Hotel. A friend of mine gave them to me. All you have to pay is the taxi-fare and the wine with dinner. Even the meal's paid for.' She rose from the table, and smiled at him wickedly. 'There, that wasn't too difficult, was it?'

Bywaters sat at the table, totally unaware of the attention he was getting from the other people in the canteen. He was trying to work out how he'd contrived to fix a date with Suzy Palmer – or been cornered into it, he wasn't sure which. Nor could he decide whether or not he really liked the idea of going out with her. It would lead to a great deal of caustic remarks and snide insinuations . . . Nevertheless, maybe it'd all be worth it. But she was so – *promiscuous* didn't seem to be a strong enough word.

Another thought struck him. All this time he'd been talking to her, he hadn't been aware of her make-up, and he hadn't noticed what she was wearing. This was really quite extraordinary: usually she was as obvious as a red lamp.

Bywaters was sure that this had some significance, but he couldn't work out what it was. It worried him.

Police horses are trained to keep patient, calm and unruffled when all about them is pandemonium. Matthew Armstrong had developed this talent since he had become a medical administrator, a job that called for Solomon-like qualities of judgement and an ability to walk a tightrope which is being shaken by different factions, while arrows are being shot from all sides. Patience was something that Armstrong possessed in large measure.

He was needing it. Coincidentally, he needed it for dealing with Sister Patience Smith. Although she had been at the Midland General for a relatively short period, and although most of the sister's administrative contacts had been with the Senior Nursing Officer, Armstrong had seen enough of her to form a very favourable impression. One of her qualities, he would have said, was her forthrightness, but on this occasion she was hesitant, ill at ease and uncommunicative. She sat on the other side of his desk, her nervousness betrayed by the way she plucked at a handkerchief. Armstrong was being as patient as a glacier: there was nothing else he could do.

Now at last it seemed that Sister Smith had found the determination to explain why she had asked to see Armstrong.

'I've thought it over for weeks, Dr Armstrong,' she said. 'I didn't know whether I ought to say anything, or to whom . . . You see, it's about a doctor. I've thought about it and thought about it – ' She was clearly very distressed. 'And I can't keep it on my conscience any longer. I *must* report it.'

Good God, Armstrong thought. *She's not going to tell me one of the doctors has tried to rape her, or something?* He looked at her with a more searching eye. *Well, she is a good-looking woman. One of the senior men . . . A determined pass certainly isn't outside the realms of possibility . . .*

'A couple of weeks ago, sir, I was theatre sister at an emergency operation. The patient subsequently died, but . . . ' She didn't seem able to carry on.

'Yes?' Armstrong urged gently.

'He died, but he shouldn't have. Oh, I know I'm only a sister, and not a surgeon, but I've seen enough operations . . . '

'I'm sure, Sister,' Armstrong encouraged.

'And this one was botched. Badly, sir. The patient should never have died . . . ' Now that she'd started, she began to speak faster, with more determination. 'The surgeon botched it. He killed the patient.'

Armstrong felt suddenly cold, and tired. Whether she was right or wrong – and he had a strong feeling that she was almost certainly right – there was bound to be the most shattering upheaval. Such an uncompromising accusation from a highly experienced and responsible senior sister wasn't the sort of thing that could be swept under the carpet, even if he'd felt inclined to try it.

'He killed the patient,' Sister Smith repeated, much more softly this time.

'Who was the surgeon who did this operation?' Armstrong asked at last.

'Mr Parker Brown. You see, sir, he was drunk at the time. Mr Parker Brown, of all people.'

She burst into racking sobs.

Chapter Eight

It was as well that Sister Smith was unable to say anything more for a few moments. This gave Armstrong time to recover a little from as great a shock as he could remember sustaining. The idea of Parker Brown operating *drunk* was simply inconceivable. It was *impossible.* And yet . . . and yet . . . Sister Smith was devoted to Parker Brown. She was the last person who would accuse him without absolutely overwhelming evidence. She would be much more likely to make excuses for him, cover for him. Nor could her accusation be provoked by a lack of understanding of the operation. Armstrong would accept her judgement above that of some qualified surgeons.

Nevertheless, Armstrong knew he had to test her allegations. With a terrible sense of sadness he realised that this was only the first of a whole series of question-and-answer sessions, each one of them most probably another nail in the coffin for Parker Brown's reputation. He took Sister Smith through her story.

She noticed Parker Brown was a little slow and clumsy in the scrubbing up room, she said, but thought it was due to tiredness. Not until later did she realise he had a strong smell of drink about him. During the operation he made errors of procedure – asking for wrong instruments sometimes – and he was increasingly clumsy as, Sister Smith assumed, the effect of the drink took firmer hold of him. An operation which should have taken half an hour, took more than two.

'Who was the anaesthetist?' Armstrong asked.

'Dr Seton.'

Armstrong was aware he would get very little from him. Seton would have been much more concerned with maintaining the patient's level of anasthaesia than taking much notice of what Parker Brown was doing. Armstrong suddenly felt a thousand years old, and sick. His oldest friend . . . and he had to start up the machine that could crush him.

Armstrong reached out for the telephone, then checked the movement. He was going to call Parker Brown and have Sister Smith repeat her accusation directly to him. After all, it is a precept of English law that an accused man should have the right to confront his accuser. Then Armstrong remembered that Parker Brown was away giving a number of special lectures to a post-graduate group in the north.

'You'd beter stand down from duty until Mr Parker Brown comes back,' Armstrong told her. 'I'll speak to the SNO myself. After that . . . Well, we'll see,' he finished lamely.

Sister Smith rose. 'Yes, sir.'

'In the meantime, talk about this to no one.'

'Of course not, sir.' She paused. Her fragile composure seemed on the point of cracking again. 'I'm sorry, but I really didn't know what to do. I haven't slept . . . I did do the right thing, telling you, didn't I, sir?' she pleaded.

He nodded. He couldn't actually bring himself to speak in case his voice gave him away.

John Smith sat in his wheelchair near the open balcony door of the Day Room, looking out across the darkening countryside. The deep blue of the near-cloudless night sky merged into the violet blackness of the far-off mountains, while away to the left was a strange fitful orange-yellow light that briefly illuminated the base of distant clouds. He couldn't make out what it was for some time, and then recognised it as the reflected glow from some blast furnace. Close to it, the air would be acrid, sulphureous; and the heat almost unbearable. From a distance, it was beautiful. Less than a mile away brilliant blue-white lights flickered on and off as cars sped along the motorway, their headlights disappearing behind trees and embankments before bursting into view again. John sighed, weighed down by a loneliness even heavier than that of an orphan.

A soft hand touched his. Although he had not heard her come into the room and close the door behind her, because he had been so lost in his own thoughts, he knew it was Alison.

'That was a very sad sigh, for such a lovely night.' Her tone was bantering, but there was an element of genuine concern.

He answered obliquely. 'I hoped you'd come and see me again, although I knew you must be busy.'

'Not *that* busy.' She paused, knowing that they were on the edge of dangerous ground. If they did not think carefully before they spoke, they might say unguarded things that could lead them into quicksands. So she just said: 'Leg giving you any trouble?'

He smiled and shook his head. 'Though if I keep complaining that it aches, will you come and see me?' Then before she could answer he said, 'Yes, it is a lovely night.' He, too, was aware of the dangers of incautious remarks that might lead to commitments.

John turned and looked at her fully for the first time since she had joined him. She was wearing a close-fitting, dark-coloured, lightweight linen dress with a fairly deeply cut, rectangular *décolleté*. (That is how he thought of it; not as a *décolletage*.) He was quite sure it was not the sort of dress she normally wore in the hospital, particularly without a white coat: it emphasised her good figure and long, slender legs. Equally, her perfume, subtle and insistent at the same time, was hardly the sort of thing she would wear for working in the hospital in daytime. The diffused light from the ward behind her outlined her profile in silver, and John was acutely aware that Alison was a beautiful young woman.

Paradoxically, the fact that she was obviously interested in him, as he was in her, made him feel even sadder rather than happy. Involuntarily, he sighed again.

He caught her eye, and answered her unasked question. 'Oh, "Thoughts that do often lie too deep for tears". Funny, I managed to remember that: the last line of Wordsworth's *Ode on Intimations of Immortality*.' He looked reflective. 'I was feeling sorry for myself. Nobody knows me, nobody wants me. The story in the local paper hasn't brought any reaction. Nobody's reported me missing. It's as if I didn't exist. I feel so . . . *alone*.'

'But you're not!' Alison's reply was quick. Too quick. She regained her calm, outwardly, at least. 'It's summer. Perhaps you were going on holiday, and you're not expected home for a fortnight, a month even.'

'I hadn't thought of that,' he admitted.

'You'll see. Somebody'll be calling about you before you know it. And when that happens, you'll start getting your memory back. Yes, you'll hear from your – ' She paused almost imperceptibly. ' – from your relations, or friends.'

The thought should have cheered them up. Instead, they

both looked at each other with a sense of loss. John reached out and took Alison's hand, then gently pulled her towards him.

The evening had started well. Bywaters had been agreeably surprised when he called for Suzy in a taxi. ('Of course a taxi. You're going to drink with dinner, aren't you?' she had said.) She was wearing a cloak over a long dress; Bywaters could see a white lace collar above the cloak, which reassured him. He wouldn't have put it past her to wear something really outrageous. Her make-up, which although still pretty extravagant by most standards, was less extreme than usual for her. Bywaters' spirits lightened: maybe it was going to be a successful evening despite all his misgivings and uncertainties.

When they went to the taxi, she took his hand and put his arm inside hers. Abruptly, with a shock as sharp as a blow, he was aware that his hand was pressing, and being pressed, against her breast: beneath the raw silk of the cloak was only the thinnest of dress materials. It was quite deliberate on her part; there could be no mistake. He was conscious of every slight movement as they walked to the car, every vibration, almost of the heartbeats beneath the breast. Inside the car she sat with the length of her thigh pressed hard against his. The journey to the hotel seemed very short.

The Wharton Towers was a new hotel full of plastic, stainless steel and fluorescence. It had every modern convenience, but very few old ones, like character and comfort. It boasted, among other amenities, a Balinese bar, a Hungarian restaurant, a Far West grill room, and what appeared to be an underwater cocktail lounge. There were no Balinese, Hungarians, or cowboys on the staff. Most were either Spanish or Greek.

Among the hotel's clientele were a number of rich and powerful people, who thought of themselves as influential as the Establishment, but the real Establishment went to the Grand. Another difference between the two hotels was that the Grand was where you would stay with your wife, the Wharton Towers with someone else's.

Bywaters found that the Towers irresistibly reminded him of an old joke about a certain London hotel, where couples who were manifestly not married to each other rushed off to double rooms. An unaccompanied visitor, only too aware of what was going on behind each locked bedroom door, walked into the street where two coupling dogs were reeling about the pavement in a six-legged gavotte. The visitor turned back and called to the reception clerk: 'I say, the hotel's sign has fallen down.'

The hotel had an air of raffish randiness. The head porter could be relied on to supply any service a guest might need: he could even find a masseuse who could do massage. It was not the sort of place anyone went for a quiet drink, or a delicate, gourmet's meal. A woman who agreed to go to the Towers with a man virtually served prior notice that she was willing: no one accepted an invitation there to say no. So, Bywaters entered the place with a subconscious air of expectancy.

The main entrance hall was fairly full of men who qualified on sight for the adjective 'self-made'. Many of them wore dinner jackets, all of them were dressed in aggressively expensive clothes. Their wives, mistresses and girlfriends were all out of the same plastic mould – some of them out of it rather longer than others. They wore jewellery that was overt evidence of their men's prosperity, while their cleavages and iron-hard, pull-together-and-push-up bras gave false testimony of their men's virility.

When they got to the door of the main banqueting hall, Suzy turned her back to Bywaters and unbuttoned her cloak for him to take it from her. As she slipped it from her shoulders, she didn't bother to give him the cliché over-the-shoulder look. If she had, he probably wouldn't have noticed it. Under the cloak she was wearing a white lace top, buttoned at the back of the neck, but completely open all the way down to the top of her long black skirt. An odd thought flashed through Bywaters' mind. He remembered that the Japanese find the sight of the nape of a woman's neck extremely erotic, and for once he understood them. The long gentle curve from the back of her head to the waist was unexpectedly exciting. Then, as she turned to move into the hall, he saw the front of the close, form-fitting lace top. It was a wide weave, and most revealing. Whenever she moved, first one part then another of the areolae of her nipples showed darker behind the white tracery of the lace. Men's heads turned sharply; woman's lips tightened as they looked at Suzy. She seemed to be enjoying the effect she was creating. Bywaters was not.

There was a second shock awaiting him. In the centre of the banqueting hall, rising out of the middle of the concentric circles of tables, was a boxing ring. The Wharton Towers, like some rather more celebrated hotels, occasionally put on boxing shows. 'Fashionable' audience paid inflated prices for tables and meals, and sat eating and drinking while the boxers tried to do each other injury.

It was a nightmare evening for Bywaters. A different sort of nightmare from the discothèque: different, and much worse. The sight of liver-faced men stuffing themselves while two young men slammed into each other nauseated him. Most of the men in the audience looked like prime candidates for the coronary club, and he could feel no sympathy for them.

Suzy joined in the shouting, the urging of one man to bruise and wound another, to smash him to the ground . . . Somehow her cheering did not have the same quality as the other spectators', but Bywaters' perception was dulled by the entire occasion, and he failed to notice the difference. Nevertheless, he did vaguely realise that although Suzy appeared to be drinking steadily during the meal, he himself had drunk by far the major share of the wine. Perhaps he was trying to deaden his own sensibilities, because he was suffering an agonising dichotomy. He found Suzy exciting, attractive, desirable; he found himself imagining her naked body and. . . . He pulled himself up sharply. How could he feel like this – despite her powerful sexual magnetism – for a promiscuous, brazen, obvious woman with an apparent streak of unpleasant cruelty in her make-up?

The turning point came during a lightweight fight between a spidery West Indian who was trying to box, and a chunky, pale-skinned Scot who knew only one thing: to keep moving forward, head down, swinging his arms. Eventually a wild swinging right hammered the West Indian high on the temple. His legs went rubbery, his arms dropped. A left hook opened a bad cut on the darker-skinned man's eye. Again that clumsy, but powerful right whistled through the air. It caught the damaged eye, and jerked the negro's head like a mad tango dancer's. The effect was like flicking a soaking-wet sponge, but instead of water, blood sprayed across the ring and on to Bywaters' table. A few drops spattered on his face, others left a trail on the white tablecloth, next to his plate.

'I've had enough,' he said grittily to Suzy. 'I'm going. You can come and I'll see you home, or stay here, as you like.'

She shrugged. 'I might as well come with you. This is all rather boring, anyway.' She smiled a brilliant, false smile. 'After you, Neville darling.'

It almost stopped him in his tracks. Now he came to think of it, that was the first time she'd used his name. He hadn't used her name at all . . . he hadn't called her anything, from the first moment he had spoken to her. He wondered why.

'Are you coming in for coffee, or something?' Suzy asked with no particular emphasis as the taxi pulled up outside the small block of flats where she lived. It had been a silent, slightly hostile journey back from the hotel. This time there had been no small intimate pressures of thigh on thigh, hand on breast. She kept her cloak tightly closed across her.

Bywaters hesitated.

'What's the matter?' she said when he didn't reply. 'Worried about your reputation? You can't be worried about mine. And I won't attack you and tear your trousers off or anything. You could probably do with a black coffee, after the wine you drank,' she added sourly, but not unfairly. Bywaters found she was beginning to irritate him again, and he decided to refuse, and go straight on home.

'Yes, all right, I will, thanks,' he said, to his own astonishment.

As she opened the door to her small flat he didn't know what to expect. Certainly not the neat, unextravagant, quietly tasteful apartment. Suzy seemed to read his thoughts. 'What did you expect? Nineteenth century French brothel, all red plush and gilt? Sit down. I'll get the coffee going.'

While she was away in the kitchen, Bywaters looked at the records neatly stacked by the hi-fi. No pop, no Mantovani or Sinatra; only classical. But even her choice of that was surprising. Opera: Wagner, Verdi, Puccini, Richard Strauss, Mozart; symphony and chamber music: Beethoven, Bach, Albinoni, Mussorgsky, Sibelius. There was no Tchaikowsky, Bywaters noted, and he wondered if it indicated a lack of sentimentality.

Her books confirmed the character the choice of music suggested. Among the authors Bywaters remarked were Thackeray, Tolstoy, Proust, Sartre, Gunther Grass, and several Shakespeare plays in the Arden editions. Bywaters was quite thrown at first, but then he shrugged. Because a woman was promiscuous, or worse, didn't necessarily mean she was uncultured, even if she were unfastidious.

There was a slight noise behind him. He turned. She was bringing in the coffee on a tray. She'd already changed out of the see-through lace top and long skirt, and was wearing a housecoat. It was decorous, and unrevealing. 'I thought I'd slip into something more comfortable,' she said, with deliberate over-emphasis of the old cliché. 'More comfortable . . . for you,' she added without the trace of a smile.

They sat at opposite ends of the settee: near enough to be able to talk quietly, but far enough apart to avoid any accidental physical contact. At first their conversation was tentative and platitudinous. They chose their subjects with exaggerated care, avoiding anything that might cause the least contention. Then Bywaters remarked that she seemed to have artistic tastes – her musical preferences were entirely classical – and yet she worked on computers, which would suggest she was more scientifically inclined.

'Bach,' she said. 'Isn't his music mathematical in its precision and development? And have you ever studied the structure of late Verdi operas? Anyway, a computer is only a tool, to make life easier for you – as long as you remember that you run the computer, and the computer doesn't run you. Besides,' she concluded, 'who says that art and science are incompatible? Look at Leonardo da Vinci . . . and Vanbrugh.'

Bywaters smiled and held up his hand.. 'All right, I'm convinced.'

This Suzy Parker, with only Bywaters to see her, was so utterly different from the noisy, over-sexed, shameless and mindless bitch she was in public that he could barely believe it was the same woman. He remembered, for instance, the Suzy who refused to help Betty Galton, and who had been sneeringly rude to him; the Suzy, provocatively dressed, shouting raucously amid boozy spectators '*Hit* him! Finish him off!' And now . . .

Once again she seemed to read his mind (or was it simply that there was a strong empathy between them?). 'I was just thinking about those boxers,' she said. 'What a terrible, brutalising way to earn a living. So degrading. And in front of all those screaming . . . ' She couldn't find the word, and gave an indeterminate gesture.

'You were doing a fair amount of shouting yourself.'

Her eyes became hooded, and she looked down. 'So I was,' she replied without inflection.

The coffee was good. When Bywaters finished it, he was abruptly aware that he was at the moment of decision. He stood – unnecessarily – to put his cup on the dining table, instead of the coffee table in front of him.

'Well,' he said. Suzy gave him no help. 'Well, I'd better be going, I suppose.'

'Whatever you like,' she said, still with nothing in her tone to give him the least indication what she was thinking.

He moved, reluctantly, towards the door. She rose and walked over to join him. For a long moment they stood there, just looking at each other. Bywaters felt a hot rush of desire. In his mind's eye still strong was the image of her in the revealing lace top; the earlier memory of her running through the rain, her blouse plastered against what seemed to be her naked breasts, was clear to the last detail. As he looked at her, he visualised himself zipping open the front of her housecoat, leaving her naked, then taking her body in his hands . . . He reached out to take hold of the zip – then instead he took her hand and shook it.

'Goodnight,' he said.

She looked up at him, eyes wide with disbelief. Her surprise left her moist lips half parted, a perfect invitation to him to kiss her goodnight.

'Goodnight,' he repeated, and went out quickly without touching her again.

It was difficult to say which one of them was the more astonished.

What's worrying me so much,' John Smith told Dr Bauer, 'isn't so much that I've lost my memory, but the reason I've lost it.'

'And what's that?'

'I've got something pretty terrible to conceal. It must be, to make me lose my memory like this,' He moved uneasily in his wheelchair.

'Not necessarily,' Bauer told him. 'You may not be trying to *hide* something, but to hide *from* something. Escape from it. It could be something quite banal.' John Smith started to say something, but Bauer pressed on. 'Quite banal to other people – even to yourself in other circumstances. It could be the loss of a loved one, for example. '

'Somebody died? I hadn't thought of that.'

'Or went away. It could be a business problem.' Bauer gave a rare smile. 'Do you know what, statistically, is the greatest single cause of a "nervous breakdown"?' John shook his head. 'Moving into a new home. Buying it . . . arranging all the finance, getting all the repairs and redecorations done, the furniture delivered . . . '

'You're not suggesting that's made me lose my memory?'

'I don't know what has made you lose it. I was merely trying to show you that one man's simple nuisance is another man's last straw.'

'We're not making much progress, though, are we? None, in fact?'

Bauer gave a dismissive wave of his hand. Privately he agreed with John, but saw no point in admitting it. He said as encouragingly as he could manage, 'There's no time scale for this sort of thing.' He pressed a bell-push and rose, to indicate that this session in his consulting room was over.

A nurse entered. 'Take Mr Smith back to the ward, please, Nurse.' She moved forward to the wheelchair. Before she pushed John out of the room Bauer said, 'If we don't start making progress fairly soon, there are other techniques we can try.' John looked alarmed. 'Nothing to worry about, I assure you,' Bauer told him. John was not totally reassured.

Five minutes later in the Day Room John was outlining this latest session to Alison. 'All that's bad enough,' he concluded, 'but there's still been no enquiries for me, no one reporting me missing. I mean, after that local paper story, you'd think that at least some nutcase might contact the hospital.'

'I've been speaking to Dr Armstrong. We think we should give the story to the national press and television. With your permission, of course.'

John said nothing.

'It's the only logical thing to do now. Besides, if someone can say who you are, and where you come from, it should help your recovery,' Alison added.

'All right,' he said at long last. 'But although I keep saying I'm worried because no one has come forward to "claim" me, now it comes to it, I'm not at all sure I want anyone to.' He looked at her long and hard. 'You realise what's happening, Alison, don't you?'

'I hope someone does turn up and say who he is,' Doreen Holland said.

'He's not a difficult patient,' Sister Washington replied, 'although it would be nice to get our Day Room back. Every time I look in there they seem to be having a *tête-à-tête*.'

'It's not only that, Frances, as you well know. I can see the most fearful trouble brewing.'

Sister Washington looked around to make sure they were not overheard. 'You think so, too?'

'It's obvious,' said Doreen, who knew (from personal experience) a great deal more about emotional relationships between the sexes than some unperceptive people gave her credit for. 'They're in love.'

'And love's a wonderful thing,' concluded Sister Washington, 'but not between a doctor and patient.'

Armstrong rarely went through the main entrance hall of the hospital. He normally entered through a small, Doctors-Only door by the car park, and left by the same one. The main hall was not on his usual tracks.

Equally so, since his departure from the Midland General for more lucrative pursuits, Arnold Godfrey Capper visited the main entrance of the hospital less than rarely. So, the mathematical odds against Armstrong and Capper actually meeting in the hall were quite astronomical. Nevertheless, at the very moment of the one day in ten that Armstrong was passing through the main hall, Capper was at the reception desk, asking for him.

'Dr Armstrong, sir! What a bit of luck! Just the man I want to see!' he said in a voice that was clearly audible above all the hubbub of arriving and departing patients, crying children, ringing telephones.

Armstrong looked around for escape. 'I'm very busy, Capper,' he said.

'This'll only take a moment,' Capper said. Then, in a hoarse stage whisper he added, 'I fixed you up.'

The entire entrance hall went silent. Ears homed in on Capper like radar antennae swivelling to pick up an enemy aircraft. Armstrong cleared his throat and said 'You'd better come along to my office.' As he set off with the lavender-suited Capper beside him looking affable and conspiratorial at the same time Armstrong felt horribly guilty. It was no good having a clear conscience: he knew he *looked* suspicious, and no amount of protestation would convince anyone to the contrary. There flashed through his mind an incident which had lain dormant in the recesses of memory, forgotten since he was a schoolboy.

It happened at his rather well-known public school, during morning assembly, when the entire school congregated for prayers and hymns, under the basilisk eye of their fearsome Head.

The school had a small choir which sang in the school chapel, and at morning prayers to give the rest of the school a lead. This choir stood at one side of the dais at the end of the hall, the Head and housemasters at the other. Armstrong was in the choir.

On this morning the school were singing 'Onward, Christian soldiers' (it was the sort of place where cold showers were warmly recommended), and had just finished the first verse. As everyone took a deep breath to dive in for the second verse, a boy next to Armstrong broke wind. It was a noble trumpet blast, mellow but powerfully penetrating. It rolled out across the assembly hall like a note from a gigantic *alpenhorn* reverberating among mountain peaks. It stopped the second verse of the hymn dead in its tracks. The entire school listened spellbound..

All eyes turned to the choir. The young Matthew Armstrong was going pink, a positive Day-Glo pink. The culprit (if the boy who had produced this prodigious sound could be considered culpable) looked a picture of shocked innocence.

The school finally recovered sufficiently to essay the next verse of the hymn, but between the second and third verses there was an expectant hush, and everyone turned to look at young Matthew Armstrong again. When at last the choir filed from the hall, past the Head, he gave Armstrong a look that burned like a thermic lance and hissed 'Animal!' (The school never sang 'Onward Christian Soldiers' again until Armstrong left. He was also instantly given a nickname it would be unfair to repeat here.)

As Dr Armstrong, Medical Administrator of the Midland General, strode along the corridor with the egregious Capper, he recalled that nightmare occurrence at school. He swept through his secretary's empty office and into his own. Capper followed cheerfully.

'A beautiful little Alfa Romeo, Dr Armstrong,' Capper said. 'That's what I've found for you. And it's a bargain, because the owner's being given a new car by – well, let's call him her fiancé, if you see what I mean,' Capper said with a wink.

Neither of them heard the outer door of the secretary's office open, and someone enter it.

Six more ears were now drinking in the conversation.

'And who is she, exactly?' Armstrong asked.

'Her name's Miss Pepper. Katherine Pepper, but everybody calls her Kay, sort of short for Cayenne Pepper 'cos she's such hot stuff,' Capper said with a horribly dirty chuckle. 'She'll be contacting you some day this week, during office hours. It has to be daytime, on account of her working nights. She *says* she's an actress, when anybody asks.'

'I'm beginning to have second thoughts about all this, Capper,' said Armstrong.

'Everybody feels like this at first, but trust me, Dr Armstrong, sir. Did I ever let you down when I was working here?' The stupendous effrontery of this prevented Armstrong from answering. 'This little lady's got the very thing you want, believe me. I can guarantee satisfaction. You won't get another chance like this.'

'I'm not sure that I want one.'

'Highly risible, sir. But just you wait till Miss Pepper shows it to you, and you get your hands on it . . . I mean, all you have to do is give it a trial. No obligation.'

'All right, Capper, we'll see.'

Capper put on an utterly unnerving professional smile, shook Armsrong's hand, and hurried out through the door directly into the corridor. In the secretary's office, Miss Fletcher, Bywaters and Knight stared at each other in stark astonishment.

Wallman looked across his desk at Alderman Percy Tindall with marked dislike. Tindall stared back at him with equal distaste. The reason for their mutual antipathy was their basic similarity: both were determined, ambitious men, although Wallman was by far the more subtle and cultured of the two. This difference, however, only accentuated the unspoken animosity. Wallman did not like being reminded what he had come from; Tindall did not like seeing what he could not become.

'I still don't understand what you want from me, Mr Tindall,' Wallman said. His avoidance of the title 'Alderman' was deliberate, and Tindall knew it.

'Then I'll spell it out again,' Tindall replied. 'My boy was injured in the crash with that bloody titled parasite's son. He – '

'But he wasn't admitted here – your son, I mean,' Wallman interjected.

'No. He felt all right then. It's only since, he's been suffering with headaches, and shock. He's home in bed; our family doctor's seeing him.' Tindall seemed fractionally less sure of himself for a moment, then he recovered. 'I'm not here about Harold – my son – but about Lord bloody Trenchman.'

'I take it you're not here because you're concerned about his progress,' Wallman said. The sarcasm was not lost on Tindall, and the flash of naked hate that he gave Wallman briefly shook even that normally steel-plated man.

'There was allegations made that Trenchman was drunk when he hit my son's car,' Tindall said. 'The police sergeant told me he was going to ask for a blood test. Well, I've been to the station to find out what's going on, and now they say there won't be any blood test because there wasn't any blood samples. Why was that?'

'I'm not sure I need to tell you, or that I want to tell you,' Wallman said after a pause.

'Don't you try that with me, doctor,' Tindall said venomously. 'If you won't talk, somebody in the hospital will. It's a big place. And if I have to, I'll bring up the matter at the next meeting of the Area Authority.'

'I wish you wouldn't frighten me like that, said Wallman, looking as terrified as a battleship. 'To stop you making a nuisance of yourself inside this hospital and out, I'll tell you this: blood specimens were taken, but were accidentally destroyed. By then it was too late to take new ones: the patient was being transfused and was being given anaesthetic. Good day.'

Tindall did not move. 'There's something going on here,' he said, slowly. 'It's the Old Boy network operating again. The Establishment closing ranks. By God, I can smell the whitewash from here. The fix is in, to save Trenchman from his just deserts.'

'I'm very busy – with patients. So if you'll please go . . . '

Tindall pushed back his chair. 'It's a cover-up. Maybe it's just you, sucking up to His Lordship's father, maybe there are others in it. But rest assured of one thing: whatever it is, I'll find out all right. I'm an expert in dirty politics.'

'I'm sure,' Wallman said, giving a thin-lipped smile.

'So just watch your step, Doctor Bloody Wallman.'

'Mr Guy Wallman, actually, but only to my friends.'

Tindall slammed the door behind him. Wallman looked thoughtfully at the closed door for quite a long time.

As Alderman Tindall strode out, down the corridors, he passed Alison Moxey, who had some newspapers under her arm. Both were so pre-occupied that neither noticed the other.

Alison found John Smith in bed in the ward, finishing breakfast. She showed him the newspapers. Some had his photograph on the front page, others inside. They all carried a caption something like 'Do You Know This Man?'

'Somebody you know, a relation, or somebody, is bound to see it,' Alison said. John nodded. Neither of them looked very cheerful.

Two hundred miles away, a woman opened her morning paper. When she saw the photograph, she started, and read the story with it.

'So that's where you are, darling,' she said, out loud.

Chapter Nine

It was a pleasant day. Although it had been hot and close for an hour on each side of midday, a heavy shower had cleared the air, and sharpened the smell of grass that had been cut before the rain. John Smith, as he was still known – for the moment, anyway – sat in his wheelchair near a bed of geraniums and carnations in the quiet gardens of the Midland General.

Alison, in an olive green dress that somehow made her look very Latin, came along a gravel path then across the grass to him.

'Do you like gardening?' she asked.

'I like gardens, but not gardening,' he said without having to think about it. She took his hands, turning them over and looked at the palms. 'No, they're not gardener's hands.' She smiled. 'I know one thing about you: you do a sedentary job. Not a mark on them. So, you could be . . . a lawyer, architect . . . ' She pretended to think.

'Dr Bauer's been all through that. I don't seem to have any specialist knowledge at all.'

'You could be a writer.'

'Or a dancer,' he suggested.

'You don't have the legs.'

It was his turn to smile. 'Thanks very much. All right, how about gigolo?'

'You don't have patent-leather hair, either.'

'Don't you think you'd better let go of my hands?' he said gently. 'I think people are looking.'

'I could always pretend to be taking your pulse.' But she released them, nevertheless. 'You sound cheerful today,' she said after a moment.

'I've been thinking, and I've . . . well, come to a sort of rationalisation of my position. I'm not at all sure it's a bad thing, not knowing who I am. All my troubles, and pains, and regrets, and disappointments – they're all wiped out.'

'So are your happy moments. And all the other people in your life.' She hesitated. 'Your loved ones . . .'

'I thought of that. But I don't *feel* there is anyone like that in my life. If I really loved somebody, surely there'd be some vestigial feelings? Some emotion deep down would stir, wouldn't it?' He looked directly at her and said: 'I can't believe that I have any feeling in my past like – ' He broke off, as a porter, pushing another patient in a wheelchair, came round the rowan trees and along the gravel path towards them.

Whether John would have broken off anyway, or whether it was just because he didn't want to be overheard, Alison could not guess. When the others had gone out of earshot again, she said, 'I suppose there isn't anyone who hasn't said, at some time or other, "If only I could start all over again." Well, you've got your fresh start. But it's a terribly high price to pay for it.'

'I don't think so,' he said quietly.

'Look, John. Are you sure you're not mistaking . . . oh, I don't know . . . gratitude to me, dependence . . . for something else?'

'Yes, I'm sure.' He paused. 'What you were saying about everybody wanting a fresh start. Have you ever wanted one?'

Alison nodded.

'Do you have a husband?'

'I'm married,' she said with unexpected harshness.

'Sorry. It's none of my business.'

'I want to tell you. I'm married, but I don't have a husband. He stopped being that a long time ago. And I stopped being a wife.' There was silence that seemed interminable.

'Oh, God. What are we going to do?' John said with sudden desperation.

'Is that you, Capper?' asked Julie Fletcher on the telephone.

'Who's calling?' came the cautious and muffled reply from the other end.

'Dr Armstrong's secretary.'

'Oh, hello, Julie,' said Capper, his voice becoming clearer (as he took the handkerchief from the mouthpiece) and less guarded. 'How's your – '

'Hold on, please,' she interrupted. Then: 'I'm putting you through.' There was a click on the line. This was caused by Julie Fletcher pushing down the receiver rest of her telephone . . . and then letting it up again. Her own telephone had not left her ear.

'Capper?' said Armstrong. 'This doesn't seem to be a very good line.' (It was not an unreasonable comment. There were two extra telephones connected to it: Julie's and the switchboard operator's.) 'This young woman, Miss, er, Pepper.'

'Oh, old Hot-Stuff, Cayenne Pepper. You seen her yet?'

'No. That's what I'm ringing you about. I have a very busy week ahead of me, and I don't think I'll be able to see her for the next two or three days. So if you'll please let her know . . . '

'Rely on me, Dr Armstrong. It's not the sort of thing you want to plunge into if you can't give your mind to it. In the meantime, I'll see she doesn't do any deals with anyone else.'

'That brings me to another point. I should insist on a thorough examination before I came to any final decision.'

'Anything you like, Doctor.'

'No offence, Capper, but there are cases where there's been something wrong and people have had some very unpleasant shocks long after – '

'Say no more, Dr Armstrong. If it puts your mind at rest . . . But I ask you, sir. You know me. Would I try to flog you damaged goods?'

'Since you put it like that, Capper: Yes, you would.'

There was no answer to that, so Capper rang off. And so did Armstrong. And Julie. And the switchboard operator.

Bywaters wondered if there wasn't midsummer madness in the air. He was aware of the Alison–John Smith situation, and now there was his own relationship with Suzy Palmer. He was by nature a fastidious young man. Since he was also a very personable young man and a well-considered surgeon, he had no trouble acquiring women friends, but the fact that he had been engaged twice, and that he had been intimate with a number of young women did not mean he had no discrimination. Suzy Palmer, however, was utterly unlike any of the women with whom he had had affairs. Going out with her had defied all logic and sense. She had been as changeable and unpredictable as a whirlwind; he was probably the only man she had been out with at the hospital who hadn't slept with her – and although he still couldn't understand why, he wasn't sorry that he hadn't. Now here he was, taking her out again. He had simply walked into her office and said. 'I'm off tomorrow afternoon. Would you like to come out with me?' She said 'Yes,' and that was that.

Their outing was an unusual one. Some fifty miles from the hospital was a small and not very well-known stately home, and all the better for its relative anonymity. It had a few excellent pictures – Constable, Reynolds, a small Van Dyck and a reputed (and probably genuine) Rembrandt. There was a Grindling Gibbons ceiling in the music room, and Capability Brown had laid out the gardens in return for some unspecified favour by the original owner of the house.

During the summer occasional small chamber music concerts were given there, and Bywaters offered to take Suzy to a Bach recital. She was delighted with the idea.

The quartet was hardly up to Amadeus standards, but the musicians were young and enthusiastic, and clearly loved the music they played with such application. Their freshness and devotion more than compensated for any technical shortcomings; the music room itself was beautiful and seemed to add something to the performance.

After the concert, Bywaters hired a boat and they drifted lazily on the tree-boardered lake. Suzy briefly discussed the concert with Bywaters, but then spoke hardly at all. He quickly fell in sympathy with her mood, and stayed silent, just looking at her. This time she was dressed unremarkably, apart from her elegance: an unrevealing lime-green shantung suit. Her make-up was still more pronounced than Bywaters would have liked, but as he studied her – she seemed oblivious of his scrutiny – he became aware for the first time of the delicate symmetry of her bone structure and the smoothness of her skin.

She was half-sitting, half-lying across the seat at the back of the boat, looking across the lake towards a small artificial island with a gazebo. A few swallows were swooping above the structure. At the same time, two swans took off with a clatter of wings from the surface of the water near the boat – clumsily at first, then with increasing grace as they became airborne, to fly to the other side of the lake. Suzy hardly seemed to notice them. The descending sun was behind her, at first

Bywaters could not see her expression. As she turned her head he saw with a shock that tears were filling her eyes, and beginning to run unheeded on her cheeks.

He was deeply moved by this private, silent sorrow, and intensely curious about it; but he knew, without knowing how he knew, that it was not the moment to ask her what was wrong. He looked away, to give her time to recover.

Driving back to town an hour later he wasn't sure whether he had taken a wrong turning. 'What's that signpost say on your side?' he asked her. She opened her bag and took out a pair of big, square glasses. She put them on to read the signpost.

'Shardthorpe, two, on the right; Caswell, four, straight ahead.'

Bywaters drove straight on. After a moment he glanced sideways at her. 'I didn't know you wore glasses.'

'I don't much, especially indoors. I can see all right to read, and work. But everything's all blurred more than ten yards away.'

Bywaters laughed with unexpected relief. Now he understood why she had seemed to ignore him – looked right through him was how he thought of it – those times in he canteen. Why she had done the same thing in the discothèque. She wasn't drunk or drugged that night after all: just myopic.

'I didn't realise I looked so funny,' Suzy said coldly.

Bywaters explained, without mentioning his former suspicion, how he had thought she was cutting him dead. 'When all you were seeing was a . . . lampstand or a tall potted plant.'

It was her turn to laugh. 'Not quite that.' It was a pleasant laugh, and Bywaters felt happier than he had done for days.

It made the next hour all the more incomprehensible and unbearable. He took her to a small riverside pub for dinner. Although they sat outside at tables under bright Continental-style umbrellas, they could only have been in England. They had just started the meal when Bywaters said: 'You know, the English countryside is marvellous. There's a sense of timelessness, permanence about it all.' He smiled gently. 'You get the feeling that if we came back in ten years, or twenty, it'd all be exactly the same. I know that's pretty unlikely, but at least that's the impression it gives.'

He returned to his cold beef salad, and so didn't see the change come over Suzy's face. He wasn't aware of anything until he noticed that she was drinking much more wine than usual. Then she had an unpleasant row with the waitress in which she was utterly in the wrong. The poor girl was quite shattered by Suzy's behaviour: the pub didn't get that sort of customer. It took all Bywaters' tact and self-control to smooth over the incident.

Before the meal was over Bywaters was wishing furiously that he'd never taken her out. She was behaving outrageously, speaking in a loud, affected voice, catching the eye of other men and looking at them provocatively. The whole performance was like a caricature of an amateur tart. Perversely, the quieter and more unreactive Bywaters became, the more it seemed to provoke her into stupid extravagances of speech and behaviour.

Maybe she really is unbalanced after all, Bywaters thought. *Well, hard luck. I don't have time to straighten out neurotic young women, even attractive ones.*

Bywaters drove her home without a word. Suzy herself didn't speak until they arrived at her home. She turned to him and said: 'Coming in? I mean, you've taken me out and then given me dinner. I suppose you consider you're entitled to . . . ' She didn't finish.

'Entitled to what?' he said coldly.

And, in two simple, flat words, she told him.

Bywaters got out of the car, went round and opened the door on her side, and took her to her front door. As she opened it to go in, he said with suppressed anger born of bewilderment and anger 'You need help. You ought to see someone.'

She checked and looked at him. 'It'd be a waste of time.' She waited, but Bywaters wasn't coming in. 'Looks like you need help more than I do.' She shut the door.

The morning after he returned from giving the series of lectures to the post-graduate group Parker Brown went straight from his home to the scrubbing-up room of Theatre A, where he normally operated. He knew his first case was a lung resection: the day's schedule – like the schedules for the other days he had been away – was made out before he left.

He spent what always seems to the layman to be an inordinate time scrubbing up, but Parker Brown's old professor had graphically demonstrated the difficulties of doing a thorough scrub-up. He had the students cover their hands with lamp-black, and scrub up blindfolded. When they took off the blind-folds, most of them were shocked to see what unwashed dark streaks and patches still remained on their hands.

As he was finishing, his theatre sister appeared, already

gowned and masked. Parker Brown did a double take. 'Who are you?' he asked brusquely.

'Sister Milne, sir. Good morning.'

'Where is Sister Smith?'

'She's off duty for the time being, sir.'

'She's not sick, is she?' Parker Brown asked incredulously. The idea of the indestructible Sister Smith being sick clearly seemed most improbable to him.

'I don't think so, sir. Dr Armstrong and the S.N.O. arranged for her to stand down for a while, and I was told to replace her. That's all I know.'

'Well, don't stand there gossiping. Let's get on with it,' Parker Brown said.

Sister Frances Milne – an attractive, but no-nonsense Newcastle-born Geordie – smiled behind her mask and helped Parker Brown into his gear.

Dennis Porter and Terence Leakey assisted Parker Brown with the lung resection. (Bywaters was in another theatre, pinning a neck of femur; Alison Moxey was performing a hysterectomy on a woman of forty who had seven children and so would hardly miss the parts Alison was removing.) Sister Milne performed adequately for Parker Brown: she had neither the prescience of Sister Smith or her predecessor, Sister Wallis, nor quite their authority yet, but she was calm and sensible. There was every indication she would soon reach their level of high competence. Parker Brown was pleasurably surprised. Only when his operating schedule was over did he allow himself to wonder about Sister Smith. He set off for Armstrong's office, a white coat over his theatre green.

When Armstrong told him what Sister Smith had accused him of, he could not believe his ears.

An hour later, Armstrong, Parker Brown and Sister Smith met officially, and she repeated her allegations. She was white, and understandably under great strain, but she faced Parker Brown squarely.

'I can't believe you're being deliberately vicious, so I'll be charitable and assume that you've lost your senses,' he said. It was his idea of being placatory.

'That settles it, I'm afraid, William,' Armstrong said after Patience Smith had gone. 'I'll have to pass on her complaint. You'd better get in touch with the Medical Defence Union immediately.'

'She *must* be mad,' Parker Brown said. 'She'll forget all this before it goes any further.'

But Sister Smith didn't. She was dtermined to see it through to the bitter end; to the final ruin of Willian Parker Brown.

At six o'clock the Doctors' Common Room was always fairly full. Some doctors were relaxing after a long spell on duty, others were preparing for the rigours of the night. A group of surgeons – Bywaters, Knight, Alison Moxey, Leakey and van Kroll among them – were again discussing Parker Brown's Day, as the epic performance was now called. 'I tell you, man,' said Leakey, 'at the end of the day he was still doing stitches that gave me a headache just to *look* at.'

'I'll never know why he did it,' said Knight. 'He must have had a rush of blood to the head.'

'I must say it seemed quite extraordinary to me,' van Kroll said, enunciating carefully. 'The whole thing was obviously premeditated. But why?'

Barbara Kennedy had joined them. 'To prove something.'

'Parker Brown doesn't have to prove anything to us,' Alison said.

'I meant, prove something to himself,' Barbara said, and moved on, leaving a small pool of thoughtful silence behind her.

There is an old saying that when four women play bridge, the first one to get up and go is very courageous . . . because the others are going to talk about her when she's gone. In fact, the principle is true about most groups. When Alison Moxey decided she ought to have a last look round the wards, she had not got out of the door before comment began about her and John Smith. It wasn't bitchy gossip; most of the doctors were genuinely concerned for her and the risks she was running to her career. Bywaters beckoned to Barbara Kennedy to come back and join them.

'Can't you have a quiet word with Alison?' he asked. 'Half the hospital knows about her and that amnesia patient.'

'Why me? She's on your service, not mine.'

'But you're a woman. And a psychiatrist. It'd be easier for you.'

Barbara Kennedy laughed hollowly. 'Any psychiatrist will tell you that "love" is the one obsession you can't simply "talk" about.'

'I suppose Alison's best chance is that Smith gets his memory back and realises he has a wife and six children,' van Kroll suggested.

'Not really. It'd be much better if a wife recognises him from the newspapers, comes here with the six children . . . and takes him home.'

'In the meantime, I still say you ought to have a word with her,' said Bywaters. 'Poor old Alison's making a thorough exhibition of herself, and in public. She's headed for trouble.' He moved off.

'Bloody hell!' said Knight, as soon as Bywaters had gone out of earshot. 'Look who's talking! You seen the way he's been chasing after the hospital bicycle?'

'Who?' said Leakey, mystified.

'Suzy Palmer. You know, the sex bomb from the computer section.'

'Ah. But why do you call her –'

'Hospital bicycle?' asked van Kroll, whose English was much more idiomatic than Leakey's. 'Because anybody can ride her.'

Barbara looked at Greg Knight. 'Do you know what you are, Greg?' He looked up, surprised. 'A shit. S. h. i. t.,' she said.

'What's *got* into everybody in this place?' he asked plaintively.

Armstrong could not remember when he last felt as depressed as he did now. He had recently heard the first whispers of the Alison Moxey situation, and someone else had told him that Bywaters looked as if he were on the point of making a resounding fool of himself over some worthless woman. Armstrong wondered how on earth he had agreed to hiring someone like Suzy Parker had turned out to be. But that was as nothing compared with the inevitable scandal that would erupt soon.

Armstrong *knew* that Parker Brown would never operate drunk. But Sister Smith's evidence was so strong; her certainty absolute. And she was a completely unhysterical woman. So perhaps Parker Brown *might* . . . He dismissed the thought, angry with himself. The lesson, though, was clear. If he, Armstrong, had suffered a moment of doubt, others who didn't know Parker Brown as well as he did would be ready to believe him guilty.

But the calamities of the day were not finished. There was still a most unpleasant shock to come: something that would cast a shadow over one of the hospital's leading members.

'I'm making an official complaint,' said Alderman Percy Tindall.

Tindall had arrived unannounced, and without an appointment, but he had made such a noisy fuss in Reception, and then in Armstrong's outer office that Armstrong had decided that seeing him was the easiest way out. Tindall had to pay a price: even a man as thick-skinned and insensitive as he was flinched at Armstrong's barbed and acid remarks. But not for long. He soon returned to the attack.

'It's about Viscount Trenchman,' Tindall said. 'There was a definite conspiracy to keep him out of trouble.'

It so happened that Armstrong was well-informed about the accident and the possibility of a charge against Trenchman. A couple of nights previously he had gone to dinner with friends he had met during the period he was contemplating marriage with Frances Hallenbeck. One of the other guests there was the local police solicitor, who asked after Trenchman, and explained his interest.

Armstrong decided to keep this information to himself for the moment.

'Really, Alderman,' Armstrong said. 'What sort of conspiracy? And who were the people involved?'

'Dr Wallman, mainly. Him, Viscount Trenchman, his father, and all the other chinless wonders – his parasite friends.'

'And what did all these people conspire to do?'

'I told you – keep Trenchman out of trouble. Stop him getting what he deserves.'

'Oh, really, do you have any idea how ridiculously improbable and, frankly, rather petulant, all this sounds?' As soon as he uttered the words Armstrong regretted them, but Tindall had sorely rubbed him up the wrong way. The other man's reaction soon destroyed Armstrong's regret.

'Don't come your bloody lah-di-dah public school superiority with me,' Tindall said savagely. 'You and your class think you're – '

'And don't use that tone of voice in my office,' Armstrong said with a voice like broken glass. 'You came storming into the hospital, made yourself offensive to the Reception staff and my secretary, and forced your way in to see me. I will have no more of it, *Alderman*, and unless you behave in a more responsible manner, I shall ask you to leave immediately.'

Tindall breathed deeply. Outwardly he got himself under control, but there was no mistaking his enmity. And, after all, he knew he had the trump card to play at the end.

'When Trenchman hit my son's car he was drunk. Witnesses

said he swerved across the road for no reason. He'd just been to a party and – '

'And everyone at the party said he had very little to drink,' Armstrong interrupted.

Tindall looked briefly surprised, but he didn't ask Armstrong how he knew. 'They would, wouldn't they? His own pals aren't going to shop him. But he stunk of liquor when the police got to the accident, and he still stunk of it when he was brought in here. I smelt it myself.'

'Trenchman explained that. There was a broken bottle of whisky in his car. In fact, the police found it when the car was taken to the police car pound.'

'Well, that was to be expected, wasn't it? I mean, any of his friends could have dropped one in there for him.'

'Yes. Well, even if this . . . extraordinary . . . story of yours had any semblance of truth about it, I fail to see how that affects Mr Wallman.'

'He got a phone call from Earl Dellamayne, Lord Trenchman's father. Here, at the hospital.'

'And you, of course, know what they said.'

'I can make a pretty shrewd guess. "You cover for my boy, and I'll see you all right." '

'That sounds just like Earl Dellamayne,' Armstrong said dryly, but Tindall refused to be drawn.

'That's why your Dr Wallman broke the bottles with the blood samples in them. So it couldn't be proved that Trenchman was pissed when he was driving. The young bastard. Well, they're not going to get away with it. Especially Dr Arse-crawling Wallman.' Tindall's temper was bringing out his vulgarity again.

'Look,' Armstrong said, not unkindly. 'I can understand your feeling upset if your son was injured in the accident, but you have only the flimsiest of circumstantial evidence to suggest – '

'Oh, no, I haven't,' said Tindall. The virulent hatred in his voice was plain. 'Wallman took a bribe.'

'Alderman Tindall, I must warn you – '

'It's no secret. It's in the paper. Haven't you seen it?' He pushed a couple of newspapers across the desk. As Armstrong studied the marked paragraphs, Tindall said 'Dr Wallman's just got a big fat grant from the Ghazarossiam Foundation. And who's chairman of the trustees who hand out the cash? Earl Dellamayne, Viscount Trenchman's father. Not bad payment, just for "accidentally" spilling a blood sample, eh?' Tindall stood up. 'Of course, I haven't got the style and all that lah-di-dah public school carry on,' he said, giving an insight into his rancour. 'I'm just a common public servant who went to an elementary school and had to earn my living when I was fourteen. But as a matter of *courtesy*, I'm informing you first that I'm making an official complaint to the Area Authority about Dr Wallman corruptly receiving a consideration to help Viscount Trenchman avoid a prosecution. Maybe the police'll do something about it, maybe they won't, but believe me, the Area Authority will. I'll see to that. I'll *have* Dr Wallman, I promise you.'

'I'm afraid the present treatment has been completely without success,' Dr Bauer said to John Smith. He was visiting Smith in the ward at the end of the day. Earlier, they had passed another completly sterile session. 'We still know nothing about you, and frankly, the way we're going I can't say we ever will. So, I think the time has come for us to consider a different form of treatment.'

John looked at him guardedly. 'What sort of treatment?'

Bauer did not answer directly. 'As you know, your subconscious has erected a barrier between your consciousness and some painful or unpleasant experience in the past. It has created this . . . locked door . . . for your mind to shelter behind. So far, we have been unable to unlock that door, or even to force a chink in it so we can see what is behind it.'

'Look, doctor, I understand my condition, so forget all the picturesque imagery and just tell me what it is you want me to do.' John was unusually irritable, but Bauer was not put out. It was a normal progression in the relationship between psychiatrist and patient.

'I'd like to try narco-hypnosis. That means I should give you a small, controlled dose of something like what used to be called the truth drug. It would put you into a state of very light hypnosis – little more than a sort of pleasant drowsiness, really. This might make it easier for us to unlock that door, let us see what it is you are trying to keep hidden. If you'll forgive the imagery again,' he added, straightfaced.

John looked dubious, and said nothing. Finally Bauer said: 'How do you feel about it?'

'I don't know.'

'Which means you do not like the idea. That's natural enough.

But John, *why* don't you like it? Is it because you are afraid of the actual technique, or because you are afraid of being cured?' Bauer rose. 'Think about it. There's no hurry for you to decide.'

He was still thinking about it, and was no nearer a decision, when Alison came to see him.

'Dr Bauer's been to see me,' he said at once. 'He wants me to have narco-hypnosis.'

'Yes, he told me he was considering it.'

'Alison, what should I do?'

'I don't know. It depends how you feel, what you want.'

'You know what I want.' They both paused for a moment. 'The trouble is, I'm afraid that if I get my memory back, I may lose everything else. But if I don't get it back, what sort of future is there for . . . for me?' he said eventually. 'I mean, my leg's nearly better, isn't it?'

'Not quite yet.'

'It's only a question of time. I can get about perfectly well with the crutches right now. I'll soon be fit enough to be discharged, won't I?'

'*I'll* decide when you're fit to be discharged,' Alison said with a smile; but being brought face-to-face with a thought she had been deliberately avoiding gave her a sudden sick feeling. 'Besides,' she said, trying to hide her concern, 'discharge you to where?'

'Excuse me, Doctor,' said Doreen Holland, who had come up to the bed unnoticed. Alison and John had been so involved with each other they had not even heard Doreen's discreet cough.

Alison turned her head. Doreen had an extraordinary expression on her face that Alison could not dicipher. 'Yes, Staff?'

'There's someone asking to see Mr Smith. She says his name is Barry Pennington, and she knows him.'

'Barry Pennington?' Alison said with stupefaction, as if she should have recognised the name, but didn't. John himself was shaking his head in disbelief. The name obviously meant nothing to him: it struck no chord. Perhaps that would come later.

'Who is the visitor?' Alison asked eventually.

'She says she's Mrs Pennington,' Doreen said.

The shock of this quite stunned Alison.

'Hello, Barry,' came a voice from the end of the cubicle.

A small, mousey-looking, plainly-dressed woman, apparently

five or ten years older than John, started walking towards the bed. As she got nearer, her smile became radiant, and she held her arms open.

'I've been so worried about you. I'm so glad you're all right, my darling,' she said.

He looked at her, not knowing what to say, or do.

'Don't you recognise me now? I'm your wife, Mary.'

Alison thought: *His wife? Her?*

Chapter Ten

All day Bywaters had tried to avoid doing what he had really known was inevitable. At lunchtime he had spent rather longer than he should have done in the canteen, and he contrived to look inside it two or three times during the afternoon. All in vain. So now, he was forced to admit there was only one thing left. He went to the administration section.

'Is Suzy Parker here today?' he asked Lorna Meadows, in charge of the department. It was a simple direct question, but it had cost him a great deal of reflection and inner debate to decide on it.

Lorna Meadows managed to check an expression of surprise. 'No, she's got a couple of days off.' She paused, and said as expressionlessly as she could: 'Is there anything I can do?'

Bywaters shook his head and went out, into the corridor. As ill-luck would have it Knight and the objectionable Geoffrey Nollet were passing. 'Hello, been to see our Suzy?' Knight said cheerfully, not really meaning it.

Bywaters, his thoughts elsewhere, replied automatically: 'She's off for a couple of days.' The other two looked at him sharply.

'Lorna Meadows mentioned it,' he explained. 'That's why the computer's behind with payments again. Because she's away.' It sounded over-emphatic and lame. The three of them walked along the corridor together.

'I hope you're not getting mixed up with her,' Knight said awkwardly. He was trying to be nice; he hadn't forgotten Barbara Kennedy's remark to him. 'She's a bit of a . . . well, the sort of woman you don't want to get mxied up with. You know.' It wasn't the most sparkling of conversations. Knight turned off towards Blood Alley, the corridor to the Pathology Department. Nollet stayed with Bywaters, who could well have done without him.

'Yeh, everybody knows what she it,' Nollet said. 'All you can get from her is trouble.' He thought for a moment. 'I don't know, though. I suppose she's all right if you want a quick one. Better than paying for it, anyway.'

Bywaters felt an almost overwhelming desire to throttle him, slowly.

That quickly passed, leaving a sick feeling of despair. He knew he was on a disaster course, heading for misery and humiliation – he knew it, but couldn't do anything about it.

John Smith (or Barry Pennington), Mary Pennington, Doreen Holland and Sister Washington were all in the Sister's Office. It was self-evident that the reunion of John Smith and his wife could not be continued in the ward. Once inside, Mary Pennington went over as if to kiss John (Alison *couldn't* think of him as Barry) but instinctively he withdrew from her. She was hurt at first, but managed to smile understandingly.

Alison was studying her closely. She seemed from a different world from John's: there was an element of . . . ordinariness about her. It was not simply her chain-store clothes, her village-salon hairstyle that gave this impression. Of course there was nothing wrong with that. It was simply that John's own clothes, his general air, breathed a different level of life. Even all that was explicable, but there was the apparent age inequality as well. Alison pulled herself up sharply. Her judgements were very subjective, she told herself. She should remember that some men are only at ease with more motherly women, who want to protect them. John could easily be one of them; that might be Alison's attraction for him – the fact that she was authoritative and sure of herself . . .

She pulled herself together. 'Thank you for the use of your office, Sister. I'll let you know when Mrs Pennington leaves,' she said pointedly. Sister Washington nodded, and indicated to Doreen to follow her out. Doreen did it with the greatest reluctance: she was bursting with curiosity to find out about John Smith, or Barry Pennington. So was Sister Washington, but she controlled it better.

'I'll stay for the moment,' Alison said with more assurance

than she felt, 'just to make sure – ' She couldn't bring herself to say *your husband* – 'he's all right.'

'Of course,' Mary Pennington said.

Gently she explained to John that they'd been married nearly ten years. They lived in Manchester, and the reason she hadn't known about John being missing was that she had been away from home – in Scotland to see her aunt. 'You remember Aunt Jenny?' she said. John shook his head miserably.

'I expect you'd been on one of your trips to London when you had the amnesia attack, dear,' Mary said. She turned to Alison. 'Barry often goes off to London on his own to see a show, that sort of thing. I don't like London very much, and I know he'll enjoy himself better if he doesn't have me to worry about.'

Alison nodded, unable to speak. She felt she couldn't stand much more of this. 'I'm sure you'll be all right,' she said to John with a dreadful attempt at a smile. Mary Pennington didn't seem to notice it. Alison hurried out. As soon as she closed the door behind her, she leant against the wall, feeling shattered.

Inside, John was staring hard at Mary Pennington, trying to strike some spark from his memory, but without success. *Maybe this is why I lost my memory,* he thought, *I was trying to escape from my wife.*

'Were we having a row before I went off to London?' John asked.

'Oh, we had our little differences, Barry, but no more than any normal, happily-married couple.'

A quarter of an hour later Doreen Holland appeared from the ward kitchen with two cups of tea on a tray. 'I'll just take these in to them, Doctor,' she said to Alison, who was sitting at the Nurses' Station. 'I expect they could do with it.'

'No, Staff, I'll do it,' said Alison, taking the tray. Doreen was so completely thrown by this unexpected move that she couldn't think of any arguments until Alison had already disappeared into Sister's Office again.

'Thank you very much for the tea, doctor,' Mary said. 'As soon as we've had it, Barry will be coming home with me.'

'I'm afraid he's not fit enough to be discharged yet,' Alison said immediately.

'But he can walk quite well with his crutches, and I'm sure you could do with his bed. I can take care of him at home, just like I've always done.' She smiled lovingly at John, who sat, whitefaced and immobile. 'Besides, I'm sure his memory will come back much more quickly back in his own home, among all his familiar things.'

Alison knew she should accept now that whatever it was she might have hoped for, was over, finished. To try to hang on was only prolonging the pain, not the pleasure. That was the irrefutable logic of the situation.

'So will you be kind enough to ask the nurse to find Barry's clothes for him?' Mary Pennington said.

Emotion overruled reason. 'I really think it's up to him to decide. Frankly, I don't think he should leave now, but if he wants to . . . '

'Well, darling?' Mary Pennington asked, looking at him lovingly.

When Parker Brown's wife had died he moved from their home into the large mid-Victorian house he now lived in. It was in a sadly neglected state when he bought it, cheaply, and he threw himself into redecorating it – with professional help, of course – every spare moment away from his deliberately assumed heavy workload. It was excellent therapy for him, and now he had a handsome house which was rather more grand than one would expect even for a man of his ample, but well-earned, income.

A number of housekeepers, with the assistance of daily helps, had tried to satisfy the exigent Parker Brown, and failed. After all, he was a precise surgeon, and a Virgo to boot. For those who believe in astrology, it explained all.

Armstrong, who was having dinner at Parker Brown's home, realised with some surprise that the present housekeeper, Mrs Florence Minchin, had been in Parker Brown's employment for something more than two years. And, oddly enough, Armstrong had seen her but briefly, not more than a half a dozen times. Something else nagged at the back of his mind, but he couldn't identify it. Nevertheless, it would come to him, he was sure.

Mrs Minchin quietly removed the dishes which had contained an excellent lemon sorbet, and put the coffee tray on the table. Armstrong regarded her casually, then with awakened interest. For the first time he really saw what an attractive woman she was. She was tall, almost as tall as Parker Brown, and her plain, but well-cut black dress tended to disguise her full figure. He guessed her age as at a little over forty. The dress, Armstrong decided, was much more expensive than first appeared. He almost thought: *Too expensive for a housekeeper*, but quickly dismissed the thought as unworthy. He examined her more closely, and became aware of her large eyes and potentially sensual mouth.

Good God! Armstrong suddenly said to himself. *How on earth didn't I notice before what a . . .* vital *woman she is.* The answer was, Armstrong knew, that she had deliberately tried to disguise the strong physical side of her nature.

Then finally, Armstrong found the missing piece to the puzzle. Parker Brown and Mrs Minchin never referred to each other by name, or title. She did not call him 'Mr Parker Brown', or 'sir', he did not call her 'Mrs Minchin', or 'Florence'. Bywaters and Suzy Palmer had the same sort of anonymous reticence, except for the one occasion when Suzy deliberately called him 'Neville' to shock. The difference was that while Bywaters and Suzy used no names because of their lack of a relationship, Parker Brown and Florence Minchin . . . Armstrong speculated on what they called each other when they were alone.

Occasionally, in the past, Armstrong had wondered about Parker Brown's sex life. He was vigorous still, Armstrong was sure, but interest in, and opportunities with, women had seemed limited. Armstrong wondered no longer.

'Have you ever thought of getting married again, William?' Armstrong said, with such innocence that Parker Brown instantly suspected him. He stared hard at Armstrong, thought hard for a long moment, then replied.

'No,' he said. And that subject of conversation was as closed as a bank on a Saturday morning.

Armstrong remembered the reason for the quiet evening together and became grave. 'William, this wretched business with Sister Smith. I'm afraid I've had to forward the papers to the Area Authority and the GMC. What with that, and this other complaint by Alderman Tindall about Wallman . . . ' He sighed. 'Have you any idea what has prompted her to make the charge against you?'

'I've thought about it, of course, but I still cannot conceive what was in her mind.'

'Your relatonship in the past, at – where was it?'

'Parkway Hospital.'

'Yes. Was there anything . . . ?' He left it.

'Our relationship was always completely professional, and nothing more. I never saw her outside the hospital.'

Armstrong sighed. 'Is there any possibility that you . . . weren't at your best when you operated on that man?'

'I shall not say that I am *always* at my best. Only a mediocre surgeon is *always* at his best. But I was far from my worst when I operated on that man Wingate. No one could have done any better; no one could have saved his life.'

That was unequivocal enough. The trouble was, in the face of Sister Smith's evidence and the unarguable fact that Wingate was dead, would the General Medical Council believe him?

Armstrong was quite certain they wouldn't.

Normally patients were discouraged from being out of bed late at night, except to go to the lavatory, but although it was nearly midnight, John Smith was by the open window of the unlit Day Room, looking out across the balcony to the distant skyline again. Sister Edwards was on night duty. She was once described by Capper as being a tougher disciplinarian than a Foreign Legion sergeant allergic to sand; but she allowed Smith to stay there. The news of John Smith's wife, Mary Pennington, was common knowledge in this wing of the hospital now, and his mental agitation was easy to imagine. (Sister Edwards, like everyone else who had come into contact with John Smith, still couldn't bring herself yet to think of him as Barry Pennington.) There was no point in keeping him in bed, where he would only stare at the ceiling, and Sister Edwards didn't want to drag a tired duty doctor out of bed to prescribe sleeping tablets. John Smith would soon feel tired wthout that.

'Hello. I couldn't sleep either.' He didn't have to turn: he recognised Alison's voice at once. He'd been hoping she'd come back to see him. She walked over to the window, closing the door behind her.

'Well,' she said, then paused, not knowing quite how to go on. Then: 'I suppose you feel relieved, in one way, to know who you are, even if you haven't got your memory back.' She forced herself to smile.

He nodded. They sat there in silence for a long time.

'But . . . She's just some stranger who's walked in and said she's my wife,' John burst out desperately. 'I don't know her. I couldn't just go off with her like that.'

'It's only natural. For the moment she *is* a stranger. But when your memory starts to come back . . . '

'I don't want it to come back if it means I'm married to her and I can't see you again.' A little awkwardly because of his foot, he stood, and took her hands in his.

'You think that now,' she began, but he interrupted.

'I tell you, she's a *stranger*. I don't *feel* married to her. How can I! I'm in love with you.' He pulled at her, and unresisting, she came into his arms. For one fraction of a second she was aware that she was standing on the edge of a precipice, but she deliberately closed her mind to the dangers.

'You mustn't say that,' she said with patent insincerity.

'I lo*ve you*,' he said again. 'Alison . . . '

'You know how I feel about you,' she said softly, her lips close to his ear.

The light clicked on with brutal unexpectedness, leaving both of them feeling suddenly naked.

Parker Brown stood in the doorway. He spoke quietly, but there was a terrifying edge to his voice.

'Dr Moxey, I'd like to see you in my office.'

Earlier, Parker Brown had been conscious of his own problems; he knew he wouldn't be able to sleep easily. So, he had decided to drive Armstrong home then go on to the hospital to see a couple of post-operative patients. Purely by chance he had noticed the empty bed, and had asked Sister Edwards where the patient was. She quite openly said she had allowed him to go to the Day Room. She had no idea that Alison Moxey had joined him there, otherwise she would have tried to cover for her.

The long silent walk to Parker Brown's office was like an interminable walk to the gallows. Once she tried to say something, but he silenced her with a look.

'I thought you had more sense,' Parker Brown told Alison as soon as they walked into his office. 'You've been a doctor long enough to know the dangers of becoming involved with a patient. Particularly a patient in a highly emotional, disturbed mental state.'

'I didn't want to become involved, sir,' Alison said. 'I tried to avoid it.'

'Not very energetically,' snapped Parker Brown.

'I'm sorry, but I can't help it if I've fallen in love with Mr Smith,' she said helplessly.

'You mean with Mr Barry Pennington, a married man. As soon as you realised what was happening you should have asked for someone to take over the case. Apart from that,' Parker Brown continued, brushing aside Alison's attempt to speak, 'you're keeping a valuable hospital bed tied up for a man who doesn't really need it. Well, that's easily arranged. Porter can take care of Mr Pennington, and discharge him.'

'No, sir.'

Brown fixed her with a stare that in normal circumstances would have instantly scared her into silence. But for the moment Alison was as much in the grip of an obsession as Bywaters, although she would have called it something else; and Bywaters would have denied he was. Such is the nature of that particular obsession.

'I beg your pardon, doctor?' he said.

'He's my patient and you have no right to take his case from me.'

Parker Brown gave a short bark of acid amusement. 'I have both the right and the reason for exercising it.'

'Sir, you said yourself he's in a badly disturbed state. If we're suddenly separated like this, and he's sent off home to a place he doesn't know with someone who's a complete stranger to him . . . And quite honestly, his leg still does need some attention.'

Parker Brown moved round his office, not taking his eyes off her as he did. It was a full minute before he spoke.

'Very well. I'll trust in your basic commonsense, and let you resolve the case. *Every* aspect of the case, do you understand?'

'Thank you,' Alison said with some dignity.

'But one more exhibition like tonight's . . . ' He did not have to spell out the consequences.

Silicones, according to one book of reference, *is a term applied to compounds of the general formula* R_2SiO, *where* R *stands for hydrocarbon radicals . . . Used as lubricants, for water-repellant finishes, high-temperature resisting resins and laquers.* There is another, more spectacular and often aesthetically more pleasing use of silicone, as anyone knows who has seen nude shows in Las Vegas and topless shows in other places of esoteric entertainment. If Miss Kay 'Cayenne' Pepper had not been given the silicone treatment, she had been richly endowed by a liberally-handed Fate. She also had magnificent long legs, but quite small feet, however, and there were times during her celebrated stage act when it seemed likely that she would overbalance and topple on to her face. Or at least, on to her formidable *balcon*, which was visible an appreciable time before the rest of her when she came round a corner.

When she entered Reception she brought a temporary halt to all activity there. She was wearing a skirt that was little more than a pelmet, and a nylon jersey top that looked as if it had been sprayed on with a miserly hand. She was irresistibly evocative of a set of footballs in an elastic bag.

In one major respect Kay Pepper's appearance was deceptive. It was true that she could never have caught a unicorn,* but she was a *nice* girl. She was pleasant, cheerful, and she was very bright. Bright enough to conceal the fact. Perhaps most important of all was that she was genuinely likeable. Even women liked her.

Ernie Penrose, the porter who had inherited most of Capper's money-making schemes in the hospital when he departed, rushed over to her side to ask if he could help.

'My name is Pepper. I have an appointment with Dr Armstrong.'

'Follow me. I'll take you there myself,' Penrose said generously. 'My name is Penrose. Ernest to my friends.'

'Oh, Ernie Penrose. I've heard of you.'

'I'm not surprised, even though I do say it myself. Er . . . how, exactly?'

'From Arnold. Arnold Capper. He told me all about you.'

'Oh? How do you know Arnold?'

'I'm his client.' Penrose stopped dead in his tracks.

'I say, are you all right?' asked Miss Pepper. 'You've gone all pale.'

Ernie Penrose pulled himself together. 'It's the long hours. You've got to be dedicated in this work.' He tried to look brave and long-suffering, but managed only to look constipated. 'His client?' he pursued. 'How exactly?'

She was about to explain, when Knight, Leakey and van Kroll, on their way to the wards, approached from the opposite direction.

'Good morning,' they all said. Kay favoured them all with an across-the-footlights smile.

'Can I help you?' asked Knight. It was a question that she was asked several times every day, by complete strangers.

*According to legend, unicorns could only be caught by a virgin sitting under a tree. There are no authenticated instances of the capture of a unicorn, but whether this was due to a shortage of trees or virgins is not recorded.

'It's all right, thank you,' she said. 'This gentleman is taking me to Dr Armstrong's office.'

That silenced everyone for a moment.

'Dr *Armstrong*?' said van Kroll.

'I have an appointment,' she explained.

'You're there,' said Knight. 'I mean, here. The office.' He indicated a door, marked with Dr Armstrong's name, leading to his secretary's outer office. Pepper turned up the candle-power of her smile, flashed it at all of them in turn, then knocked on the door and entered.

'Bloody hell,' said Knight. 'If that's the bird Capper's fixed up for Armstrong . . . '

'He'd better keep on taking the tablets,' Leakey finished for him, with his grand-piano grin.

Later that day, a day in which the hospital had buzzed like a jar full of bluebottles, Barbara Kennedy and Bywaters walked into the cafeteria and saw Armstrong cheerfully eating a Welsh rarebit – an indication of an unnatural insouciance. They looked at each other significantly and went over to join him. Armstrong was drinking tea with his rarebit, which was one encouraging sign, at least. He might be going potty, but not potty enough to drink canteen coffee, Bywaters observed. They had been with him only a moment when Leakey and van Kroll appeared and joined the party.

The three younger men looked at Barbara expectantly. After a moment she coughed with some embarrassment and said in a suddenly loud voice, which she managed to control fairly quickly: 'Er . . . interesting young woman, the one who came to see you this morning.'

Armstrong looked up, surprised. 'A lot of young women came to see me this morning. It was my out-patients day.'

'Miss Pepper,' prompted Leakey.

'Oh, her,' said Armstrong. 'I thought you meant a patient. You noticed her, did you?' Since this was tantamount to asking a group whether they'd 'noticed' the brass band in the chapel nobody answered.

'Who was she?' said van Kroll, who was not English and so not inhibited about asking.

'Capper arranged it, actually,' said Armstrong, not answering directly. 'I suppose you've all heard, but I'd be glad if you kept it to yourself for the time being. Of course, sooner or later I shan't be able to keep it secret any longer, but in the meantime . . .'

The others all nodded; then there was a fusillade of worried glances around the table as Armstrong tackled his rarebit again. He looked up, and everybody suddenly looked nonchalant again. 'I must say, I'm very excited by the prospects. It's been a long time since I went in for anything quite like that. I mean, it's not your ordinary, run-of-the-mill old banger.'

This produced a strained silence that was almost painful in its intensity. Fortunately Armstrong was too occupied with eating to seem to notice it. Then everyone spoke at once.

'Do you think – '

'Are you sure – '

'Is it really – '

'Dr Armstrong – '

Just as abruptly, everyone stopped again. There was a great exchange of 'After you' gestures, all of them abortive. Armstrong seemed blissfully unaware of the consternation he was causing.

'Actually,' he said, and everyone's attention became riveted on him as if he were about to announce the winner of the Irish Sweep. 'Actually, it's not definitely fixed up yet. I mean, not *definitely*. We agreed that I should have a week's trial, see how it goes.' He smiled modestly. 'After all, it's been a long time since I tried anything quite like that. I want to make sure I can cope. I don't want to do myself any damage.' He rose, and smiled at them all. 'Good morning.' And left.

A man who is chasing a woman but doesn't want to admit it to himself can produce the most contorted rationalisations for encountering her. He can persuade himself, for example, that their meeting was completely fortuitous, even though he has been prowling about in front of her house for hours

Bywaters at least did not try to delude himself. He deliberately set out to contact Suzy Palmer, and admitted it to himself. He remembered the address of her block of flats, called Directory Enquiries and hung on while the phone rang for a seeming eternity. When he was given her number he called it on four seperate occasions before she answered.

'This is Neville Bywaters,' he said. 'Are you doing anything this evening? Would you like dinner, or something?' The silence that followed this was so long he thought they had been cut off. 'Hello? Are you still there?' he said.

'Why? I mean, why do you want to take me out?'

'I'm not sure,' he said slowly. 'Perhaps . . . I dislike failure, and misunderstanding . . . '

'You sure you don't just want – '

'No!' he said sharply, before she could finish. 'Look, I enjoyed that last time, the Bach chamber concert, the afternoon on the lake . . . '

'So did I,' she said, almost too softly for him to hear. 'Until . . . ' she added, but he didn't hear that.

'I'll call for you at seven,' he said and hung up. He hurried out of his consulting room, and nearly knocked over Geoffrey Nollet, who was passing.

'Terribly sorry, my dear chap,' he said. Nollet looked at him blankly. It was the first time since he'd been at the hospital someone hadn't said: 'Get out of the way, you stupid fool.'

When Suzy opened the door to Bywaters, he caught his breath. She looked utterly different from the woman he'd seen about the hospital so often: even from the cool young woman who had gone to the concert with him. This time she had unmistakeable *class* about her. Her hair was neatly coiled and pinned up at the back of her head, revealing her slender neck. She was wearing a tan blouse with matching slacks and a light suede jacket: the evening had turned cool. Bywaters was thrown off balance again. She was as unpredictable and changeable as the wind. Maybe that was her attraction – or part of it, anyway.

She had been on the phone in the bedroom when he called. 'My mother,' she explained afterwards. 'She rings two or three times a week to make sure I'm all right.'

'Are you eating enough, are you keeping your feet dry . . . ?' he said.

'Something like that.' She paused. 'She writes, too; long letters. She's marvellous.' If a shadow passed across her face Bywaters didn't notice it, and it was quickly gone anyway.

'I was thinking of taking you to The Woolpack, but I'm not sure they'll let you in wearing trousers,' he said, as he led her to his car.

'I'll take them off, then,' she said, but there was no sexual implication; they both laughed.

In fact, there was no difficulty at The Woolpack, which was fairly choosey about who was let in, but didn't operate hard and fast rules. Suzy, looking as she did on this occasion, was admitted without hesitation; but in one of her tarty dresses and make-up she would have been told politely and firmly that they didn't have a table.

It was a quiet drive out of town and across open country to the restaurant which had started life as a rather dull roadhouse, and then acquired a brief reputation as a rendezvous for dirty weekends and nights. When wickedness became easier and more fashionable, the place went downhill, becoming seedier and seedier until even illicit sex couldn't make you forget tattiness. It was purchased by a retired RAF officer who risked his entire gratuity on redecorating and refurbishing the place. The first thing he did was to put in enormous picture windows on the west-facing side of the building. He reasoned that most people would come for dinner, and the marvellous view across the countryside towards the sunset would be a handsome bonus. Then he established the principle that he would give the finest possible food and service first, and worry about the cost second. It was a good formula: after a shaky start, The Woolpack prospered. And anyone who came away from dinner there feeling less than marvellous either went there with indigestion, or without a companion, or both.

Certainly Bywaters and Suzy were in a happily euphoric mood when they left – and it was not due to alcohol: he always took great care about his intake when he was driving. There was a strange, comforting empathy between them; and there had been no hint of the sudden sadness which sometimes overtook her, no abrupt and inexplicable surge of temper. He turned on the car radio, recognised almost instantly that the music was Richard Strauss's *Death and Transfiguration*, and switched to another station. Julian Bream was playing the blind composer Rodrigo's *Concierto de Aranjuez*. Fortunately it was the last vigorously dancing movement, for the preceding *Adagio* is almost unbearably sad. That music, and the *Courtly Dances* from Britten's *Gloriana* which followed saw them back to town, and to Suzy's home.

When they pulled up in front of the block of flats she said 'I'll make you some coffee' – a plain statement of fact in a neutral tone suggestive of nothing. A refusal would have been pointless, giving the remark a significance it did not have.

Her behaviour once inside the flat could not have been more innocuous. She flung her coat on to a chair in the corner of the living room, and went straight to the kitchen. This time, however, she did not go to 'put on something more comfortable' while Bywaters played a record of a Mozart string quartet, then sat relaxed on the wide settee.

When she returned with the coffee tray, and bent over the low table to put it down, he was all at once aware of her figure. In The Woolpack, with other people near them and the constant attendance of the waiters, there was little sense of intimacy. While they were there he looked at her, spoke to her, but did not *see* her as he saw her now. Surely Suzy could not be unaware of the sudden rush of blood he felt as she sat beside him, not quite touching him. He remembered how, on that first occasion, she had held his hand tight against her breast, and he ached to touch it again now. Bywaters found the whole situation weird. He desired this woman beside him, she was known to be a sexual creature herself, she had tacitly indicated her readiness . . . and she was clearly provoking him the way she leaned back, making the thin blouse pull tight over her breasts. And yet he couldn't bring himself to – no, that wasn't it: he didn't *know how* to make the next move, the gesture that would establish the essential first physical contact between them. His anger rose, because somehow he felt it must be her fault he was behaving like a schoolboy on his first serious date.

Suzy leaned even further back against the settee, and took a deep breath, slightly arching her back. He looked at her breasts, and knew she was aware of him staring at them. As he continued to look, he saw the nipples harden and become more prominent against the thin tan blouse. Her mouth opened slightly, and the tip of her pink tongue ran round them slowly to moisten them.

The impulse to take her in his arms was irresistible. He leaned towards her – but then the record came to an end with a noisy scratching. Bywaters took a deep, uneven breath and got up to turn off the player. After a moment Suzy rose, too. She went over to him and leaned against the wall. 'You've got quite a reputation at the hospital,' she said. There was an edge to her voice that stung him. He looked up sharply.

'So have you,' he said. She flinched slightly, but then her mouth twisted into a wry smile. 'Ah, but I deserve mine. You don't deserve yours.'

For a moment he misunderstood. 'Why? What is my reputation, then?'

'You've got the reputation for being quite a man. What do you do? Get them drunk first? Or is going out with women just a cover?'

She reached behind her head, and unpinned her hair so

it fell about her shoulders. Very slowly, she unfastened the top button of her blouse. Then the next one. The deep cleft between her breasts was emphasised by the light coming from beside and below. Slowly again she rubbed the first two fingers of her right hand up and down the cleft, looking at Bywaters with a faintly mocking smile as she did it.

His mouth felt very dry.

Still without haste, she stretched out her left hand, took his right one, and pressed it against her breast, hard. It broke the spell which had seemed to bind him in complete passivity. He pulled her towards him and kissed her on her parted lips, attacking her rather than caressing her with his own mouth. His hand felt for her blouse to unbutton it, but she pulled away from him, and ripped it open herself with both hands, effectively leaving herself naked above the waist. Her breasts rose and fell with her quick, almost gasping breathing. It was, Bywaters thought, one of the most erotic sights he had ever seen.

Their love making was hungry, almost brutal from the outset, and gained in frantic intensity. At one moment, for no longer than a heartbeat, Bywaters suddenly wondered *How many other men have been on this settee?* . . . and loathed himself for even thinking it: it made him even more violent in his sexuality – to the point that he was only dimly aware of Suzy's nails raking his back, and her deep, indrawn sighs.

Bywaters was an experienced man, a sensitive and understanding one; but the uncontrolled tempestuousness of their assaults on each other's bodies blinded him to something that subsequently hit him with shattering force. At first he did not want to believe it, but the more he thought back, the more certain he became. He looked down at her, naked, her eyes shiny with the tears that were welling on to her cheeks, and with some indefinable emotion.

She was not the experienced, promiscuous young woman he had imagined her to be.

Quite the reverse.

Chapter Eleven

As Bywaters lay beside Suzy while they both relaxed after the violent mental and physical upheaval of their love-making, he began to understand a great deal that had baffled him before. He did not understand everything at once, of course, but he grasped the general pattern, and the finer detail became progressively apparent to him later. Suzy's lack of experience had produced this strange protective aura, which made it difficult to make the first positive sexual move with her. Her overt hyper-sexuality was a deliberately assumed façade, the boldest of bold fronts, but behind it was a timid naïvety. It explained the strange reactions of some of the doctors who had taken her out: they hadn't made love to her after all, but couldn't possibly bring themselves to admit their failure with someone who appeared to be so basically sexual. Paradoxically, her blatant provocativeness and *outré* dress, which made it seem that she was determined to be an amateur whore, turned out to be her greatest defence. The man expected the most effortless trip to bed of his life – probably visualised himself even having to fight her off a little. But when it came to it, there was some strange and powerful emotional barrier between him and Suzy. But who was going to admit he hadn't made it with *her*, of all people?

Bywaters realised that he had managed it only because she provoked him beyond endurance – with, he suspected, behaviour of which she had only a theoretical knowledge. That extraordinarily arousing gesture of the fingers between her breasts . . . he was certain that she did not fully understand its implication for herself, and it did not come from experience.

He did not want to consider the natural corollary: that she had provoked him so deliberately because she wanted *him*. He didn't have that sort of unpleasant conceit.

She kissed him gently, then with increasing warmness, driving out all thoughts of anything but her exciting body. She came closer to him, held him – rather inexpertly, but perhaps all the more exciting because of it. They were on the bed now, which was wider and more comfortable than the settee. Here he no longer had the least thought of any other man in her life.

They made love again, slowly, gently, exploringly, affectionately. . . . This time he was certain without the least possible doubt of her inexperience. There were moments when she had to ask him what to do, how to respond; and delicately, patiently he guided her. Once she cried out with what he thought was pain, but she pulled him closer to her with desperate need.

When once more they lay quiet, unmoving, she caught him looking almost unbelievingly at her body from her feet – one foot resting on the other – up her legs; looking caressingly at her body, her breasts; and brushing the nipples with the lightest of touches of his sensitive fingertips; looking at the fine curve of her delicate neck before leaning forward to kiss her without passion but with love.

She turned her head and hid her face in the hollow of his shoulder.

'What's the matter?' he asked.

'I'm . . . it's the way you look at me. It makes me feel shy.'

'After what we've . . . ?' He laughed.

She nodded, her face still hidden, but he could feel she was laughing, too.

What he had meant, of course, was that it was odd she should feel shy at being looked at after their ultimate intimacies. It occurred to neither of them that he could have meant it was ludicrous that she should be shy, considering the way she dressed – revealingly, provokingly, often more erotically than simple nakedness.

For the moment Bywaters did not ask himself why this strange, unsophisticated girl should have acted so wildly, so blatantly with other men.

For the moment.

There is a well-known hospital story about a doctor who knocked on the door of a private room, and waited until the woman patient said 'Come in'. He then told her to undress completely and gave her a most searching examination. When it was over, the woman laughed. The doctor asked why.

'Why did you bother to knock?' she said.

Wallman, accompanied by Doreen Holland, knocked on the door of the private room, but demonstrated his authority by entering without waiting for an answer.

Lord Trenchman was sitting up in bed, reading S. J. Perelman's *Crazy as a Fox*. He put down the book as Wallman and Doreen entered.

'I'll have to stop reading that,' he said. 'Every time I laugh it hurts my ribs.'

Wallman smiled, then took the latest X-rays and intravenous pyelogram from Doreen. Apparently they were encouraging, for he nodded with satisfaction. Finally, he took the chart from the end of the bed and studied that.

'Well, you seem to be coming along nicely. Your ribs are knitting satisfactorily, the slight infection you had has cleared up, and we saved the damaged kidney. It's functioning quite well.' He looked closely at Trenchman's face. 'There'll be hardly any scarring on your face. One or two little white marks for a while, but they'll probably disappear eventually.'

'You did a good job. I'm grateful.'

'No need for that. All part of the job. Staff, how's his appetite?'

'Very good, these last couple of days, sir.'

'Is there anything you need?' Wallman asked Trenchman.

'Not really. They're taking jolly good care of me. Oh, by the way, my father was in yesterday. He asked after you.'

Wallman turned to Doreen. 'Thank you, Staff. I'll see you in a moment.' Doreen nodded and went out of the room.

'I was . . . busy operating,' Wallman said after she'd gone.

'He mentioned the grant. I'm glad. I'm sure you deserve it.'

'Uhuh,' Wallman said flatly.

'Nobody told me: was anyone else hurt in the accident?'

Wallman shook his head. 'You were the only casualty we admitted.' If there was an evasion in what he said, Trenchman didn't notice it.

'Good,' he said eventually. Then: 'I still can't understand how it happened.'

'I shouldn't worry about it too much,' Wallman said mechanically.

'Er, how long will it be before I can leave?' Lord Trenchman asked.

'Not long. And the less you think about getting out of here, the quicker it'll be.' Wallman nodded and started to leave. As he got to the door, Trenchman called to him.

'Mr Wallman.'

'Yes?'

'I wasn't drunk, you know.'

Wallman didn't know what to say, so he just nodded, and went out.

As he came out of the lift on the ground floor, Wallman met Kirby.

'I want to see you right away.'

'I have patients waiting.'

'This won't take long.' As Wallman started to interrupt, Kirby pressed on: 'Think of it as an emergency case that's just come in. Because, in a manner of speaking, that's just what it is.'

Inside the office, Kirby came straight to the point. 'I have to make a preliminary investigation into Tindall's complaint about you. I've seen the papers, and I'm afraid it looks rather bad. You know I'll do my best to cover for you, but – '

'There's nothing to *cover*.'

'I expresed myself badly. I'll do my best on your behalf, but the circumstantial case is very strong. Tindall's obviously got his sources inside the hospital, because he knows that you said Trenchman was fit enough to give a specimen of blood, *then* Earl Dellamayne telephoned you, and after that you broke the specimen bottles.'

'Accidentally. *I* wasn't even holding them. And I'm not at all sure that the phone call from Dellamayne *did* come through when you say it did.'

'I didn't say it did. Tindall's sources do.'

'Even so,' Wallman said impatiently, 'it's all a bit far-fetched.'

'Added to that, there's the grant from Dellamayne's foundation.'

'It's not *his* bloody foundation, for God's sake! It's the Ghazarossiam Foundation!'

'But it's well known he makes the decisions, and the other trustees just rubber-stamp his recommendations. And the award couldn't have been worse timed, from your point of view. Oh, yes, congratulations on the grant.'

Wallman glared at him. Kirby probably wasn't trying to be sarcastic . . . or was he? Anyway, that was a minor point now.

'So, with one thing and another, it does seem rather black.' He paused. 'And that's not all.'

'Come on, what else is in the complaint?'

'Apparently when Dellamayne phoned the night his son

was admitted, he asked for you *by name.* As well he might. Since he knows you . . . ' He looked sideways at Wallman, who seemed carved from stone. Kirby went on: 'Even that's not the end of it. I don't know how Tindall found out – waiters, servants, journalists, perhaps – but he also knows you met Dellamayne for lunch to canvas for his help in getting the grant. That clinches it: the whole thing looks very much like a mutual back-scratching operation at best, a bribe at worst. It's a very solid case . . . '

Doreen saw Alison Moxey in the corridor near the Day Room, and bustled over towards her like Doris Day preparing to tackle Rock Hudson, but Sister Washington intercepted her. 'Not now, Staff,' she said.

'But – ' Doreen began.

'Not now.'

Doreen took a second look, and saw that Alison's attention was fiercely concentrated on something or someone in the Day Room. 'Mrs Pennington?' Doreen asked. Sister Washington nodded.

Mary Pennington was showing John Smith a photograph. 'This is our little home in Bramhall,' she said.

John looked hard at a blurred picture of the back of an ordinary semi-detached suburban house. Mary herself was in the garden, smiling uncertainly at the camera. It seemed to have been taken five years or more ago.

'You took it yourself, but you wouldn't trust me with the camera,' she explained. 'Do you remember?' He shook his head miserably, but she wasn't upset. 'Never mind, darling, it'll all come back in time.' She looked at him with a coy mock-seriousness that made his flesh creep. 'But I really think you ought to come home now. I need you; I can't manage on my own, you know. Not properly.'

'Yes, I understand,' John replied. 'But . . . ' He was floundering badly, but Alison recognised the signs and quickly entered the Day Room. She greeted them as if she hadn't been waiting outside, watching, all this time. Then, with deliberate casualness, Alison asked a question.

'Mrs Pennington, there's something we're all curious about – I'm sure it would help Dr Bauer, the psychiatrist . . . ' Mary Pennington looked at her sharply. 'What work does . . . Mr Pennington do?'

'Oh, Barry doesn't work,' she replied with her over-sweet

smile. 'My father left us the house and enough money to manage on. Not a lot, but adequate. I don't need a great deal for myself, you see. I'm a stay-at-home. Barry's the one who likes to go and do things.'

The reply lay like a stone between them. John – Barry – was a parasite on his older, less attractive wife? Alison suddenly felt sick; and it was clear that John himself was shaken by this news.

'I don't do anything at all? No part-time job, even some unpaid work?'

Mary Pennington shook her head. 'There's no need for you to, darling.' She looked at Alison. 'Doctor, I'd be grateful if you'd do what you can to persuade Barry to leave here. I'm sure his leg's well enough for him to come home. He'll be much better with me: I can look after him, like I did when he broke those three ribs.'

'How did I do that?' he asked, before Alison could say anything.

'You were knocked over when a young woman skidded on her – what do you call those bicycles with engines? – oh, yes, a moped.'

Alison rose. She couldn't bear to see this strange woman's possessiveness, to have to acknowledge her rights over John, and to suffer the fact that she knew him intimately – better than he knew himself; while Alison herself loved him without knowing him at all, and with no rights over him.

'You will tell him to come home, won't you, doctor?' Mary Pennington repeated. Alison nodded and went out.

'Next time I come, darling, it'll be to take you home, where you belong. And don't worry: I know it's going to be a little strange at first. But because I love you, I'll give you all the time you need to recover, and for us to get to know each other again. You know I won't make any . . . demands on you until you're ready. I'll sleep in the spare room until you want me. I'll respect your feelings, darling.'

John looked at her aghast. He had not thought for a second of sexual relations with her. He looked at her with new eyes, and tried to imagine himself in bed with her, making love to her . . . and his flesh crept. Her declaration, meant to reassure, only horrified him. Mary seemed unaware of his reaction as she gathered up her things, kissed him on the cheek, and went out.

'Next time, darling,' she said.

He watched her go, a haunted look on his face.

Although it was a bright afternoon, the Doctors' Common Room was as gloomy as an undertaker's anteroom.

Bywaters sat by himself, white-faced and drawn, clearly so lost in his own agonising thoughts that no one risked going and speaking to him. Barbara Kennedy was about to, then saw his eyes, and decided to leave well alone.

All morning he had been in an euphoric glow after his night with Suzy, and the fragile tenderness of their parting. Then, he had encountered her in the corridor, talking to Dennis Porter. With a shock he saw she was again wearing her flamboyant Egyptianate make-up, and one of her more revealing dresses. There was a bigger shock to come: He increased his pace to go to speak to her, and he was almost certain she had seen him coming when she leaned forward and kissed Porter with a long, open-mouthed kiss. She pulled away just as Bywaters drew level, looked at him and said: 'Oh, hello, Neville. Sorry, I can't make it tonight. I've got another date.'

She put her hand in Porter's arm and walked off without a second look. Porter glanced over his shoulder at Bywaters and gave an apologetic shrug. Bywaters couldn't blame him; but in any case, he was stunned, and felt very little – like a soldier who has received a mortal blow yet is unaware that he had been wounded. The pain comes later.

By the time he had recovered, both Suzy and Porter had disappeared.

Armstrong and Parker Brown were speaking quietly in a corner. Parker Brown was telling him that he had received the official notification from the General Medical Council's Disciplinary Division of the date of the hearing of the charge against him.

'Does anyone here know yet?' Armstrong asked.

'Only you, Matthew – and Sister Smith, of course – but I expect it'll be common knowledge soon.'

'Have you informed the Medical Defence Union?' Parker Brown nodded. 'I did it the day you told me what Sister Smith had said.' He shook his head in bewilderment, like a wounded bull in the ring.

Bauer, who always looked serious, was with Alison. Fortunately for her, she was not in Parker Brown's direct line of vision, and in any case he had his own problems. Otherwise, he might well have guessed what was making her look so sombre, and resolved the situation by removing John Smith from her care.

'Certainly the arrival of Pennington's wife doesn't seem to have done him any good,' Bauer said. Alison looked at him blankly. 'Who?' she asked.

'Pennington. The amnesia patient,' he said without impatience. (Alison, of course, still thought of him as John Smith.) 'His reactions are illogical, too – '

'If there's such a thing as logicality in psychiatry,' said Barbara Kennedy, who happened to be passing and heard that one sentence. Neither of the others reacted. Barbara grimaced and walked on. It was one of those days.

'I've spoken to the wife,' Bauer continued. 'She couldn't help me with the problem. Or didn't want to,' he added. 'She seemed rather resentful of me – although I expect that was only the usual uneducated person's customary attitude to psychiatrists: a general reaction to us all rather than a particular one to me.'

'What help were you hoping to get?' Alison asked.

'Some indication of the area of stress which caused the amnesia. But according to her, he had no problems, sexual, financial or professional. It's a pity we weren't able to use narco-hypnosis. It might have solved everything for us. As it is . . . ' He left it in the air.

'She wants to take him home.'

'No reason why she shouldn't, as long as he continues treatment there. But one thing is quite certain about the case.'

She looked questioningly at him.

'We haven't heard the last of this: not by a long way.'

The day had seemed interminable to Bywaters, and everyone who had come into contact with him had found him either absent-minded or abrasive. He had become increasingly difficult as the time drew nearer to the end of office hours for the administrative staff. Finally, he had gone down to the computer section, waited until Suzy came out of her office. He took her arm and said, 'I want to talk to you.' She was going to protest and struggle, but one glance was enough to see that he was utterly determined. He would not be put off by a noisy scene, not even here in the hospital.

He took her into his consulting room, pushed her towards the chair, and shut the door behind them.

'What is all this?' he asked. 'What the hell's got into you?' For a moment she was going to say 'All what?' but that would have been too ingenuous.

'Look, just because you've been to bed with me doesn't mean you own me,' she said.

'No, not just because we've been to bed together. But because there was more to it than that. You know it, and I know it.'

'You don't own me,' she said again, with something like sullenness.

'Yes, I do. Or at least, I own a small part of something inside you; and since last night, a tiny part of me belongs to you. We both gave, and accepted.'

'Oh, come on,' she said with attempted casualness. 'We had sex . . . ' (Before last night she would have used the coarsest of expressions to try to shock him, put him off, but she could not bring herself to speak like that to him now.) 'We had sex . . . It's happening all over, all the time.'

'Not like last night.' He waited, but she did not try to deny it. 'And today, you look like *that* again . . . ' He gestured towards her dress. She started to make a movement of something like modesty, as if to cover her breasts. She checked it almost at once – but not before he had noticed. 'Then you behave like a tart with Dennis Porter, who you don't even like much, and you do it where I'll be sure to see you. For God's sake, what's the matter with you?'

'What's the matter with me,' she repeated, with such unexpected bitterness that Bywaters, who thought he was beyond shock, nevertheless was taken aback.

She fell into a brooding silence. Bywaters did not try to press her for an answer. He sensed now that she would tell him eventually, without any more encouragement. She sighed, and said at last, 'I suppose I owe you an explanation, if I don't owe you anything more.' He sat down at the desk, facing her.

'Neville,' she said softly, 'I –'

His bleeper sounded.

It set up the most agonising conflict he could remember since he had joined the hospital. His deeply engrained training and professional instinct was to answer the emergency call for his help; his natural instinct and emotion cried out to him to ignore it. The bleeper sounded inordinately loud in the room. He *could* ignore it . . . They'd get someone else . . .

He reached out for the phone and dialled 'O'. As he did he said to her, 'We'll finish this later.' He did not hear her say as she went out: 'It *is* finished.'

The Day Room was full of patients watching television, and even Alison, in the grip of what used to be called 'unrequited love', the worse sort of overwhelming obsession, could not bring herself to ask Sister Washington to give up her office, where she was catching up on paperwork, for a purely personal, non-medical, talk with John Smith. Infatuated as Alison was, she had not totally lost all sense of propriety. Not yet. So, she was compelled to talk to him sitting at his bedside, keeping her voice low with an enormous effort.

'I don't want to go off with a stranger, someone I've known for far less long than I've known you,' John said to her in an uncertainly controlled voice. 'Someone I don't . . . feel for the same why I feel about you.' Somehow he could not say 'love' here in the ward.

'Oh, hell,' Alison said. She blew her nose hard so she wouldn't cry. Because once she started . . . She pulled herself together.

'I don't want to go with her, but what else can I do, at least to begin with? I don't have a job, I don't know anything. How would I live?'

Alison was on the point of saying that she could manage to keep both of them until John could establish himself (how?) but instinctively she realised it wasn't the moment.

'And you're married, yourself,' he said.

'You can forget my husband. That was over before you came into my life.'

'There's your career.'

'That wouldn't be affected.' *Unless your wife complained to the GMC*, she thought, but once again she stopped herself saying too much.

'And I suppose I owe my . . . my wife something, some loyalty, even though I don't *know* her. She seems so devoted to me. If I left her . . . ' He paused, then burst out, 'But even the very idea of . . . ' It was his turn to stop short, but Alison guessed what he was thinking about – sexual relations with Mary Pennington.

The strain of speaking in a low voice, keeping from touching each other, trying to look self-controlled while suffering these deep, searching emotions, was almost too much for them. 'I don't *want* my memory back; I don't want to be Barry Pennington, and be *looked after* by her. She smothers me. Oh, dear God, what a mess! What are we going to do?' He looked at her desperately, but she was silent. 'Alison?'

Armstrong hoped that this new day would not be overcast by the general gloom and *Angst* that had seemed to affect practically everybody for the past forty-eight hours. Quite unwittingly he was to provide a little light relief himself, although he was unaware of it, and would have been flabbergasted if he had known what his colleagues were thinking.

He was walking along the corridor between his consulting room and the wards, talking to Tony Callie, the new young houseman physician, when Kay Pepper bounced along the full length of the corridor towards them. It was an awe-inspiring sight. Tony Callie unaccountably thought of the sound of galloping horses, and could not work out why until much later. (It was because the sound of horses' hooves is made by knocking two coconut shells together.)

'I must see you, doctor,' she said breathlessly. 'I'm in trouble.'

Already? thought Callie. *He's only known here –*

Armstrong coughed noisily. 'If you'll just come along to my consulting room . . . Er, Dr Callie, I'll see you in a moment.' Armstrong took Kay Pepper's arm without any ulterior motive other than to guide her to his consulting room, but Callie thought enviously *I'd like to get* my *hand in there . . .*

As Armstrong and Kay walked quickly to his room, Callie, keeping a respectful distance, strained his ears trying to hear what she was saying. In fact, she was telling Armstrong: 'I know I said it'd be perfectly all right for you to have it for a week but I got my dates mixed up. I have this engagement in this club up north, and I can't get there and back in time if I don't have my car.'

It was an innocuous enough statement, but Callie, unfortunately heard only part of it.

I know I said it'd be perfectly all right . . . but I got my dates mixed up . . . in the club . . .

Armstrong and Kay were in the consulting room only a few moments. If he'd known how easily the situation could have been resolved, Armstrong wouldn't have bothered to leave the corridor. It was a pity he did.

He reassured her that he was perfectly willing to let her have her car back. Kay thanked him, bobbled over to the door and opened it. Callie was just outside, ostensibly waiting for Armstrong, but with his ears in overdrive. Knight was with him, full of the misinformation Callie had just given him, and waiting to see if there was anything more to be learned.

'You can't imagine how relieved I am, Dr Armstrong,' she

said in a voice like honey dripping off a book of Patience Strong's poems. 'A lot of men would have been very nasty and told me to get lost.'

'I can't believe that,' he said politely. 'Now, if you'd like to call at the hospital first thing tomorrow . . . '

Her face fell. 'Tomorrow?'

'Well, call at my house this evening, if you prefer. We can do it then.'

'You're super! I was so worried!' Kay said. And because she was a 'theatrical' and they do that sort of thing, she gave him a big, fat, lipstick-leaving kiss on the cheek. She turned quickly, setting up a series of intricate and complex body vibrations that were quite indescribably delightful. She gave Knight and Callie one of her lighthouse smiles, piped a 'Hi!' and tripped away down the corridor.

'Do you suffer from adenoids, Dr Knight?' said Armstrong with a voice like a Russian ice-breaker.

'No, sir,' Knight blurted.

'Then why are you standing there with your mouth open in that offensive manner?'

Knight shut his mouth with an audible snap. He was thinking *Wait till I tell the boys about* that!

'That's healing very nicely,' Parker Brown said. 'It's almost completely better. By the time you've had some more physiotherapy, you won't have the least trace of a limp. What games do you play?'

'I'm not sure,' said John Smith.

'No, of course not. Although from your muscular development, I should say you are reasonably athletic. Dr Moxey, a moment, please.'

While he and Alison went towards the Nurses' Station of the ward, Doreen Holland settled John Smith back in bed, then picked up his patient's file and X-rays to put them into the wheeled records cabinet that was pushed round the ward with doctors when they were visiting patients.

'I see no reason to keep him in hospital any longer,' Parker Brown said flatly. 'He should be discharged without delay.'

'But sir: you said you'd give me time to resolve the case. In your own words, "every aspect of the case". Well, his leg may be better, but . . . ' She hesitated.

'When I said that I did not give you carte blanche to keep

him here until he's an old-age pensioner. Now I'm giving you a direct instruction – '

'Excuse me, sir.' Sister Washington's interruption was like a last minute reprieve at the gallows to Alison.

'Sister Lester in the I.C.U.* is calling. She thinks Mr Gregory, your mitral stenosis patient may be collapsing.'

'I'll speak to you later,' Parker Brown said to Alison, as he hurried from the ward. Alison felt sorry for Mr Gregory, and at the same time she was grateful for the interruption. It gave her a little more time. But would it be enough?

'There's a telephone call for you, doctor,' said Doreen.

Alison picked up the phone on the nurse's desk.

'Hello?' came a woman's voice. 'Dr Moxey?'

'Yes?'

'This is Mary Pennington. I'm coming to collect my husband tomorrow. Will you see his things are ready, please?'

The phone at the other end clicked and went dead.

'Can you tell me whether nine-oh-seven-five is engaged speaking or out of order, please?' Bywaters asked the operator – a man, as it was night time.

'Hold on, please.' After a moment he came back on the line. 'The phone's off the hook,' he said. 'But there's somebody in the house. I could hear them moving about. I'll put the howler on, then perhaps they'll replace the phone.'

If a phone is left off the hook, deliberately or accidentally, the exchange can make the phone give an ear-piercing 'howl', and draw the subscriber's attention to it.

'No, don't bother,' Bywaters said hurriedly. 'I'm just going round there now. I'll see to it. Thanks.'

The number was Suzy's. When it gave the engaged signal for more than an hour, Bywaters guessed she'd taken the phone off the hook, but before setting off for her flat he wanted to make sure. Now he knew.

'I'm going to lean on this bell until you answer,' Bywaters called through her letter box, and finally Suzy capitulated and let him in. After all, she had to tell him sooner or later. Perhaps when he did know he wouldn't want to see her again anyway.

They sat well apart in the room: 'Sit over there, Neville, please. *Please*, or I won't talk to you,' she said. He was about

*Intensive Care Unit.

to argue, but there was a note of hysteria in her voice. It was going to be difficult enough, telling him. If he touched her the sheer physical excitement would distract her, and she wouldn't be able to go through with the explanation. So, he forced himself to sit quietly in an armchair while she sat on the edge of the divan. She got up, then sat down again half a dozen times before she started speaking. He had never seen her acting like this, and, for that matter, looking like this, either. She had on the unrevealing housecoat, and almost no make-up. It made her appear very young, very defenceless, and quite beautiful, as opposed to desirable: her skin was naturally smooth and clear, her bone structure delicate. Bywaters wanted to reach out and take her in his arms, but he knew it would only delay the explanations.

She didn't know how to tell him, how to start; but eventually she chose the best way: straight out, in the simplest terms.

'I've got a congenital heart defect. I don't have long to live.'

They both sat there silent, unmoving.

'So, I've been making the most of the time I have left. A short life, and a merry one . . . ' She gave a dreadful smile that wrung his heart. Once she had started, it became increasingly easy to tell him the entire story: it came pouring out. Her father died of heart trouble when she was a child. In her teens Suzy suffered from 'growing pains'. When she was old enough to be told, her mother explained that she had this congenital heart defect – the one that killed her father.

'What is it exactly?' Bywaters asked.

Suzy shrugged. 'She told me once, I think. I don't remember. The name doesn't matter. We went to doctor after doctor . . . Every time my mother would come out from the surgery I'd only have to look at her face to know . . . '

'Darling, there's been enormous progress in heart surgery, even in just the past few years. I could arrange for you to see the best man – '

'No!' she said loudly, shocking him into silence. 'So many times I've allowed myself to hope again, and then been disappointed. Each time it's got harder to take. I'm reconciled to it now. I'm not going to open that old wound any more. *No, Neville!*'

He looked at her, and knew it was useless to argue.

'I said I'm reconciled to it now, although sometimes . . . ' Her thoughts were far away. 'I had a boyfriend. He was the first to . . . you know. They say you either love or loathe the first man. I loved him . . . Mother insisted that he had to be told, but I couldn't do it. I was afraid of how he'd react when he knew. So, she told him for me. I was right to be afraid: I never saw him again.' She faltered for a moment, but managed to steady her voice. 'Mother's been wonderful to me: if only you knew . . . But, a few months ago I decided to . . . live, while I was still alive. You know – drink, sex, the lot.' She paused, a faint look of disgust on her face. She pulled herself together. 'So I left home. Besides, I could see how the strain of waiting was affecting mother, too. She tried everything to stop me, but it wasn't fair to her for me to stay.'

Incidents he thought he had forgotten sprang back into Bywaters' memory. Now he understood why Suzy had sounded so bitter when she said to Nurse Betty Galton: 'You've got plenty . . . ' She was thinking, 'You've got plenty of *time.*' And why Suzy had suddenly changed from a happy young woman to an unpleasant shrew at the riverside pub that night. He had touched the rawest of nerves when he talked of the sense of timelessness and permanence of the countryside. What had he said? 'You get the feeling that if we came back in ten years, or twenty, it'd all be exactly the same.' He'd thought her unbalanced at the time. Well, it was enough to unbalance anyone.

'The trouble is,' Suzy was speaking again, 'I *thought* I was reconciled to it, but I'm not. I'm *not.*' She started to cry. Bywaters went over to her and put his arm around her. Her crying increased. 'Everything's changed,' she sobbed.

'What's changed?' he asked softly.

'I've fallen in love with you.'

Chapter Twelve

Armstrong, Parker Brown, Wallman and Kirby were seated around the table of the hospital conference room, where so many careers had been decided; lives, too. In this room young doctors had been selected to join the hospital, others had been given promotion; some had been given the opportunity to resign before stern action was taken. Patients' lives and deaths had been discussed without their knowledge: hope offered and hopelessness accepted.

Now, by unhappy coincidence, two senior surgeons were under a cloud at the same time.

Wallman's case was the less serious because the evidence was all circumstantial and indirect. Kirby made this point when he reported on his enquiries to Armstrong, Medical Administrator, Parker Brown, Senior Consultant Surgeon, and Wallman, the person against whom the complaint had been made. 'My enquiries have been inconclusive, as far as the hospital is concerned. The difficulty it that there was a great deal of activity in Casualty the night Lord Trenchman was admitted, and it is impossible to determine the strict chronology of the relevant events of that evening. In addition, whether the Ghazarossiam Foundation's decision to make the grant to Mr Wallman was made before or after the night of the . . . er, incident cannot be established satisfactorily.'

'Why not?' asked Wallman.

'Because if Earl Dellamayne *had* corruptly arranged for you to get the grant in return for "helping" his son, he's hardly likely to admit it anyway. So, there is no direct evidence to support Alderman Tindall's allegations. The trouble is . . . ' He paused for effect. 'In your profession it seems that frequently you are not presumed innocent until proved guilty, but presumed guilty *unless* you can prove your innocence.'

'Which in this case, is going to be difficult,' Armstrong said heavily. Although he was feeling moderately sympathetic to Wallman, in the forefront of his mind was his deep concern for Parker Brown.

'Charming,' said Wallman.

'What would really get you off the hook,' said Kirby, abandoning his Establishment style of speech for a more comfortable colloquialism, 'is if it could be proved that Trenchman wasn't drunk. But your difficulty there is – why did he swerve right across the road like that for no reason at all – unless he was drunk?'

No one had an answer to that.

'Oh, by the way,' Kirby added, 'I had a call from a local journalist who'd got wind of the complaint. I managed to persuade him he'd be running all sorts of risks of libel suits if he tried to write anything. And Tindall isn't the most popular of men: I can't imagine anyone putting himself at risk for Tindall's sake.'

'Nevertheless,' Armstrong said, 'this is going to be a "No smoke without fire" situation unless we can clear it up somehow.'

Parker Brown at last rumbled into life. 'The whole damn thing's ridiculous beyond words – an unpleasant farce dreamed up by some pestiferous politician who has no conception of the pressures of work in Casualty.' He looked at Wallman. 'I wouldn't blame you if you punched the blasted man on the nose.'

Wallman stared at him in astonishment.

'Of course, Mr Parker Brown doesn't mean that literally,' Kirby said with that cold smile that did not touch his eyes. He didn't want to see Parker Brown and Wallman becoming too friendly. 'Now, I understand that the representative of the Medical Defence Union is coming here to see Mr Parker Brown about the complaint against him to the General Medical Council.'

Wallman was even more astonished than before. 'What's that?' he asked.

'Oh, I'm sorry. Hadn't you told him?' Kirby asked Parker Brown with an insincerity that could have been cut with a blunt knife.

'No, but it doesn't matter. It'll be public knowledge soon enough,' Parker Brown replied.

'As far as I'm concerned, it won't be mentioned outside this room until it *is* public knowledge,' Wallman said levelly.

It was Kirby's turn to be astonished . . .

Mary Pennington, a determined smile on her face, walked into the ward. 'Good morning, Sister,' she greeted Sister Washington. 'I've come to collect my husband and take him home.'

'Oh, yes,' Sister Washington replied. 'If you'll just come to my office.'

'Why?'

'Oh, the usual formalities before we discharge a patient.' Mary looked at her steadily, and for the briefest flash Sister Washington saw something hard and steely in her make-up. No, that wasn't quite it: a sort of uncontrolled determination . . . But the expression was gone so quickly that Sister wasn't sure that she really saw it. As they moved off to the office, Sister Washington nodded to Doreen, who hurried to a phone.

Sister Washington was unaccountably inefficient on this particular morning. She could not find John Smith's patient's file, or any of the other documents for completing the discharge of a patient. Mary Pennington sat quietly for a while, but finally Sister's continued fiddling and shuffling with papers made her fidget. She started to speak when the door opened.

'Good morning, Mrs Pennington.' It was Alison Moxey. 'I believe you're here to take . . . Mr Pennington home.'

'That's right. And we've quite made up our minds. You have no right to stop us.'

'Stop you? We're not going to try to stop you . . . Sister, have you completed the documents?'

'I was just about to start, doctor, but I can't find them.'

Doreen appeared in the doorway, looking far too innocent to be genuine. 'I have Mr Smith's . . . I mean Mr Pennington's documents here, Sister.'

'I'll deal with it,' Alison said, taking the folder. She nodded to Sister Washington, who went out without another word.

'Now,' said Alison, sitting at the desk and opening the folder, 'what's your husband's full name?' This time she had no difficulty in saying 'husband'.

'Barry William Pennington.'

'Date of birth?'

'February nineteenth, nineteen thirty-three.'

Other straightforward questions followed. Mary Pennington answered them all without difficulty or hesitation.

'Well, that seems to be that,' Alison said with a bright smile. 'We'd like to keep him a little longer, but I'm sure you'll take very good care of him. Like when he had those broken ribs.' She smiled again, but Mary Pennington did not respond. 'Three, wasn't it? On the left?'

'That's right.'

Alison nodded slowly, looked at Mary, then reached for the phone.

'Are you calling the ward, doctor?'

'No. The police.'

The meeting in the conference room was nearly over. There was nothing more to say about the Tindall complaint, and they had gone on to consider other hospital problems, like the use of agency nurses in the Intensive Care Units. Although they were needed to keep the unit personnel up to strength, it sometimes caused resentment among the hospital staff. Nurses felt a natural jealousy of the agency girls, who were being paid twice as much or more than the staff nurses, for precisely the same work. In fact it was not uncommon for the higher-paid agency nurse to work under the supervision of a hospital nurse. The only solution was for the Government to increase nurses' pay, but the chances of that were less than the chances of income tax being abolished.

As the three men moved to the door, Armstrong said: 'I wonder if it would help things if Mr Wallman handed over the case to another surgeon.' The other two, still thinking of the nursing difficulties, looked at him blankly. 'Lord Trenchman,' Armstrong elucidated. 'It might take some of the steam out of the situation.'

'It's too late now,' Parker Brown said. 'The lid has already blown off.' It was obvious he was right, and no one commented.

'Tindall seems almost pathologically determined to prove that Trenchman was drunk, and Mr Wallman covered up for him,' Kirby said.

'Wasn't Tindall's son injured in the accident?' Armstrong asked. Kirby shrugged. 'Not seriously, anyway. He was at home for a couple of days with a headache or something.'

Parker Brown didn't seem to hear any of these last exchanges. 'I wonder . . . ' he said at last. 'Kirby, I want you to make one or two discreet enquiries.' He explained his theory, and what the enquiries were to be. The others listened to him with increasing interest and respect.

Alison's hand was still on the phone. Mary Pennington had not spoken for almost a minute.

'He isn't Barry Pennington; he isn't your husband,' Alison said coldly. 'He's never had broken ribs. When bones break and then heal, they leave unmistakable permanent traces that show up on X-rays. I checked with the Regional Authority in your area. They keep very full records, you know. There *was* a patient named Barry Pennington who was from a road accident with broken ribs, but he wasn't anything like John Smith. And there's one other very important fact. Barry Pennington died eighteen months ago.'

Until now Alison had remained eminently calm and self-controlled. Now she permitted herself the luxury of letting go.

'I hope you're pleased with what you've done. You badly

upset my patient, made him extremely unhappy and even more confused. God only knows what psychological damage you may have caused.'

Mary Pennington's face was utterly expressionless, but tears started streaming down her face. It was an uncanny, unsettling sight, and Alison's sudden access of pity for her was modified by a certain unease.

'The last thing I wanted to do was hurt him,' Mary said in a flat, toneless voice. 'It's true I don't know him: I'd never heard of him before I saw that story in the paper. But I felt so sorry for him. He had nobody; nobody wanted him – but I did . . . He reminded me so much of my Barry. For a while, I almost thought it *was* him. I know it sounds silly, but when Barry died, I couldn't take it in. I thought he'd come back, some day.' She paused. Her eyes were blank, seeing not the Sister's office, but something from another time, another place. 'I could give him love, and a good home. He wouldn't have to work . . . I could make him so happy. He's such a lovely man, handsome and kind. I'd do anything for him.'

Alison tried hard to resist the feeling, but she was becoming increasingly sorry for this drab, distraught creature.

'Doctor, please don't tell the police. My mother's still alive; she has a weak heart, and if anything happened to me . . . ' It wasn't the usual whine from someone trying to plead their way out of trouble with the nearest lie to hand. Alison felt (correctly) that Mary Pennington was telling the truth about an ailing mother. Alison withdrew her hand from the phone. Mary saw the gesture, and realised the implications.

'Oh, thank you, Doctor,' she said. She took a handkerchief from her handbag and dabbed at her eyes. She looked a mess: her hair was straggly, and two long strands were hanging down to one side; her nose was pink and shiny from blowing it vigorously and her eyes were pink-rimmed from the tears. The idea of this dreary woman with the elegant, handsome John Smith . . . Alison marvelled at her pretensions until she realised that Mary Pennington's life wavered uncertainly between reality and fantasy. She was speaking again.

'Look, Doctor, you don't *have* to tell him I'm not his wife. Oh, I *know* I can make him happy once he comes with me! We can keep it a secret: no one else need know . . . ' She now had the face of a cunning peasant, cruel and selfish, and basically stupid.

Alison thought deeply, then regretfully picked up the phone again. She asked for the police.

'What have the police got to do with this?' Mary said with thin bravado. 'I haven't done anything illegal. What can they charge me with?'

'That's up to them. But that's not why I'm calling them. Mrs Pennington, you need help: supervision and treatment.'

The police came on the line, and Alison spoke to them briefly. As soon as she put the phone down Mary spoke again.

'You say it's to help me, but I know why you're doing it. *You* want him, don't you? You want him for yourself. You're acting all cool and decent and superior, but inside you're no different from me. You don't want him to get his memory back, because *you* want to keep him.'

It struck home: there was some element of truth in what Mary Pennington said. Alison *did* want John, and she, too, might descend to deception to keep him if it came to it. The only difference between them was one of degree.

She shivered, afraid.

Afraid that she was involved in something that would ruin her. And that now it was too late to escape.

Parker Brown slowly stripped the gloves from his hands, then began to take off the rest of his operating theatre clothes. It had not been a long or particularly difficult schedule, apart from a very tricky and unrewarding – from the point of both the surgeon and the patient – operation on a pancreas, which required both patience and a certain ability to be a contortionist to get at the seat of the trouble.

It was only mid-afternoon, and already he felt tired, tired, tired through to the very marrow of his bones. The prodigies of the famous Parker Brown's Day seemed an age away.

'Why did you do it?' came a voice beside him.

It took Parker Brown a moment or two to react, 'Do what?' he said, beginning to bristle because he thought there was an implied criticism of his surgery.

Wallman was entering the scrubbing-up room after his own operating. He came over to the next washbasin to Parker Brown before replying, so he would not be overheard.

'Why did you take my side like that about Tindall's complaint? And that wasn't a bad idea you came up with.'

'Really,' said Parker Brown with rusty irony. 'You're very kind.'

'I wasn't trying to be sarcastic,' said Wallman. 'I wondered why you did it, in view of our past . . . ' He hesitated. 'Trouble.' It was a magnificent understatement, considering how he and Mrs Helen Grant had conspired against Parker Brown.

Parker Brown took so long to reply that Wallman thought he might have made a serious tactical error in reminding him. 'For two reasons,' he said at last. 'First, I am always against ignorant, evil-minded people making baseless complaints against doctors who try to help them or their relatives. Paranthetically, by the same token,' he continued, beginning to gather momentum like a battle cruiser coming under full power, 'I have no time or sympathy for inefficient, incapable, inconsiderate and inattentive doctors. Second,' he went on without stopping to draw breath, 'you are no doubt aware that I am not an animal lover.' When Parker Brown was in one of these moods, the best thing – the only thing – to do was stand back and let him drive straight on through. Which Wallman did. 'In fact, I believe that dogs are an abomination: ambulatory culture beds of viruses and parasites that foul footpaths, parks and public places. However, animals have one admirable quality that civilised man does not. Animals of the same species very rarely kill each other when they come into conflict. As soon as one of them acknowledges defeat and turns tail, the battle is over. The victor does not pursue the adversary and destroy it.'

Wallman did not reply. He had to swallow the fact that he had been defeated by Parker Brown on that previous occasion and had run away. Now the older man was underlining the quality of his victory.

'By the way,' Parker Brown asked, 'did you marry that woman?'

'Mrs Grant? No, there was no need,' he replied with a wry smile. 'Besides, she didn't strike me as the ideal doctor's wife.'

'She wouldn't have been marrying the ideal doctor.' Parker Brown couldn't resist the riposte.

What it all boiled down to was that Parker Brown was a big man. He had thoroughly defeated his enemy; now it was forgotten: he bore no long-lived malice. And he had a tremendously strong sense of justice.

That is why he felt so shattered by his theatre sister's inexplicable accusation.

'Why didn't you tell me before?' John Smith said anguishedly. 'I've been going through agony, thinking of having to go and live with her.'

He and Alison were in Sister Washington's office. Alison had given some thought to where she should tell him about the outcome of that last interview with Mary Pennington, and the office combined privacy with the right degree of professional impersonality. And it was an 'official' talk.

'I couldn't be sure until today she was lying. I knew you hadn't ever broken any ribs, but she may have been exaggerating, and not just lying. People often talk about "broken ribs" when they are badly bruised. And it took time to get the information through from the Regional Authority.'

'You must have known how I felt,' John said, sounding briefly a little like a spoiled child. 'You could have – '

'What about how *I* felt!' Alison said sharply. 'Can't you imagine how terrified I was of losing you? All the time I knew there was a good chance she was lying, but I had to guard against too much hope. I prayed it'd turn out all right, but I had to keep telling myself . . . ' Her voice broke.

'Darling, I'm sorry,' John said after a moment. 'I didn't mean to sound selfish. It's just the tensions, and pressures of the moment . . . ' His voice was on the edge of becoming shrill. 'I can't go through a situation like that again.' He took a couple of deep breaths. 'Alison, what are we going to do?'

'I don't know, yet.' She looked at him intently. 'John, are you sure you're not . . . over-dramatising what you feel for me?' She smiled wanly. 'Patients often do think they're in love with their doctors.'

He took her hand. He was calm again now. 'Alison, you're the first woman I've loved. My life, all the life I know, started when I came here. Whoever I was doesn't exist any more. I've never loved anyone else.'

She looked worried. 'That's just it: I'm the first woman you've met since you became John Smith. That other man, the man you were, hasn't stopped existing: he's only lost. One day you'll get your memory back, and you'll be that man again – that man who's known other women, who has a wife, perhaps. Children.'

He shook his head violently. 'I told you I didn't feel married to Mary Pennington, and I was right. I don't feel that I have anyone I loved, really loved, in my past. You'd know a thing like that, wouldn't you?'

Alison, for all her scientific training, was a romantic. She wanted to believe he was right. And after all, maybe he was. But she couldn't just leave it there. 'And when you get back your memory, when that other lost man is found, you may feel quite differently; you may change your mind; you may not love me at all.'

He got up and moved round the desk to her side. 'If there's one thing of which I'm certain . . . Listen,' he said. 'I've lost my memory for facts about me, my past, that's all. Not my tastes, my feelings.' He smiled gently. 'I like coffee, not tea . . . Dickens, not Trollope . . . Buffet, not Lowry . . . I don't think that if . . . when I get my memory back all that's going to change. But what about you, and your husband?'

'It's over. It's all with yesterday's seven thousand years.'

He recognised the quotation. *'The Rubaiyat of Omar Khayyam.'* Then his face became serious and worried again. 'I can't stay here forever. I've been fit enough to leave the hospital for days. What happens now?'

Armstrong put much the same question to Alison, Parker Brown and Bauer jointly at a meeting in his office. Although John Smith wasn't Armstrong's patient, he was causing administrative problems. His presence in the hospital had provoked press reaction and one unbalanced woman into action. Both Smith and the hospital had to be protected against any repetitions. 'The first thing to settle,' Armstrong said, 'is his physical and mental states: his fitness or otherwise to be discharged. Dr Bauer?'

'If he's an amnesic, clearly he isn't fit in absolute terms, although whether he is fit enough to be discharged is another matter.'

Armstrong stared at him. It was always fascinating to hear Bauer use precise English like that while speaking with his unmistakable accent. 'Is he fit to be discharged, as far as you are concerned?'

Bauer thought for a long moment and said simply: 'No.' Then he added quickly: 'But I don't have a spare bed for him. I'm overloaded with modern psychiatric casualties: depressed women who have lost drive, purpose and a sense of identity in modern faceless and characterless communities.'

'Very interesting,' Parker Brown said with a voice that grated like a bastard file. 'Can we get on and leave the philosophical exposition for a more suitable time? Like when I'm not here?' Bauer looked at him, quite unruffled.

'Alison?' Armstrong said.

'His leg's mended enough for him to be discharged,' she said in a small voice.

'So he doesn't need a hospital bed.' Armstrong was leaving her with no room for manoeuvre.

'Exactly,' said Parker Brown. 'In any case I have already decided to have him discharged.'

'Where to?' asked Bauer.

'We don't want him here,' Parker Brown went on, ignoring Bauer. 'He's taking up a bed, and he's causing trouble.' He stared hard at Alison, who dropped her gaze.

'Dr Bauer does have a point, William,' Armstrong said mildly. 'Discharge him to where?'

'That is not our concern. It is a matter for the Social Services. Although if you want my opinion, I think he should be in a mental institution.'

'No!' Alison said loudly – too loudly, and too emphatically. She did something she hadn't done for years. She blushed. The deepening colour started at her neckline, then slowly spread hotly up her face.

There was a long silence, broken at last by Alison, who was the one finding it most unbearable. She launched into an appeal for keeping John Smith at the hospital, for a while, at least. She knew she was being too emotional and her voice was too high-pitched. But like a child who knows it is being naughty, and so perversely behaves even more naughtily, the knowledge of her lack of control pushed her into even more excesses. Armstrong looked at her with compassion, Bauer with interest, and Parker Brown with the most unnerving look of all: utterly without expression.

When she had finished Bauer said: 'I am inclined to agree with Dr Moxey that it would be better to keep Smith here. This is the only environment he knows, and so the only place where he can have any sense of security. Furthermore I should like to try narco-hypnosis as other techniques have failed to help restore his memory. At least I have established some sort of rapport with him. If he goes somewhere else, the treatment will have to start again from zero. It would be a waste of time.'

'I'm inclined to agree with Dr Bauer,' Armstrong said, looking at Parker Brown.

'I'd like to speak to you alone for a few minutes,' he replied.

'I have said all I have to say,' Bauer said. He nodded to the others and left without another word.

'Wait outside, please, Dr Moxey,' Armstrong said, not unkindly.

She did not have to wait long.

As soon as she returned Armstrong told her, 'Mr Parker Brown has decided that, in the best interests of the patient, he will be allowed to stay in the surgical ward until further arrangements can be made.'

'What sort of arrangements?'

'Transfer to the psychiatric wing, for example.'

Alison was delighted.

'I have also decided,' Parker Brown said, 'that also in the best interests of the patient, and the hospital, that another doctor will treat him.'

'But – ' Alison began.

'There will be no discussion,' Parker Brown cut her off. 'You will no longer treat John Smith, you will not see him socially. You will do your best to avoid him.'

Alison knew that this was the one occasion when she should keep quiet. If she kept her head now she could sort it all out when the situation had cooled down. She took a deep breath.

'Do you understand?' Parker Brown said . . . and Alison's fuse blew.

'What gives you the right to interfere in my private life?' she said.

'Apart from any considerations of professional ethics, *Doctor,* the right as your superior in this hospital. While you are a hospital doctor, you are subject to its discipline.'

Alison's last self-control went.

'Then perhaps I don't want to be a doctor here,' she said with passion.

For a long while after Janie Hart was killed, time and time again Bywaters made determined efforts to revisualise the last, and only occasion he had made love to her; the last moment of the last day he had seen her. He wished he could have made more of the brief moments they had been together; tried harder to be aware of every last detail of her appearance, every tone of her voice.

Now, in love again, he was going to lose the person he loved.

The only difference was that this time he knew it in advance, and it was killing him.

The old wounds Suzy had inflicted on him were no longer hurting. He knew that her immoderate and immodest behaviour, her apparent excesses, were really completly out of character. That incident in the corridor when she kissed Dennis Porter was meant only to drive Bywaters away from her, a small pain to save him from a greater one later. She wanted to avoid any emotional involvements, and thought that this was the best way to shatter any relationship between them.

He lay on his side, propped up on his forearm. The bed was uncovered: the summer night was warm. Suzy, naked like him, lay sleeping beside him, her hair half across her face and on the pillow. Her smooth skin shone golden in the light from a low-wattage bulb in a converted oil lamp. An artist could not have arranged things with greater effect. Bywaters felt a sudden access of enormous tenderness for her; he felt tears pricking at the back of his eyes.

Their lovemaking this time had been like nothing Bywaters had ever known, because of this dark shadow over her. All true lovers – not casual sexual partners – swear 'this is forever', and believe it when they say it. Suzy and Bywaters, though, knew it could not be forever, even if they loved each other until the day – He would not take the thought beyond that point. He tried to thrust it away – but how can you deliberately *not* think of something?

When they came to bed his awareness was sharpened because he wanted to be conscious of every tiny physical sensation, every shade of emotional feeling. He traced the outline of her face with his finger, then kissed her softly, searchingly at first, then more hungrily. There was the taste of salt on their lips, salt from their tears. Like a million women before her she said: 'It's all right. I'm crying because I'm so happy.'

He kissed the delicate hollow at the base of her neck, and she sighed deeply. When he stroked her body softly and gently, she lay still for a moment, then began to tremble violently. She pulled him towards her, whispering into his ear, then flicking the tip of her tongue into it.

They were preternaturally conscious of each other, of every tiny contact between them, from their closely-pressed lips down to their legs, twining and intertwining.

At the end, she said with a shuddering gasp 'Oh! I never knew it could be like that!'

He looked at her face and saw with a shock that her eyes were open, studying him. Her lips parted gently, and she moved towards him to kiss him once more.

'I've come to a decision,' he said.

'You're going to make coffee?'

He smiled. 'In a minute. I meant, I've decided to make an honest woman of you.'

She pretended to misunderstand, or perhaps she really didn't know what he meant. 'Make an honest woman of me? What are you going to do? Stop going to bed with me?'

'I want to marry you, Suzy.'

She became suddenly very serious.. 'We don't have to. We can go on like this, whenever you want, for as long as you want, or as long as you can put up with me. Or until I – '

He put his hand on her mouth. When he took it away she said: 'Neville, darling. It'd be a mistake. How could we marry, knowing it was going to end?'

'It always ends like that, sooner or later.'

'Look, they already know about us at the hospital. With my reputation . . . ' she smiled wryly, 'being your mistress is one thing, your wife another. You can bear to know your mistress had been to bed with other men; and no one blames you for having a mistress who's had other lovers. But a wife . . . that's different. If I were your wife, even though there have only been a few men, every time you looked at another doctor at the hospital you'd wonder if he . . . ' He shook his head. 'Oh, yes. Even if I told you honestly, the ones who have – '

'No!' he said. 'No, I don't want to know.' He paused, and touched her lips with the tip of his finger. 'I love you, and I want to make the commitment to you.'

'That's not how you make a commitment, darling,' she said with an insight he did not expect. 'Besides, marrying me would ruin your career. They all think I'm a certain kind of girl, the kind of girl you don't marry. They'd take you for a fool.'

Bywaters was about to speak, but she added quickly: 'I told you before: I'm yours when you want me, and for as long as you want me. But I won't allow myself to become a burden to you. I won't marry you, darling: that's final. I love you too much.'

It had been a beastly day, Armstrong decided. He was looking forward to getting home, having a long soak in the bath and listening to what he called 'rubbish music' on the radio, while his mind was switched off. Then he would have a leisurely dinner, and continue his reading of *A la Récherche du Temps Perdu* in the original French. Armstrong was rather proud of his French, not without reason.

He walked towards the small Staff Only door leading to the car park, his step becoming lighter.

But he had one more hurdle to leap before he could go home.

'Good evening Doctor,' came a familiar voice, heavy with reproach.

Standing in the corridor near a small writing room that seemed to be empty – seemed – was Arnold Godfrey Capper, looking like an advertisement for dishonesty.

'You'll have to excuse me, Capper,' Armstrong said firmly. 'I'm in something of a hurry.'

'I'm not surprised,' Capper replied. When he was a humble employee of the Midland General Capper had a peculiarly privileged position vis-à-vis Armstrong. It was the sort of relationship that occasionally exists between a private soldier and a very senior Army officer. They have served together in the same regiment in all parts of the world, and while the officer has slowly mounted the promotion ladder, the soldier has resolutely remained where he was always destined to remain: one rank below acting unpaid lance-corporal. The soldier is permitted a familiarity with the brass hat that even RSMs would fear to take.

Now that he had left the hospital Capper felt himself entitled to a man-to-man, even more egalitarian, approach to Armstrong. 'I'm not surprised you're in a hurry,' Capper said critically. 'I can quite understand you don't want to talk to *me*.' Armstrong looked at him, bewildered. 'But it's not good enough, Dr Armstrong. I want my cut.'

For one quite wild moment Armstrong wondered if Capper was talking about some surgical operation he was waiting for, but immediately dismissed this as a figment of a tired imagination.

'I've heard from Kay Pepper, and I understand you've changed your mind.'

'Who? Oh, her. No, that's not quite accurate,' Armstrong declared.

But Capper, renowned for his Niagara Falls style of conversation, was not stopped that easily. 'Now be fair, Doctor. You asked for a right sporty little number, and I produced Miss Pepper, who had exactly what you was looking for. She let you have a go at it for a week, absolutely free . . .'

'Not quite a week,' Armstrong interpolated. He felt he should say something.

'But wasn't it a new sensation? Didn't it make you feel ten years younger? Twenty?'

'It was very pleasurable, certainly,' Armstrong conceded. (And undoubtedly he *had* enjoyed driving her Alfa Romeo sports car.)

'Then if you changed your mind, that's not my fault. I provided what you asked for, Miss Pepper's ready and willing to give it to you, at the right price . . . You can't just back out now. At least, not without paying some sort of compensation for her lost business and my lost time. Blimey, while she was messing about with you, Doctor, if you'll excuse the expression, I could have fixed her up with another customer. Now we're both out of pocket.'

'Yes, I see. There's only one thing wrong with all that, Capper. I haven't backed out. Miss Pepper had to go north, and we agreed to talk things over when she gets back. I'm still very interested.'

'Say no more then, Doctor. Accept my apologies. I should have known you'd play fair. It's just that in this business, you meet some very dodgy types. It's proper undermined my well-known faith in mankind. So you'll be seeing her again as soon as she gets back.'

'I shall.' Armstrong started towards his car, then checked. 'By the way, Capper, have you tried it yourself?'

'Only once. I felt that before I offered something like that, I ought to have a go at it myself. I don't mind admitting it nearly frightened the life out of me. I'm not used to that sort of thing. I thought I was going to break something vital. And the way I got bounced about! I couldn't stop trembling for a couple of days afterwards.'

'Really,' said Armstrong with a certain smugness. 'I must say I enjoyed it – and more each time.'

'Then you won't mind coughing up when the time comes, eh, Doctor?' said Capper, his cheerfulness restored by the thought of approaching money. 'I'll be in touch, as the bishop said to the actress.'

He and Armstrong went their separate ways. Behind them, rising like twin moons over the horizon, two heads slowly appeared over the partition wall of the apparently empty waiting room and peered through the glass panel first in one direction, then in the other. Although it was an impromptu performance, it was remarkably well synchronised. So was everything else the owners had just been doing, for that matter.

The heads belonged to Ernie Penrose and ancillary worker Phyllis Forrest respectively, who had been doing an advanced biology tutorial.

'Cor!' said Phyllis.

'Bloody hell!' said Ernie Penrose, who was rather more articulate.

The medical staff at the hospital were all thoroughly aware of the (erroneous) story about Armstrong and his explosive dolly bird, but the full extent of his alleged involvement had not percolated to the ancillary staff. However, now that Penrose and Phyllis were cognisant of the story, it would go through the hospital's below-stairs, as it were, like a petrol-fed forest fire.

Next day when Armstrong came to the hospital he was greeted with such a variety of knowing, sideways, shifty, admiring, confidential, leering, surprised, and many other kinds of looks that he thought everyone had gone stark, staring mad.

Some of us suffer traumatic experiences that we never forget, even if we recover from them eventually. We keep recalling the last moments when we knew that the rending, tearing crash was inevitable. Some relive that two-second eternity before the gun went off and completely changed one private world.

Finally the pain dulled even if the sense of outrage never completely dies. When Bywaters walked into Casualty, returning to duty after a meal break, he stepped straight into a disorienting nightmare that sent him staggering off his psychological balance.

One of the hospital's ambulances, returning with a non-urgent case of abdominal pain, knocked down someone in the forecourt of the hospital.

The casualty was admitted by Gregory Knight, When he came out of the cubicle, he left the curtain open, then saw Bywaters arriving. He checked, then on impulse, turned back and pulled the curtains closed.

'What's the matter?'

'Nothing. She's all right.'

'Who is?' There was obviously something wrong. Bywaters' heart started pounding. He hurried forward to the cubicle. Knight hesitated for a second, then stepped aside, cursing himself for his own clumsiness.

Bywaters entered the cubicle. Lying on the table, her face white, her eyes closed, was Suzy Palmer.

'Oh, dear God, no,' he said in a voice of utter despair. All of a sudden he was back three years, looking at the body of Janie Hart, his heart dying with her on the table. His head spun.

After some time – he had no idea how long – he became aware of Knight's voice.

'Neville, she's all right. Just unconscious, nothing serious. Listen: she's *all right*!'

'All right?' Bywaters said at last.

'Mild concussion, I should think – that's all. I've examined her myself; no sign of any damage. Blood pressure normal, all reflexes, everything okay. If the head scan shows nothing, she'll be back tomorrow.'

Bywaters' heart began to slow its racing. His head cleared. 'Thanks, Greg,' he said. He was suddenly aware that Knight had really tried to stop him worrying. Which meant that Suzy had been right when she said that everybody knew about them.

A sudden thought hit him with shattering force.

'I'll take over the case, if that's all right with you,' he said.

Knight hesitated, but Bywater's tone gave him little chance to refuse, and Bywaters was the Senior Casualty Officer on duty. 'Why not?' he said.

Bywaters picked up the patient's admission sheet. 'I want an E.C.G., full chest X-rays and an arteriogram of the heart,' he said, scribbling on the form.

Knight looked at him blankly.

'But she's only . . . ' He tailed off. 'There's nothing wrong with her.'

'We'll see,' Bywaters said. 'We'll see.'

When Bywaters received the E.C.G., chest X-rays and arteriogram he took them to his consulting room where he studied them alone and in silence for a while. He did not need to ask expert opinion from any cardiologists at the hospital, any more than a surgeon needs the assistance of an orthopaedic specialist to recognise a fractured femur on an X-ray plate. The message from the three sources was clear and unmistakable.

He stood up, still holding the X-ray plates and the strip of cardiograph paper. Then, with a terrible gesture of rage, he flung them against the wall of the room.

Chapter Thirteen

A hospital ward late at night is not a place for anyone without steady nerves who doesn't have to be there. There are strange, unexplained, scary noises: sudden short coughs, sighs, moans . . . A creak, and a soft, unidentifiable – to the unaccustomed ear – rustle and padding as a patient gets out of bed to go to the lavatory, trying not to wake the others . . . A distant door slamming and the sound of hurrying feet . . . A lift clicking and whirring into ghostly life without warning or apparent cause. Experienced night staff learn to accept these sounds and ignore them, like a good watchdog that sleeps soundly although the central heating is giving odd thumps and gurgles, but becomes instantly alert the moment there is an unusual scratching at the door.

A Night Sister or Nurse will make notes, or read up text-books for an examination, while a sort of inbuilt automated alarm system ignores the normal night sounds, but reacts instantly to an unprogrammed noise.

Sister Edwards looked up sharply. The entrance door to the ward was swinging. Alison Moxey had just entered quietly on rubber-soled shoes.

'Yes, doctor?' Sister Edwards asked, keeping her voice low.

'It's all right, Sister, I'll manage,' she said. 'I know it's late but I want to speak to Mr Smith.'

'Mr Parker Brown has left orders that – ' Sister Edwards began, but Alison walked straight past without another word.

As she expected, John was not asleep; he was lying on his side, staring at the dark window at the bottom of the cubicle. 'I hoped you'd come back,' he whispered.

When he had put on a dressing gown they went quietly to the Day Room. Sister Edwards was no longer at her desk.

Inside the Day Room, they stood facing each other, just touching each other's hands without daring to hold them properly.

'I know you're not supposed to come and see me, but I've missed you,' he said, his voice strained.

'And me . . . ' She couldn't say more, but it was enough. They stood, unmoving, looking at each other, for a timeless moment. Without speaking, without more than the barest touch, they were aware that they were sharing a deep, common emotion which had no need of words or gestures.

'You'd better go,' he said. 'I don't want you to get into trouble. 'Please . . . '

'Not yet. John, listen. This is why I've come to see you. I've got it all worked out.' She spoke with mounting urgency. 'Where I live, there's a bigger flat that's going to be available in a couple of weeks – it's a married couple and they're moving out – and I can have it. We'll move in, together, and you'll be able to leave hospital and be a psychiatric out-patient . . . '

'But your career; this business of doctor and patient . . . ?'

'You won't be my patient. And besides, who's going to complain to the authorities?'

They both knew the answer to that one – *Your wife, if it happens you're married* – but chose to ignore it. They brushed aside other questions with awkward answers, too, like how he would earn his living eventually . . .

'Oh, dear God,' he said quietly and took her into his arms.

There was an old superstition in the First World War that the safest place to be was in a shell-hole, because shells never hit the same spot twice. This philosophy persists, but it was equally as false then as it is now. By the same token, lightning frequently strikes the same place more than once.

Now, lightning struck in the same place for a second time. Alison and John had been caught alone in the Day Room at night by Parker Brown once; and now, at the moment when appearances were at their worst, he caught them again.

The light snapped on.

'Go back to bed, sir!' Parker Brown said to John in a voice like a whiplash. He looked absolutely terrifying. 'Sister Edwards, see he goes there, at once.' Parker Brown stood aside to allow John Smith to leave the room. Sister Edwards was just behind him, in the corridor. She looked like a jailor ready to escort a prisoner back to solitary confinement.

John hesitated. 'Now!' Parker Brown hissed.

John looked at Alison, then walked out without another word.

When he had left, Parker Brown addressed himself to Alison.

'You will report to me in my office at eight thirty tomorrow morning. In the meantime, you are relieved of all duties in this hospital until further notice.'

He turned and walked away.

Bywaters sat morosely in the canteen, with a cup of cold tea and a piece of soggy, rubbery toast covered with a layer of sickly marmalade that looked more like engine grease than orange preserve. He was alone at his table.

A hand touched Bywaters on the shoulder, then someone sat beside him. There was a smell of a familiar perfume. He turned his head, and looked at Suzy without expression.

'Good morning, darling,' she said. 'They've discharged me. Wasn't that the stupidest thing, getting knocked down by an *ambulance*!' She laughed. 'When will you be off duty? When shall I see you?'

'Never. It's over,' he said flatly.

She looked at him, uncomprehending. 'What?'

'Never. It's over,' he repeated.

'What's happened?'

'When you were brought in, I had a full examination done: X-rays, arteriogram, E.C.G., the lot. Suzy, I know exactly what's wrong with you.' He stood up. 'What did you expect? I had to find out sometime. So, it's finished. Goodbye.'

He left her sitting there, her eyes enormous in her strained, white face.

Alison's meeting with Parker Brown, with Armstrong there in his capacity as Medical Administrator, was short and utterly humiliating. Apart from what he said, Parker Brown's manner, his tone, was excoriating.

'Your behaviour has cast serious doubt on your judgement and your reliability. I am appalled that a surgeon of your ability and potential could be so wantonly stupid, so shamefully oblivious of all sense of propriety, duty and obligation. Your lack of self-respect and respect for your profession has been execrable. You will carry out no further duties at this hospital until Dr Armstrong and I have decided what action is required. Furthermore, do not delude yourself that you will go and speak to Mr Smith this morning. I have given orders that you are not to be admitted to the ward. That is all.'

Alison nodded, unable to speak. She turned to go out.

'As far as I am concerned, Dr Moxey, I shall move for your dismissal from this hospital.'

Parker Brown had not recovered from the distastefulness of that meeting when he undertook his second unpleasant interview in two days. This one was at the chambers of Howard De Soutter, Q.C., at the Inner Temple. Fenton, the Area Authority solicitor retained by the Medical Defence Union for Parker Brown, had suggested De Soutter to represent him at the Disciplinary Committee's inquiry into Sister Smith's charges.

De Soutter was a very busy man; at least as busy as Parker Brown himself, and could not be expected to find the time for a journey to the Midland General simply to confer with a client. Or if he could, it would cost the earth.

De Soutter's room in chambers was magnificent, quietly expensive in a massively mahogany-furnished way. One entire wall of the large room was occupied by a formidable law library of leather-covered books. De Soutter himself looked as if he had come out of the window of a very expensive tailor, except that very expensive tailors don't have dummies in their windows. He was tall, with firm, regular features and a well-trained voice, the sound of which did not displease its owner. He exuded confidence, power and authority.

Parker Brown loathed him on sight.

'I've studied the papers very carefully, Mr Parker Brown,' he said firmly. 'You have a remarkable record. Remarkable. Now, don't deny it,' he added, holding up his hand.

'I have no intention of denying it. It *is* a remarkable record.' Normally Parker Brown wouldn't have been quite so outrageously immodest, but De Soutter irritated him. It hardly presaged well for their relationship. De Soutter looked briefly disconcerted at Parker Brown's retort, but he recovered almost instantaneously with professional expertise. Fenton gave a short nervous laugh. He was overawed, almost overwhelmed, by the Q.C.

'I don't think you have a great deal to worry about, Mr Parker Brown,' De Soutter declared. 'Over the years I have had the privilege of representing a number of senior medical practitioners before the Disciplinary Committee. The atmosphere and general attitude have perceptibly changed over the past few years. There is a new . . . understanding, a new tolerance. It is true that in your case we have a certain difficulty with the . . . ah . . . unequivocal evidence of a respected and experienced theatre sister. Nevertheless, in a case like this – a most distinguished surgeon, unexpectedly required to perform an additional operation after a long and exhausting day – I'm sure the committee would not take a harsh view. A gentle reprimand, possibly, but – '

'One moment.' Parker Brown's voice was sharp, insistent. 'There is one thing you appear to be overlooking, Mr De Soutter. I am not guilty. I was not drunk.'

De Soutter gave him an encouraging smile. 'I'm sure I know what is in your mind, Mr Parker Brown. Unless I'm very much mistaken, you are aware that a counsel cannot defend a client who has admitted his guilt to his counsel, unless the client pleads Guilty. Now, at a Disciplinary Committee inquiry, as it is called, there is no pleading of Guilty or Not Guilty, so that ruling does not apply. You do not have to give me that undertaking.'

'You are very much mistaken,' Parker Brown said with a venom that shook even De Soutter. 'I am not in the habit of lying, even if I can call it something else by using a lawyer's sophistry, or worse. I am a surgeon, sir, not a professional deformer of the truth. As I have always maintained, Sister Smith is lying. I am not guilty, I was not drunk.'

'In view of your very natural concern, I shall overlook certain aspects of that last observation,' De Soutter said stuffily and pedantically. He referred to papers clipped together to make a brief. 'Let us forget Sister Smith for the moment. I would remind you that the anaesthetist, er . . . '

'Dr Seton,' said Fenton, speaking for the first time.

' . . . anaesthetist Dr Seton, states that he saw you drinking in your consulting room immediately before you went to operate.'

'I had one sherry,' Parker Brown said. De Soutter gave an expressive shrug. 'Do you not have a glass of sherry at lunch, perhaps with wine as well?' Parker Brown asked.

'Occasionally.'

'Does that make you unfit to defend the liberty of your client in court, sir?' demanded Parker Brown.

De Soutter's mouth tightened. He began to boom a little. 'If I needed a surgical operation, I should accept your advice. In these circumstances, I beg you to accept mine. You say yourself you cannot suggest why Sister Smith should lie . . . ' (*if she* is *lying*, he implied heavily) ' . . . and I believe it would be wrong to attack her strongly and perhaps alienate the committee. You will be much better served by relying on the fact that you were called on unexpectedly to operate, on your distinguished record, and on my humble ability to present your case in such a way that the committee will take a sympathetic, understanding view of the circumstances.'

It was the screaming hypocrisy of the '*humble* ability' that applied the match to Parker Brown's blue touch paper. He stood and glared at De Soutter.

'It is clear that we have diametrically opposed opinions on how my case should be conducted,' he said. 'In that case, you have my permission to withdraw from representing me. Good day, sir.'

He stalked out of the room, presenting to De Soutter the most expressively hostile back he could recall seeing. Fenton made some slightly incoherent excuses to De Soutter and bolted after Parker Brown, who was managing to stamp noisily as he moved down the thickly carpeted corridor. A door opened and a young man came out, to be sent cannoning back into the room by the determined Parker Brown.

Parker Brown was about to castigate him when he stopped dead. 'I know you,' he said.

'Dominic Frayne. I was the accident case on the motorway. Catorid artery.'

'*Carotid* artery,' Parker Brown corrected him automatically.

'Will you come in, sir?' Frayne said, opening wider his door. On impulse, Parker Brown entered. Fenton arrived, still looking startled. Parker Brown introduced him to Frayne.

This was a much smaller, more functional and infinitely less expensive room, yet somehow Parker Brown felt more comfortable in it.

'I was sorry to hear about your trouble,' Frayne said.

'*How* did you hear about it?'

'I got up the papers for Mr De Soutter.' Parker Brown frowned at him. 'That means I read them, picked out the salient facts and made notes for him.' Frayne smiled. 'It's a common practice. I suppose it's like a junior doctor seeing a patient and making a preliminary study of the case for the consultant.'

Parker Brown reluctantly agreed that there was a parallel. 'You're in excellent hands with Mr De Soutter. He's an absolutely first-class – '

'He's a damned fool and a hypocrite to boot. No, sorry,' Parker Brown said, stopping Frayne's protests with a wave. 'That was quite wrong of me, and I apologise. He is your chief.'

'In a sort of way, yes. Head of Chambers.' Frayne coughed. 'What, exactly . . . ?'

'He wants me to plead previous good character, throw me on the uncertain mercy of a gang of . . . ' Parker Brown fumed. 'He can't get it through his head that I'm not guilty, and that the damned woman's lying her head off.'

'Well, of course you weren't drunk!' said Frayne, astonished. He paused. 'Still, if Mr De Soutter thinks it best to . . . ' He didn't know how to finish.

'Wait a moment,' Parker Brown said. 'How do you know I wasn't drunk? It's my word against Sister Smith's.'

Frayne looked at him blankly for a moment, as if it were a silly question. Then he gave the one crucial answer that could affect Parker Brown, the only one that could set in train a remarkable series of events.

'How do I know? Well, if you were guilty, you wouldn't try to wriggle out of it. You'd say so.'

There was a long pause.

'Mr Frayne, will you represent me?' Parker Brown said flatly.

'I'm afraid you're not allowed to approach me direct. And in any case – '

'Why not?'

'Ethics.'

Parker Brown gave a bark of contemptuous laughter.

'You have much the same sort of thing in your profession, I believe,' Frayne said, quite unruffled. 'Like seeing a patient without the permission of the patient's regular doctor. Well, I can only be approached through a solicitor.'

'Fenton, you're a solicitor. Get him to represent me, if he'll be so good.'

'But – with respect, having a man of Mr De Soutter's standing as your counsel is almost a character reference in itself.'

'I don't *need* any references from a damned lawyer. Sorry, Frayne.' The young man seemed amused rather than insulted.

'Mr Parker Brown, are you sure you're not acting on impulse and – ' Fenton began agitatedly.

'Of course I'm acting on impulse. I'm always right first time. De Soutter was *your* idea. Now, will you both kindly arrange what it is you have to arrange, and I can get back to the hospital.'

Three times going back on the train Fenton tried to tell Parker Brown that it was unwise, foolhardy even, to trust his career to a young, relatively inexperienced barrister. The third time

Parker Brown got up wordlessly and went to another compartment. The trouble was, he was beginning to think that Fenton was right, but his boats were burned.

Psychiatrists are, by the nature of their work, professional busybodies. They have to poke around in the private recesses and dark corners of their patient's minds, places where some very nasty creatures frequently lurk; they have to ask all sorts of searching questions about our very private lives. So, they are accustomed to being rather more inquisitive and insistent about their curiosity than most people, except possibly policemen and tax inspectors.

Consultant psychiatrist Barbara Kennedy did not lack courage. She had stood up to Parker Brown fearlessly – or apparently so, at least – on a couple of occasions. That terrifying man had a low opinion of psychiatrists, as he frequently made clear to everyone within earshot. In fact, she had been scared stiff at the time, so her courage was all the greater.

Notwithstanding all this, she was reluctant to tackle Bywaters about his depressed, withdrawn state recently. It was only the action of a pressure group, specially formed for the occasion and led by Gregory Knight that pushed her into reluctant action.

'I tell you, every time he walks into the ward the patients take one look at his face and they think they're booked for the boneyard. He's a bloody *drag*,' Knight said.

Wim van Kroll, Terence Leakey and Dennis Porter all nodded agreement. 'Working with him is like living in an Ingemar Bergmann film,' added van Kroll.

Barbara privately agreed that Bywaters had been particularly dreary lately. 'Do you know what the trouble is?' she asked.

'Suzy Palmer,' said Knight. 'They seemed to be getting on all right together – '

'*That* was weird,' Porter interjected.

' – but it's all turned sour.'

'She looks pretty dismal herself, man,' said Leakey.

'If you know what the trouble is, why don't one of you tackle him?' asked Barbara.

'He doesn't work with you,' Porter said reasonably. 'If he turns nasty, you won't be with him all day.'

'He won't punch you on the nose,' Knight said.

'And because you're much nicer than all of us, and no one

could refuse you anything,' Wim van Kroll said with a dazzling smile.

'Oh, shut up,' Barbara said with an embarrassed smile in one of her rare Roedean moments.

'N'kmbwe,' muttered Leakey.

'What does that mean?' asked Porter.

Leakey looked at van Kroll. 'Bullshit.'

Barbara's genuine concern for Bywaters helped her overcome her trepidation at tackling him. No one likes a snub, not even a psychiatrist. In the event, her unease was quite unjustified. Bywaters was at the stage where he wanted to unburden himself to someone, if only to inveigh against Suzy. It all came pouring out: their relationship, his interest in her despite her reputation, how she wasn't that sort of girl after all, but was acting like that because of her congenital heart disease that was going to kill her . . . and how he had finally grown to love her.

'Then she had that stupid accident, being knocked down by one of our own ambulances. Well, while she was unconscious I ran a full set of tests on her: E.C.G., X-rays, arteriogram, the lot.'

'And?' Barbara asked.

'What I found made me sick. Bloody sick.'

'But the trouble is,' said the perceptive Barbara, 'you still love her.'

There were elements in Bywaters' account that didn't fit, as he himself would have realised had he been less emotional about it. Barbara noticed it, though, and she observed Suzy Palmer herself for a couple of days. Finally, she tackled Suzy as well. By the time Suzy had unburdened herself, it was inescapable that there was something very odd about the entire situation. A niggling suspicion began to gnaw at Barbara. She dismissed it as wildly improbable; but it returned, and as an expert in unreasonable behaviour she began to think it was not so impossible after all.

The problem was, what to do about it.

At Wallman's request, Parker Brown and Armstrong were examining Lord Trenchman preparatory to his being discharged in a few days. Parker Brown was there to examine his face, the broken ribs and the internal damage they had caused, while Armstrong was concerned with the functioning of the injured kidney. They examined Trenchman, and studied all the test results and X-rays.

Both doctors agreed that Trenchman had made excellent progress.

'You'll be able to leave here at the end of the week. And you should have no facial marks worth mentioning in a couple of months,' Parker Brown said, while Armstrong nodded agreement.

Trenchman, who had been staring at him fixedly, suddenly looked astonished. 'I can't leave here for a couple of months?' he said.

'No, at the end of the week,' Armstrong explained.

'But Mr Parker Brown just said: "You'll be able to leave here in a couple of months." '

'No, no. You'll be able to leave here at the end of the week. And you should have no facial scars worth mentioning in a couple of months,' Parker Brown repeated, a little testily.

'I'm sorry,' Trenchman said politely, 'but you didn't mention facial scars. You simply said I'd be able to leave here in a couple of months. Dr Armstrong, you heard him?'

There was a long silence as Armstrong and Parker Brown regarded each other. They had no need to speak. Each knew exactly what the other was thinking.

'There are a couple more tests we'd like to do,' Armstrong told Trenchman. 'We don't want you leaving here until we're absolutely certain you're completely cured.'

'And I'm sure you won't mind two of our colleagues having a look at you, before you go,' Parker Brown said in a tone that did not admit the possibility of a refusal.

'Dr Bauer and Dr Stable,' Armstrong added. He knew who Parker Brown was thinking about. Stable was a neuro-surgeon.

Outside, in the corridor, Parker Brown said 'So that's it. I wonder if he knows?'

'Unlikely,' Armstrong opined. 'It's not even in his medical records we got from his family doctor. And I don't think he's the sort of man to take that kind of risk.'

'It rather changes things,' said Parker Brown with satisfaction. 'Now, if Kirby's enquiries turn up what I think they will . . . '

'William, it's all very well worrying about other people. I'm more concerned with *your* problem.'

For the moment Parker Brown had forgotten his own predicament. When he thought of it, he had a sick feeling in his stomach.

John Smith knew something strange was about to happen by the way Sister Washington and Doreen Holland asked him to go to the Day Room. Under their professional smoothness their manner was strained, secretive . . . anticipatory. He was surprised to find Bauer and Parker Brown waiting there.

Their first questions were innocuous, almost desultory, about his general health.

Then, unexpectedly, came a woman's voice from behind him.

'Hello, Gerald.'

John Smith turned and replied quite automatically 'Hello, Lorraine.' Standing in the doorway was a handsome rather than beautiful woman, perhaps five years older than him, deeply suntanned and very expensively chic.

'Do you know her?' Bauer asked formally.

After a long pause John Smith said.

'Yes. It's my wife. Lorraine Bartlett.'

Gerald Bartlett's memory was returning like a landscape seen through lifting mist. Images came back to him unaided, others were recalled by the skilful prompting of his wife. He was able to tell Bauer and Parker Brown his own story with only the minimum of help.

Gerald and Lorraine Bartlett lived in France, on the Côte d'Azur, where they were the concessionaires for one of the American manufacturing giants, nearly as big as General Motors. Their company, Cavenne S.A., distributed cars, motor boats, refrigerators and domestic electrical equipment. The company was established by her father who left it to Lorraine when he died.

Although it did not all emerge at the first meeting, Lorraine was the one who ran the business; Gerald had some sort of ill-defined sales and public relations capacity, but no authority. Lorraine was very much the daughter of her father.

Lorraine was in America, in Detroit, on business, leaving Gerald nominally – but only nominally – in charge of things in France when he disappeared. From what Lorraine and her private enquiry agents had been able to discover, Gerald left Nice and went to their *pied-à-terre* in London, before leaving for the north – presumably to the farm where he was born and had a happy childhood. Later his parents had gone to

Cornwall, while Gerald had a number of precarious and ill-defined jobs in the art world in London and Paris.

What was he running from? They'd had stupid marital arguments, Lorraine agreed, but they shouldn't seriously have upset him.

(Bauer suspected – rightly – that Gerald was resenting his sense of inferiority to his dominating wife, and had left as an act of defiance. However, he was able to do it only when Lorraine wasn't there; he would not have had the courage to leave her to her face, as it were.)

'I'm afraid Gerald has passed through a very bad period recently,' Lorraine explained. 'Perhaps I should have been more understanding. You see, his mother was killed in a rail accident six months ago. Then his father died.'

'We'd been estranged for a long time,' Gerald said. 'He wanted me to . . . He wanted me to become a farmer, take over from him down in Cornwall.' He smiled painfully. 'I couldn't really see myself as a farmer.'

Gerald Bartlett was telling only half the truth. His father didn't simply want him to be a farmer: he didn't want him to marry a rich woman and 'waste' his life away. The old man had a strong Puritan streak, a profound belief in the Victorian virtue of hard work. He strongly disapproved of Lorraine Cavenne, whom Gerald had met at a private viewing at a London art gallery where he was working at the time. He also cordially detested the gallery itself and the entire world of art. The estrangement from his father and lack of a reconciliation before he died, so soon after his mother's death, presumably were too much for him.

Lorraine admitted that her preoccupation with the business and her taking Gerald too much for granted were probably the cause of the domestic crises. The trip to Detroit had been the last straw.

Whether she had the insight to appreciate it or not, Bauer and the other doctors could see quite simply the situation. Lorraine had effectively bought herself a handsome, charming husband to dance attendance on her, cause no trouble, and be grateful for the luxury she could give him. But she remained very much in control: she made the decisions, she held the purse strings. It may have sounded an undemanding, pleasant-enough life for him, but its lack of challenge and real stimulus could be mind – and soul-destroying.

Even the sybaritic Gerald found it too much with the sudden

twin blows of the deaths of his parents. His life had not given him much spiritual strength and stamina, after all.

As the doctors left the Day Room so Gerald and Lorraine could be alone for a while she was promising him that she would spend more time with him, be more considerate. There was even a faint possibility that she meant it, at that moment. But Lorraine would always be Lorraine, Gerald would always be weak, dependent, hedonistic at the expense of his self-respect – except when he might have brief moments of being John Smith, or some other anonymous man. But the periods of escape would always be brief.

In the corridor outside the ward Parker Brown and Bauer encountered Alison, who was on her way to the canteen. She did not avoid Parker Brown's eye. 'One moment, Dr Moxey,' he said. She checked.

'You can go and see Mr Smith if you like,' he said. She stood motionless, shocked, then hurried away. There was a momentary reaction of surprise from Bauer, but almost instantaneously he knew that Parker Brown was right.

When Alison got to the Day Room, after persuading Sister Washington that Parker Brown had lifted the ban on her visiting John, Lorraine Bartlett was still there. She was holding her husband in her arms, comforting him, telling him that they'd be happy again, together . . .

Alison heard them, but they didn't know she was there. At that moment, they weren't even aware she existed.

'There can be no doubt, Lord Trenchman,' Armstrong said gently. 'I've spoken to your family, to some of your close friends – without letting them know why, of course – and the E.E.G. is quite unmistakable. You suffer from epilepsy.'

Trenchman shook his head. 'But I don't have fits, seizures, nothing of that kind. I'd know. I *can't* be.'

'There are many forms of epilepsy, and many degrees of severity. You've had the mildest form: you've had *petit mal* attacks,' said Wallman, who was with Armstrong and Parker Brown in Trenchman's room. 'The only symptoms are a fleeting lack of consciousness – that's all. Frequently the patient doesn't even know he's had an attack.'

'Which is what happened when I spoke to you the other day,' Parker Brown said. 'It was quite obvious to Dr Armstrong and myself you'd been temporarily unconscious while I was speaking to you. You simply missed part of what I said to you.'

'Your friends and family have occasionally noticed the same sort of thing,' Armstrong said. 'I'm sure that's what happened to you on the night of the accident. You had a sudden 'absence', lost control of the car, and never knew it had happened. I'm afraid it means you mustn't drive again – not until you've had treatment, anyway.'

'So there's something that can be done?' Trenchman said.

'I'm sorry, we should have said that at the beginning,' Wallman told him. 'Your condition can easily be controlled with drugs . . .'

'Ethosuximide, paramethadione, troxidone . . . there are a number of very effective ones. We'll soon find out which one is best for your particular case,' Armstrong said.

Trenchman sighed. 'Well, I suppose it's just as well you found out, I suppose,' he said.

'And just in time,' Wallman said with an enigmatic glance.

In a corner of the canteen Bauer sat quietly with Alison, who was trying to look calm and controlled, but without much success. She started up. 'I must say goodbye to him,' she said.

Bauer restrained her. 'He's gone. He's already left the hospital. He and his wife flew to Nice this afternoon.'

Alison stared at him with big eyes. 'But he didn't even . . . Not without saying goodbye?'

'Face it, Alison,' Bauer told her. 'It's over. The John Smith you loved is dead: he died the moment he recognised his wife. In fact John Smith never really existed.' He paused. 'It's odd. Quite fascinating. That woman who said she was his wife, Mary Pennington. She was older than him, and she said he had no need to work. She wanted to dominate him: the exact pattern of his real marriage – having an authoritative, matriarchal figure who provided for him. Perhaps Mary Pennington subconsciously recognized in him the sort of man he really is.' He waited for her to speak, but she sat still, looking miserable.

'You see what I'm leading up to, Alison? John Smith, or Gerald Bartlett, was an inadequate personality who wanted to be dominated by a stronger woman, have her take care of him.' Then, gently, 'Wasn't that your real relationship with him?'

Barbara Kennedy came and sat beside them. 'Excuse me, Alison, I must have a word with Paul.' She turned to him. 'I've got to go off for a day. I'll tell you about it later. I've rearranged my appointments, and I'll make up the time with evening sessions when I get back.' Barbara seemed to notice

Alison properly for the first time. 'Hello, what's the matter with you?'

Alison didn't answer, so Bauer did it for her. 'You heard about John Smith's real wife turning up, of course? They've left the hospital. Alison is rather upset.'

Barbara's expression turned to one of distaste. 'Good God, Alison, you only knew him for five minutes. As a surgeon you've seen, over and over again, people showing courage and strength of character when they've lost people they've loved for a lifetime. A little of that sort of courage wouldn't come amiss with you.' She stood up sharply. 'See you tomorrow, Paul.'

In another part of the canteen Parker Brown was conferring with Armstrong and other senior consultants, trying to arrange an ad hoc committee to consider Alison's case and decide whether they should either ask her for her resignation, reprimand her, report her to higher authority, or simply take no action. Reluctantly Armstrong, as Medical Administrator, agreed to chair the meeting.

At that moment Alison appeared beside Parker Brown's chair. 'Mr Parker Brown,' she said formally, 'I shall be handing in my resignation from the hospital tomorrow morning.' She spoke next to Armstrong. 'I should like to leave the hospital as soon as you can arrange for someone else to be appointed, please.'

'You can leave tomorrow. We'll manage without you until a replacement arrives,' Parker Brown said sharply. 'Deciding to go is the only sensible thing you've done since this whole sorry affair started. I only hope you have learned your lesson.'

Alison stood irresolute for a moment, then walked away, out of their lives.

'You were rather hard on her, William,' Armstrong said.

'I detest stupidity, self-indulgence, and most of all the wanton waste of ability,' he replied. 'She's better off away from here.'

'That's not very charitable.'

'I am not interested in charity. Only in justice.'

I hope he gets both at his disciplinary hearing, Armstrong thought.

Chapter Fourteen

Suzy Parker was quite baffled. There was this memo from Barbara Kennedy asking her to come to her office at two o'clock. Since Barbara had been so sympathetic and had listened so patiently to her story of how things had gone wrong with Nèville Bywaters, Suzy felt she owed it to Barbara to make an effort and turn up.

'Come in and sit down, Suzy,' Barbara said encouragingly. When she had settled, she asked her, 'Why did you say Neville Bywaters broke things off with you?'

Suzy suddenly wanted to cry, but she managed to control herself. 'You know why.'

'Tell me again. Please.'

'He did those tests, and when he found out how ill . . . Well, he knew there was no future for us, and so . . . ' It wasn't very coherent, but it was comprehensible.

'Do you know what he told me? That you'd lied to him to make him feel sorry for you, and to explain away your sleeping around, acting like an amateur whore.'

Suzy straightened up. 'That's not true! I mean, I suppose that's what he told you, if you say so. But . . . I don't understand. Why would he say that? He even asked me to marry him . . . '

'And you refused. That might confirm his suspicions.'

'That's impossible! I don't understand,' Suzy repeated. She looked bewildered and badly upset.

'He said it,' Barbara told her slowly, 'because there's nothing wrong with your heart, and never has been. You've got a heart like a diesel engine.'

'You've got it all wrong,' Suzy said, but broke off when she saw Barbara's face.

'I've seen the X-rays and the tests myself. You're perfectly fit.' Barbara's face became grave. 'I'm afraid this isn't going to be pleasant, but there's no other way.' She spoke that awful phrase that is so often the precursor to something well-meant but catastrophic in effect. This time, however, Barbara was deadly accurate: 'It's for your own good.' She picked up the phone and said, 'Send her in.'

Behind Suzy's back the door opened and someone came in.

'Darling . . . ' came a tentative voice. Suzy swung round. '*Mother!* What are you doing here?'

'I brought her,' said Barbara brusquely. 'She has something to tell you.' Mrs Palmer was having difficulty in starting: she was reluctant to talk at all, it seemed. 'If you don't tell her, Mrs Palmer, I shall,' Barbara warned.

Hesitantly, Mrs Palmer started to explain how an early fright about Suzy's health had made her overly-protective towards her daughter. Then, because she loved Suzy so much, because she didn't want her to leave her side, she began the elaborate pretence that she had this congenital heart condition. Many selfish parents pretend to be ill themselves to keep their children with them, bound by chains of anxious concern; Mrs Palmer did the opposite, telling the child she was ill, so she would want to stay under her mother's protection. She took Suzy to the doctor regularly, but always made her wait outside while the doctor gave his opinion, to 'protect' her.

As the quite shocking story unfolded, Suzy listened in horror. Her mother began apologetically, ashamed, because she had selfishly wanted to keep her daughter tied to her; but as she explained, gradually she began to justify herself. Increasingly she insisted that the whole grisly charade was for Suzy's own sake, to keep her at home with her mother where she would be safe and protected. Suzy needed shielding from a cruel world, unfair to women, from her own emotions and gullibility . . .

'God, I was that all right!' Suzy burst out bitterly.

She heard everything her mother was saying, and she understood it on the surface, yet she could not thoroughly take it in. The enormity of the stolen years, wasted away inside the soft prison of false solicitude and lies, was too much to assimilate all at once. Perhaps it was as well.

'I think you'd better go now, Mrs Palmer,' Barbara said eventually.

She rose, begging Suzy to forgive her, and in the same breath again justifying what she had done was for Suzy's protection. She even managed somehow to argue that it was love for Suzy that had prompted her into doing this, and not monstrous self-interest.

Suzy did not turn her head as her mother left. She was thinking of all the anxious phone calls and letters – anxious not because of concern for her, but in case Suzy had found out the truth, as she must one day. The sustained, calculated hypocrisy of it all made Suzy feel sick. But soon that was to pass, as she began to take in fully the implications of her changed future. She had been given an entire new life. For years she had blotted out the thought of home, family and children; now she could dare to think about them. It was too much to take in at once.

Afterwards Barbara was asked how she persuaded Mrs Palmer to come and tell Suzy the truth of her condition, and how she had tricked her. 'If you don't come and tell her, I shall,' Barbara told her. 'And you can be sure I won't spare you. I won't give any explanations or excuses for you.' Mrs Palmer was anxious to salvage what she could from the situation and explain to Suzy how she had done it, as she believed, for Suzy's own good. (That awful phrase again.)

That was the 'how' of it; but *why* did Barbara bother to persuade Mrs Palmer to come and tell Suzy? Because Suzy probably wouldn't have believed the full truth coming from a third person. Most of all, it was important that Suzy hear it from her mother so she could be free of her.

Now, there was only bitter resentment for her mother's cruel selfishness; hate, almost. But that, too, would pass eventually; understanding, if not forgiveness, would take its place. In the final analysis Suzy would realise that her mother was to be pitied as much as detested, and this change of heart would not have come about if there had not been the direct confrontation.

Barbara let Suzy sit in her office until she had recovered sufficiently from this traumatic experience to be able to face everyone again.

'I'm sorry to put you through that,' Barbara said. 'But you had to know, and there was no easy way.'

'Yes, I know,' Suzy replied. 'It sounds a bit inadequate, but . . . well, thank you. You know how I feel.'

Barbara gave one of her rare, but very warming smiles. 'I can guess. Now I expect you'll want to go and talk to Neville Bywaters. If you have any trouble with him, just refer him to me. *I'll* tell him,' she said firmly.

Suzy hurried away.

Parker Brown sat silently in a corner of the Consultants' Dining Room. Armstrong and Wallman hurried over to him.

'I've just heard from Kirby,' Armstrong said. 'He's finished his enquiries along the lines you suggested.'

'Good,' said Parker Brown absently.

'Alderman Tindall's coming in tomorrow,' Wallman said. 'We're all going to meet him. Would you like to be there?'

'I should like to indeed,' Parker Brown said, in something like his old style. 'Unfortunately I have a previous engagement: in London, before the Disciplinary Committee.'

There was an abrupt silence. Kirby and Wallman looked at Parker Brown without expression. Armstrong knew without any doubt how Kirby felt; and despite Wallman's recent friendly attitude towards Parker Brown, he wondered what he was *really* thinking . . . *really* hoping for.

The battle lines were drawn up: Armstrong, Wallman and Kirby sat on one side of the conference room table, Tindall and a sallow-skinned, thick-lipped man on the other, the two groups facing each other warily across the polished mahogany No-Man's-land. Tindall fired the first shot. He introduced his companion as 'Mr. Gambon, my solicitor.' He added, 'The reason I brought him is because I want to hear what's happened to my *official* complaint, and to advise me what action to take if I'm not satisfied with what you're doing about it.'

'Ah, yes,' Kirby said without inflection. 'I believe your son was injured in the accident, as well.' It may have sounded like a *non sequitur*, but Kirby knew exactly what he was doing.

'That's right,' Tindall answered acidly. 'Mr Gambon here is going to take care of that, too.' Gambon studied his nails.

'Since you made your serious allegations against Mr Wallman, there have been certain developments,' Armstrong said quietly. 'We now know what most probably caused the accident. Why Viscount Trenchman swerved across the road.'

'We know that already. His lordship was drunk,' Tindall interrupted. Gambon touched him on the arm.

'Lord Trenchman is suffering from a medical condition which caused him to lose consciousness for a few seconds,' Armstrong went on.

'What medical condition?' asked Gambon.

'I'm afraid it would be unethical for Lord Trenchman's doctors to disclose details of his condition to a third party,' Kirby said smoothly.

'But the condition exists all right,' Wallman said with heavy satisfaction. 'Believe me, it does.'

Gambon looked up sharply and studied the others across the table. It was obvious to him they were telling the truth, but Tindall was unconvinced. He didn't *want* to be convinced, at any price.

'You're just covering up for him!' he shouted at Armstrong, indicating Wallman. 'It's a bloody game of ring-a-ring-a-roses. He gets Trenchman off the hook, then you do the same for him. That bastard was drunk, and the Establishment is closing ranks to save him from getting his proper deserts.' Gambon touched him on the arm again, but Tindall shook off his hand. He glared at Wallman: 'You deliberately destroyed the evidence and got paid off for it. But if it's the last thing I do – '

'It may well be, if you go on like that,' Kirby said sharply. 'First, there is no evidence whatsoever that Mr Wallman *deliberately* destroyed anything. Second, there is no evidence that Lord Trenchman was drunk when he had the accident. In fact, any evidence that does exist tends to prove that he was *not* drunk. Third, the minutes of the Board of Trustees of the Ghazarossiam Foundation clearly show that the grant to Mr Wallman was decided two days before the date of the accident.' There was a heavy silence finally broken by Wallman.

'However, it is possible that too much drink did play some part in the crash,' he admitted. Tindall looked up hopefully.

'The driver of the other car in the collision had drunk . . . ' Kirby referred to notes in front of him . . . 'between five and six pints of beer, and three, possibly four, large whiskies. Your son.'

Tindall was flabbergasted for the moment, then he recovered and went over to the attack again. 'How do you know? He was never breathalysed!' he shouted.

'Because his car was on the correct side of the road, and it didn't occur to the police. Quite reasonably they were more interested in the car on the wrong side of the road,' Kirby said. 'Of course, we're not suggesting that drink was the cause of the accident, but it could have been a contributory factor. In other words, if he had not been drinking, Mr Tindall Junior's reactions might have been better and he might have avoided Lord Trenchman's car.'

'One moment,' said Gambon. 'On what do you base the allegation that Mr Tindall's son had been drinking that night?'

'Enquiries,' said Kirby nonchalantly. 'Peter Tindall is quite well known by sight in certain quarters. He always goes to the same pubs. It wasn't difficult to reconstruct his evening with . . . ' He regarded his notes again. ' . . . Miss Hilda Belling.'

Gambon shot a glance at Tindall, who avoided his look. 'I'm curious to know why you should make the equiries, Mr Kirby,' Gambon said.

Armstrong replied. 'A member of the surgical staff of this hospital had been accused of corruption and helping to conceal an offence. Mr Parker Brown, as Chief Consultant Surgeon, felt that in the circumstances the best way to protect Mr Wallman's and the hospital's interests was to gather all the available evidence in case of any legal action.'

'I'd like to say something,' Wallman took over. When he spoke it was with an odd air of a lesson being repeated. 'If there are any further suggestions that I behaved improperly in any way, or corruptly received an improper consideration for any action I performed, I shall take legal action.'

'Mr Gambon,' Kirby said politely, 'I suggest you warn your client of the dangers of repeating his allegations outside this room. It could prove very costly.'

Armstrong had the last word. 'You will be hearing from us officially, Mr Tindall, that we have investigated your complaint, and found that it was unfounded.' He smiled politely. 'I'm sure you'll be pleased to know that your suspicions were quite wrong.'

When Wallman and Kirby were alone, Kirby said, 'Tindall thinks he's very clever, but of course, he missed the point.'

'Which was?'

'That whether Trenchman was actually drunk or not is beside the point, if you *thought* he was at the time.'

'How perceptive of you,' Wallman replied coolly. 'Do you think Gambon realised that?'

'I'm certain of it.'

'That was my impression, too. But he didn't seem very keen to get involved.'

'No,' said Kirby slowly. 'After all, there was that question of the date of your award.'

'Oh, yes,' said Wallman. 'How did you know the minutes of the Board of Trustees' meeting showed they'd made the grant two days earlier? Those meetings are supposed to be very confidential.'

'Didn't you tell me yourself?' Wallman shook his head. 'Then I really can't think where I heard it,' said Kirby with wide-eyed innocence. 'I mean, I wouldn't have imagined it, would I!'

Wallman looked at him long and hard. Kirby's face was plain to read. *That's one you owe me. And some day, I'll collect.*

That was Wallman out of danger. Now it was Parker Brown's turn for ordeal.

The General Medical Council's headquarters are in Hallam Street, London, W.1., which runs parallel with Gt Portland Street, north of The BBC's Broadcasting House.

It is a slightly old-fashioned building, with a small entrance hall from which double glass doors lead to a staircase. On the first floor are the wooden double doors which lead to the Council Chamber, a large, high-ceilinged room – really more of a hall. Opposite the main doors is a raised bench, very much like a High Court judges' bench, with a witness box beside it. Behind the bench is a great, stained-glass window, with a triple plain window on each side, each window with a large extractor fan at the top, six in all. At each end of the chamber is a gallery with a clock set in the front.

When the committee used to occupy the high bench it was a terribly unnerving business to appear before it, with twelve members staring down at the doctor under inquiry. It was like appearing at the Old Bailey, or, if the 'defendant' was imaginative, before the Inquisition. These days the proceedings are much less formal and less intimidating. Square, leather-topped desks, with leather-backed bucket chairs – all rather old-fashioned – are set out in the form of an E without the centre bar, or a square horseshoe, at one end of the room, under the Members' Gallery, facing the Press and public gallery. The President and the Legal Assessor – a senior barrister – sit at the top table, their backs to a great fireplace flanked by bookcases filled with bound volumes of *The Lancet* and *The British Medical Journal.* At each end of the horseshoe is a table, set at a slight inward-facing angle. One is occupied by the counsel for the GMC, the other, nearer the doors, by the doctor and his council, if he has one.

In the middle, between the angled tables, is a single desk where the shorthand writer sits. The witness desk and chair is directly behind him, so when anyone gives evidence, he had to hurry from his desk and sit with GMC counsel, so he will not cut off the Committee's sight of the witness, and vice versa. All the tables and desks, except the shorthand writer's, have a microphone.

There is an air of casualness about the setting. It is highly deceptive.

Parker Brown and Frayne sat at the left-hand table. Parker Brown glanced round the chamber lit by the afternoon sunlight, then at each member of the committee, two of them women, all with a sheaf of pink paper on the desk before them. He looked up at the Press Gallery. It was empty. Details of treatment to a patient would be given in this inquiry, so the President had ruled that it would be heard *in camera.* Finally, Parker Brown glanced at Dominic Frayne, who was intently studying his papers. He looked so very young and inexperienced that Parker Brown suffered a deep, sick feeling to think that his career, his entire future, depended upon the ability, or lack of it, of this young man. Normally Parker Brown was massively certain of his own judgement, but for once he wondered if his impulsiveness and self-assurance had not ruined him at last.

Frayne looked up and caught Parker Brown's eye. He looked strained, for he realised how enormous was his responsibility. But he smiled bravely, and Parker Brown warmed to him. If they went down, it would be with all guns firing.

Frayne signalled to Parker Brown to rise as the charge was read out.

'Inquiry into the following charge against William Parker Brown, registered as of Elm Bank House, Middleton Tracey, MS London 1952, MRCS England, LRCP London 1950: That on June the ninth, 1976, you performed a surgical operation on Harry Wingate when you were unfit by reason of being under the influence of alcohol. And that in relation to the facts alleged you have been guilty of serious professional misconduct.'

The President looked at Parker Brown without expression and said courteously, 'Sit down.'

The GMC counsel, Eric Follett, a man of about fifty, pale from spending his life in courtrooms, rose to present the case. He had done this more times than he could remember, but this was one of the most extraordinary he had been concerned in.

'Sir, this is a charge in which information was laid by the theatre sister who assisted Mr Parker Brown at the operation in question, and the case rests almost entirely upon her testimony. Although as a general principle it can be unsatisfactory for a case to rest on one person's unsupported evidence, in this instance you may think she is a particularly reliable witness for a number of reasons which will become clear.

'The circumstances are that after a long day in theatre, Mr Parker Brown went off duty, but because of shortage of staff and other eventualities, he was required to perform an emergency operation for an obstruction of the bowel. Between the time when he left the theatre and returned to it, he drank sufficient whisky or other alcoholic drink to make him unfit to perform the operation properly. The patient subsequently died. My first witness, sir, is Dr Archie Seton.'

The commissionaire at the door passed the word to Seton, waiting in the witness room. He came from the sombre corridor into the chamber rather like a rabbit coming out of its hutch into daylight: timidly, and without enthusiasm. He studiously avoided Parker Brown's eye.

Seton was duly sworn, and taken – very nervously – through his testimony to the point where he went into Parker Brown's consulting room.

'And when you went in, what did you see?'

'Mr Parker Brown had a bottle and glass on his desk. He had a drink as I came in.'

'You mean he drank?'

'Yes.'

'Was it alcohol?'

'Yes.'

'How do you know?'

'I could smell it.'

'Let us come to the operation. How long did it take?'

'Three hours.'

'Three hours! For an obstruction of the lower intestine? Do you know why it took that long?'

'Mr Parker Brown seemed to be having some difficulty.'

'In what way?'

'He kept complaining, and muttering, and saying "Damn and blast". Things like that.'

'Thank you.' Follett sat down. Seton was not a very important witness.

Dominic Frayne rose and smiled at Seton.

'Did you actually see Mr Parker Brown drink anything from the glass?'

'No.'

'But you said he had a drink as you came in?'

'Well, yes, but I mean, what else was he doing? He'd *had* a drink.'

'But did you see him drink anything? Yes or no?'

'No.'

'Thank you. Then how do you know he *had* drunk anything?'

'The glass was used.'

'Of course. How long before you arrived in the consulting room *was* the glass used?'

'I don't know. I mean, how could I?'

'Exactly. What was in the bottle?'

'I don't know.'

'Was there a label on it?'

'Not that I saw.'

'Then how do you know that it contained alcohol, or that Mr Parker Brown had been drinking alcohol?'

'I could smell it.'

'I see. You recognised the smell of alcohol. What kind was it? Whisky, sherry, gin . . . or something else?'

'I can't be sure. The drop left in the glass was sort of straw coloured. Whisky-coloured.'

'A lot of things are whisky-coloured. Sherry, flat ginger beer, lager, cold tea.'

'But I recognised the smell of alcohol!'

'So you did. That must be a most unusual smell, in a consulting room.' Seton remained silent.

'Now, tell me if I have this right. You entered Mr Parker Brown's consulting room where there was a bottle containing something you cannot identify, and there was a used glass on the desk, containing the remains of some liquid, which you also cannot identify. You did not see him drink from the glass, but you did recognise the smell of some form of alcohol in a surgical consulting room.'

'Yes, I suppose so.'

'Now let us come to the operation. You said Mr Parker Brown kept complaining and muttering and saying "Damn and blast", things like that.'

'Yes.'

'Is it unusual in your experience, such as it is, for surgeons to mutter and swear as they operate?' This brought some muffled chuckles from other people in the room.

'Not really.'

'I didn't think so. When you were administering the anaesthetic, could you actually see the site of the operation?'

'No. The screen was up.'

'In how many operations for obstruction of the lower intestine have you been the anaesthetist?' Seton mumbled something inaudible. 'I'm sorry, we didn't hear that?'

'About a dozen. Well, six, anyway.'

'Six. And during any of those operations, have you seen the site of the operation?'

'No.'

'Not one?'

'No.'

'Six operations as anaesthetist. Would you be surprised to learn that Mr Parker Brown has performed, and assisted at, something more than six *hundred*? No more questions, sir,' Frayne said to the President.

Follett indicated he had nothing more to say to the unhappy young man, and he was allowed to leave.

As he passed Parker Brown's table he gave an apologetic look. Parker Brown nodded at him. He felt no resentment. Seton was an idiot, but not malicious.

'The next witness is Sister Patience Smith, sir,' Follett said. This simple announcement electrified the room: all eyes were on the door through which she would come – all except Parker Brown's.

She wore a plain black outfit, relieved with small trimmings of white, and a medium-sized hat. *She looks as honest as a nun*, Frayne thought, and his heart sank. Although he had not mentioned it to Parker Brown, he still had no firm idea of how to tackle her in cross-examination, which would be crucial. He knew he had to see and hear her give her evidence before he could come to a final decision, but at the moment he was devoid of any idea whatsoever of what style to adopt, and what line he should take.

Sister Smith took the oath in a small, but firm voice. Looking at her, Frayne wished she were his witness, and not the other side's. She was impeccable. As Follett led her through her evidence with consummate skill, Frayne's disquiet increased. Patience Smith was carefully constructing a tomb for Parker Brown's reputation, every word a cold marble block, each dovetailed into the next to make an airtight, rocklike structure.

She told the Committee of her long professional experience, and her association with Parker Brown beginning at the Parkway Hospital, then at the Midland General. She admired him, and was loyal to him, she said. He was one of the best, if not the best, general surgeons she had ever worked for. Until the night of the operation on Harry Wingate . . .

When she met Parker Brown in the corridor of the theatre suite, his breath smelled of alcohol. Still, it could have been one drink, so she didn't worry about it, even though it was unusual for him.

'Unusual?' Follett asked. 'How unusual?'

Sister Smith looked away. 'Fairly unusual,' she said. It was beautifully done.

Parker Brown had gone to the scrubbing-up room, she said, but disappeared after a few moments. After a while, she went to look for him. She found him in the locker room, drinking from a half-bottle of whisky. When he saw her, he threw the bottle into his locker.

'Did you say anything to him?' Follett asked.

'No. I didn't know *what* to say.'

'Did Mr Parker Brown operate on his own, or did he have the assistance of any other surgeons – apart from Dr Seton, the anaesthetist – that is?'

'Alone. There was Mr Parker Brown, myself, and one nurse, Nurse Benson. She wasn't very experienced, but Mr Parker Brown and I should have been able to manage. We had done before, in similar emergencies.'

Follett turned to the top table. 'Nurse Benson will not be giving evidence here today, sir. Shortly after the operation on Mr Wingate, she left for a post in Canada. Of course, we are not suggesting there is any connection.'

Sister Smith took up her evidence about the actual operation. It started reasonably well, but as it progressed, she said, the alcohol began to have its influence on Parker Brown. His work became increasingly clumsy and erratic.

'The intestine was badly distended with gas, but he asked me for a diathermy knife.'

'Did that surprise you?'

'Very much.'

'For the benefit of the non-medical people here, will you explain why?'

'A diathermy knife is electrically heated so that it seals the small blood vessels as they are cut. It is never used on a distended intestine where there is gas, in case it causes the gas to explode.'

'So what did you do?'

'I reminded him of the danger, and passed him an ordinary scalpel.'

'What did Mr Parker Brown do?'

He mumbled something, I couldn't quite catch it, and then took the scalpel.'

'What was the condition of the patient's intestines? I mean with regard to whether there were any adhesions.'

'There were some adhesions, certainly, but . . . '

'But what?'

'Not enough to cause Mr Parker Brown much difficulty in normal – ' She stopped dead. Too late, of course. Once again, it was beautifully done.

Her two-hour long evidence came to an end with questions about her decision to report Parker Brown.

'Why did you wait before you made the complaint? Why didn't you go to see Dr Armstrong the next day?'

'I'd known and respected Mr Parker Brown for many years. We'd worked together . . . I admired him enormously, as a surgeon, I mean. I couldn't suddenly . . . '

'Even though you knew he had operated when he was drunk?'

'Yes. I was torn. I told you. I'd known, respected and admired him for years. You don't forget that sort of relationship.'

'What finally made you decide to see Dr Armstrong?'

'One day, Mr Parker Brown went through the entire operating schedule on his own. He operated non-stop for seventeen hours, twelve operations in all, including open-heart surgery and a portacaval shunt.'

The entire room turned and looked at Parker Brown.

'Why did this make you report him?'

Sister Smith searched for the right words. 'I felt he . . . ' She stopped. 'Yes, Sister?'

'It wasn't just that he was trying to prove something, when he didn't really have to. But . . . ' Again she paused.

'Yes?'

'But . . . ' She plucked up courage, and put the last stone into place. She blurted out: 'I didn't think it was the action of an entirely balanced man. And coming after that night when he was drunk . . . '

She had effectively buried Parker Brown.

The President adjourned the hearing until the next morning.

Frayne had dinner with Parker Brown at his hotel, but neither man had much of an appetite. What Frayne had to say didn't improve Parker Brown's. 'The way the committee look at it, there's no reason for her to lie to say you were drunk, and every reason for you to lie to say you weren't. So a straight conflict of evidence is bound to be decided against you. The only way I can break down her story is not by meeting it head on. I've got to find out *why* she's lying. There must be something in your past relationship with her.'

'There's absolutely nothing,' Parker Brown said. 'I don't think I've ever seen her outside a hospital.' Frayne kept at him doggedly, but it seemed hopeless.

'There must be *some* reason. Did you ever make a pass at her? Try to seduce her?'

'Of course not!'

'I don't see why "Of course not." She's still attractive. Did you ever try to touch her, get hold of her?'

'On the contrary!'

'I don't understand.'

'One evening she came to see me in my consulting room and said she was very worried because she thought she had a lump in her breast. She asked me to examine her. I told her she'd be better advised seeing the gynaecologist, but she said she didn't get on with her, for some reason. She wanted me to do it. She was very insistent.'

'And you did?' Parker Brown nodded, slightly embarrassed. 'That was all?'

'Isn't that enough? I examined her breasts, and said I could find nothing wrong, and that was an end of it.'

'Did it occur to you that she was trying to seduce *you*?'

'Perhaps,' Parker Brown said slowly. 'But it's the sort of thing that happens once sooner or later between men and women who work together for a long time. It's meaningless.'

'I wonder.' Frayne paused. 'There must be something more, if you could remember it.' An idea came to him. 'When you left Parkway Hospital, did she expect to go with you? Did she want you to take her with you?'

Parker Brown looked as if he'd been struck by lightning. Frayne was right: there *was* something. All at once he remembered.

When he was working out his contract at Parkway before taking up his appointment at the Midland General, Patience Smith, while away on holiday, had written him two letters – hysterical, unbalanced, sexually-oriented letters. When she returned, Parker Brown took her aside and spoke to her. She apologised, excusing herself on the grounds that she had been overworking, and had been sick while she was away.

'And you've only just remembered this now?' Frayne said

incredulously. 'How the hell could you have forgotten *that*?'

Parker Brown's answer was simplicity itself. 'I didn't want to remember.'

Frayne was almost afraid to ask him the next question. The answer could mean the difference between vindication and disaster.

'About those letters . . . '

Next morning, as Frayne prepared for his cross-examination of Sister Smith he said to Parker Brown: 'You realise the dangers? If this misfired . . . '

'What have I to lose?' he replied.

Frayne began by putting Patience Smith at her ease with questions about the operation on Wingate that he knew she could answer without difficulty. Then quite unexpectedly he threw questions about the examination of her breasts. She was momentarily taken off balance, but quickly recovered. She said, as she had said all those years ago, that she asked Parker Brown to examine her because she didn't like the hospital gynaecologist. The Legal Assessor stirred a little as Frayne persisted with his questions, but before he actually told him to put an end to this line of cross-examination, Sister Smith gave one answer: 'I'm sorry, but I don't remember the details. I hardly remember the incident, it was so many years ago.'

'You were alone with a surgeon you admired enormously who was examining your breasts in the privacy of his office and you – '

'It was in his consulting room,' she said sharply.

'I thought you said you hardly remembered the incident, it was so long ago.'

She realised she had made a mistake. It showed on her face, and in the reactions of the members of the committee. Nevertheless, she recovered well. 'I wouldn't have gone to his *office* for an examination.'

It was the first tiny crack in the beautifully smooth façade she had constructed. Frayne dared to hope a little.

'You said you admired and respected Mr Parker Brown?'

'Yes, and I did.'

'You felt more than that, didn't you? When you were at the Parkway Hospital you were in love with him, weren't you? Deeply in love?'

Follett started to rise, but the Legal Assessor waved to him to remain seated.

'Mr Frayne, how does this affect the issue of whether or not Mr Parker Brown was under the influence of alcohol when he operated on that patient?'

Frayne drew a deep breath. This was the first of two great chasms he had to leap.

'Sir, this case is a simple matter of a direct conflict of evidence, and I submit I am entitled to test the reliability of this witness. It is our contention that Sister Smith is deliberately giving untrue testimony to this Committee. Now, it is the very core of our defence *why* she is doing it. We say it is because of the development of a certain personal relationship between her and Mr Parker Brown. Unless I can investigate this relationship, I cannot present what I am instructed, and what I firmly believe to be, the true defence to this most grave of charges. I should also like to remind you, Sir, that my learned friend opened the door to this line of questioning by introducing Sister Smith's relationship with Mr Parker Brown, and so I say I am entitled to question her on this point.'

The Legal Assessor nodded. 'Yes, but this is not a court of law, Mr Frayne, and legal rules of evidence do not apply here,' he said.

'Indeed, Sir,' Frayne replied. 'Otherwise I should have made observations about my learned friend's leading questions to this witness.'

The Legal Assessor's lips twitched for a moment, but he soon looked serious again.

Frayne spoke quickly. 'May I remind you, Sir, that this hearing is in camera, and before professional people. I do fully realise the seriousness of the course my cross-examination will take, subject to your ruling, and I solemnly assure you I do not take it lightly. I urge you, Sir, to allow me to pursue this line.'

The Legal Assessor frowned. He leaned towards the President, and they conferred in whispers for a moment.

'Very well, Mr Frayne, but I shall be following your cross-examination very closely. If I feel you are overstepping the bounds . . . '

'I am most grateful, Sir.'

Frayne turned towards Sister Smith. Her hands were clasped together, and her knuckles showed white.

'Sister Smith, when you were at Parkway Hospital, you were in love with Mr Parker Brown, were you not?'

'No. As I told you, I respected and admired him – as a surgeon.'

'And when he decided to leave the hospital, without taking you with him, you were unhappy?'

'I was . . . sorry to see him go. We had a good professional relationship. But "unhappy" is too strong a word.'

'I put it to you that you were much more than just "unhappy". You were *very* unhappy. You felt rejected, abandoned by the man you loved, the man you had tried to seduce by getting him to "examine" your breasts.'

'That's ridiculous!'

The Legal Assessor was fidgeting again. Frayne hurried on. 'Did you not write two letters to him, letters in most extravagant terms? Letters in which you poured out your sexual desires to him?'

'No! That's monstrous.'

Frayne searched in his papers. He found two letters, written on pink paper, and stared at them.

'You are on oath, Sister Smith. Do you still swear that you did not write two such letters to Mr Parker Brown?'

'I do swear it! And that's a cheap trick! Those letters you have – they're not letters I ever wrote. Apart from anything else, I never use pink paper.'

'No. You write on blue paper, don't you?' Then slowly, with great emphasis: 'On paper like *this*.'

And he produced two more sheets of blue paper, covered in thick, black italic writing. The letters looked old, well-folded and worn. He held them up for Sister Smith, sitting 30 feet away, to see. She stared at them, the colour draining from her face. She looked old, haunted.

'The bastard! He said he'd destroyed them!' Her voice was harsh, uneven.

'And so he had, madam.' Frayne slowly tore up the two letters: letters that he had written under Parker Brown's guidance, then made to look old by folding and refolding the previous evening.

The rest was a formality.

As they left the Council Chamber, Parker Brown told Frayne 'I can't help feeling sorry for her. Harbouring all that resentment, keeping alive all that hate, for all those years.' He shook his head. 'I don't understand it.'

'People keep love alive for even longer. And hate is stronger than love.'

'How very cynical you are, for a young man.' Parker Brown remained broodingly silent for a long while. 'I don't know how to thank you for what you've done for me,' he said quietly.

Frayne shrugged. 'You don't have to. I know how you feel. You saved my life.'

'And you just saved mine.'

Before he left London, Parker Brown made a couple of telephone calls – to Armstrong, and to Mrs Minchin, his housekeeper. Inevitably, they were both overjoyed by the news.

'As soon as you get back we'll go out and have a celebratory dinner at the Royal,' Armstrong said.

'No thank you very much, Matthew. I think I'll go straight home. Mrs Minchin will have something for me.'

And of course, she did.

Epilogue

In hospitals death is a fact of life, someone once said, without trying to be witty. Yet although staff become accustomed to death, as they must do to survive themselves, they do not become hardened to it. Surgeons sometimes operate on what they know is a hopeless case, but still feel a sense of loss and frustration when the patient dies. Nurses, to the last days of their careers, feel a little sick and empty when they strip a bed after a patient has died.

Compared with the ultimate and most awful act, dying, all other problems may seem slight; but having to bear constant exposure to death does not drain doctors and nurses of all emotion, leaving them none for anything less. Parker Brown felt genuinely sorry for Sister Smith for a long time, and it took positive efforts from his friends at the hospital and Mrs Minchin at his home to bring him out of his minor depression.

Sister Smith herself was subjected to a disciplinary hearing, but a decision was postponed for six months while she received treatment. Eventually her case was closed: no action was taken after her supervising consultant psychiatrist gave a good report. She went to South Africa where she managed to piece together her shattered career. She was, after all, a first-class theatre sister.

Alison Moxey went to Nice to see Gerald Bartlett. She told herself she had to get him back, or get him out of her system. When she saw his home, high in the hills behind Nice, with a great blue swimming pool in the immaculate grounds, smart, brittle friends about the place, their Ferraris, Jensens, Mercs and Rollses in the driveway, she knew she'd been living in a fantasy world. He wasn't going to give up all that to live in a three-room flat in an industrial town for love of her.

Three months later she married a forty-year-old accountant who had always lived at home with his mother until she died six months previously. It turned out perfectly for both of them.

When Bywaters and Suzy realised that there was no pressure on them to snatch every second of happiness, their relationship changed subtly. They still met, went out together and went to bed together, and enjoyed it enormously. But neither of them was ill-mannered enough to mention the word 'marriage'. They took each day as it came, without commitment.

Armstrong decided after all that he didn't want an Alfa-Romeo sports car. That this particular one was an open car with a less-than-perfect soft top, and there was a week of solid rain, helped him to make up his mind. The misunderstanding among the rest of the hospital staff about his relationship with the bobbly Kay Pepper was cleared up, as eventually it was bound to be. The shrewd Barbara Kennedy was the first to suspect that perhaps Armstrong had been deliberately nourishing the misunderstanding, and enjoying it.

One tiny residual unresolved question remained. Quite unexpectedly Parker Brown said 'I wonder what I *did* do with those letters?'

'What letters?' asked Florence Minchin.

'It doesn't matter,' he replied. 'Turn out the light, will you?' And she leant out of bed and did so.

Armchair bookshop

All good bookshops stock Everest titles. If you have any difficulty getting our books – or if you prefer to shop from home – please fill in this form.

To: Armchair bookshop, Everest Books Ltd., 4 Valentine Place, London SE1.

Please send me the titles ticked. I enclose a cheque, postal order or money order (no currency) made out to Everest Books Ltd.

(All prices include postage and packing. If you are ordering more than one book, deduct 10p from the price of each additional book.)

- ☐ VALENTINO – THE LOVE GOD Botham & Donnelly 93p
- ☐ LAST SNOWS OF SPRING Ken Johnson 68p
- ☐ CROSSROADS 1 – A NEW BEGINNING Malcolm Hulke 58p
- ☐ CROSSROADS 2 – A WARM BREEZE Malcolm Hulke 63p
- ☐ CROSSROADS 3 – SOMETHING OLD, SOMETHING NEW Malcolm Hulke 68p
- ☐ CROSSROADS 4 – A TIME FOR LIVING Malcolm Hulke 73p
- ☐ THE CRIME COMMANDOS Peter Cave 68p
- ☐ THE OLYMPIC MISSION Pamela Ferguson 78p
- ☐ A SPY FOR CHURCHILL Robert Vacha 78p
- ☐ PHANTOMS OVER POTSDAM Robert Vacha 78p
- ☐ HUNTERS' WALK Willis & Hart 83p

While every effort is made to keep prices down, it is sometimes necessary to increase prices at short notice. Everest Books Ltd reserve the right to show new retail prices on covers which may differ from those previously advertised.

NAME ....

ADDRESS ....

....